The Fires of Calderon

The Fires of Calderon

Lindsay Cummings

K·T· KATHERINE TEGEN BOOKS
An Imprint of HarperCollins *Publishers*

Katherine Tegen Books is an imprint of HarperCollins Publishers.

Balance Keepers #1: The Fires of Calderon
Copyright © 2014 by PC Studio, Inc.

 PC STUDIO

Library of Congress Cataloging-in-Publication Data
Cummings, Lindsay.
  The fires of Calderon / Lindsay Cummings. — First edition.
    pages cm. — (Balance keepers ; #1)
  Summary: "Eleven-year-old Albert Flynn is trained to restore balance to the
hidden earthly realms that have fallen into chaos and threaten to destroy the
world"— Provided by publisher.
  ISBN 978-0-06-227518-9 (hardback)
  [1. Adventure and adventurers—Fiction. 2. Magic—Fiction. 3. Friendship—
Fiction. 4. Imaginary creatures—Fiction. 5. Animals, Mythical—Fiction.] I. Title.
PZ7.C91466Fir 2014   2014001888
[Fic]—dc23   CIP
                                                                             AC

14 15 16 17 18   CG/RRDH   10 9 8 7 6 5 4 3 2 1
❖
First Edition

To my dad, Don Cummings, who is the reason I write.
And to my bookish dad, Patrick Carman, who is the reason
I'm able to keep writing.

Table of Contents

The Core

Belltroll

The Tower

Observatorium

Professor Asante's Quarters

Lake Hall

Professor Bigglesby's Quarters

Main Chamber

Treefare

The Pit

Library

Cedarfell

Canteen

Waterfall of Fate

Professor Flynn's Quarters

Ponderay

Calderon

The Path Hider

The Way Inside

The Realm of
Calderon

Calderon
Peak

Sea Inspire

Unknown Dangers

Ring of Gold

Forest of
Thorns

Ring of Entry

Tunnel to the Core

Tree of
Cinder

The Realm always provides the Means

CHAPTER 1

The Dead Letter Office

Herman, Wyoming, was a five-blink town. Albert Flynn knew this because it was the kind of conclusion one could only arrive at based on long hours of exceptional dullness. On his first day in Herman, Albert had taken off at a dead run from one end of town, which was marked by a mailbox shaped like a birdhouse, and arrived at the other side of town without blinking more than five times. Once, he'd done it in only two blinks, a feat that had made his eyes burn as if someone had thrown a handful of flour in his face. By day two, he not only knew about the five blinks, he understood there was a real chance that a normal boy might literally die of boredom before the summer came to an end.

But Albert was no ordinary boy. For starters, he was smart enough to make things interesting for himself, especially in a place like Herman.

And so, being a kid of small size and big imagination, he decided to jump across town, an activity that took under twelve minutes and included exactly 217 jumps, an encounter with a black cat, and a detour through a sprinkler. He decided to crawl back to the other side, a decision he would later regret as he sat on the steps of the post office picking gravel out of his palms.

It was activities like these—blinking, jumping, and crawling—that led Albert to believe that Herman, Wyoming, was possibly more interesting than he'd initially given it credit for. He'd seen and heard some unusual things on those small but important journeys.

Surrounded by a dense ring of evergreen trees, the town was secluded in a way that made it feel set apart from the rest of the world. While he was hopping past the town grocery, he found a cluster of pink, polka-dotted daisies sprouting right out of the cracked concrete. At noon, as Albert crawled on the edge of the circular forest, he could hear music on the wind that swept through the evergreen trees. Houses were brightly painted with purple and blue and yellow, and though most of them looked as if they were about to crumble from their own weight, they'd stood for as long as Herman had been a town, and would for centuries more.

The post office sat in the middle of Herman, Wyoming. It was here that Albert had spent summers before, here where he would spend the summer again. The building was small, thick, and perfectly square, the sort of place where one simply came and went without a lingering glance. Unless one wanted to stop and watch three wrinkled old men playing a game of Tiles on the front porch, one of whom was Albert's grandpa, who he called Pap.

"How's that sorting project moving along?" Pap asked from the porch. It was Albert's third day in town, and the sorting wasn't *moving* at all. Pap turned a white Tile in his wrinkled hands. His two old buddies shook their heads and smiled.

"I'm plotting strategy," Albert answered, because he couldn't tell Pap the truth: that he'd been blinking, jumping, and crawling around town when he should have been working. The dead letter office, which held all the undeliverable mail for the entire county, hadn't been touched since the previous summer. It was Albert's job to wrangle it into shape, and having goofed off for about as long as he was likely to get away with, he wandered into the dusty, old post office.

"That's the spirit," Pap said as he watched Albert move in the general direction of work needing to be done. "Show those letters who's boss."

The post office was where Albert Flynn, a short stick

of a boy with mouse-brown hair and three large freckles on his nose, found himself on his first week of summer vacation.

His dad, Bob Flynn, was the mail carrier in Herman, and summer was the only time they saw each other. Unfortunately, his dad's mail route took him miles outside of town, to all the scattered homesteads in the valley. He was usually gone all day.

To Albert, Herman, Wyoming, was a second home. He spent the rest of the year in New York City, surrounded by the constant blaring of sirens, throngs of people in the streets, and a blended family that threatened to drive him insane. Both of Albert's half brothers and his half sister were notorious tattletales who constantly conspired to blame every mistake or problem on Albert. He was eleven, they were five or six or seven, depending on the kid, and he was hopelessly out of touch with everything they did. Albert's mom was often at loose ends, dealing with three high-energy city kids, and while Albert's stepdad wasn't altogether mean, he also wasn't interested in Albert.

Summers in Herman with his real dad were the best part of Albert's life, not because he was in love with the post office (that part, unfortunately, was boring, just like school was boring to Albert)—it was because he loved the woods, the mountains, the adventure of being way out in the middle of nowhere. He wasn't just good at jumping and crawling; he was also a strong climber and an avid outdoorsman. Herman, Wyoming, suited him. And even though they weren't as close as Albert wished, he did prefer living with his dad to the city life.

Albert made the turn down a short hallway and arrived at the door to the dead letter office. Inside it was like a miniature city with its own towers of unmarked envelopes and dust-covered packages stacked to the ceiling. On his first day, Albert had made a tunnel through the unclaimed mail, wiggling his way to the other side, and there he'd sat, doing what he always did: open, read, file, and repeat. That was Albert's job. By the end of the first hour he was desperate for a promotion out of the dead letter office, and that's when the blinking, jumping, and crawling had started. He hadn't been back since.

There was a small, dust-covered radio in the corner of the room that played country music and hourly news updates. A long wad of tinfoil was duct-taped to the radio to improve the static-filled reception. When the afternoon news roundup started, Albert looked up from his work opening, reading, and sorting. They were saying something about New York, and at that very moment, New York was starting to seem slightly more exciting than opening other people's mail.

"Weather experts are reporting an unusual cloud of volcanic ash over New York City and so far, scientists are scrambling to figure out where it came from. Dr. Moritz Wilhelm of the weather bureau had this to say:

"'Seismic activity in the gulf region appears to have created an underwater plume of ash powerful enough to break the surface of the ocean. We're investigating.'

"An underwater volcano? Scientists are debating as we speak. . . ."

Albert went back to the mail, sorting and sorting and sorting, thinking about how cool it would be to watch volcano ash fall like snow back home. Maybe there would be enough to build a snowboarding jump. Maybe he could even see blobs of red lava shooting into the sky.

"Figures," Albert said, shaking his head. "I leave for five minutes and miss volcano burps. Next it'll be dinosaurs on Forty-Second Street. Just my luck."

He opened packages of old holiday presents, such as fruitcakes hard as stones that would never be eaten. (Not that they would have been in the first place. Albert knew a thing or two about bad fruitcakes.) He read letters from mothers to their sons, scolding them about not keeping in touch. He felt a little awkward reading other people's mail, but that was the job. These were dead letters and packages with no return address that had never found their point of delivery, and it was Albert's job to examine them like an archaeologist. If he could find a full name or a return address inside, he would send the item back from where it had come. If not, the contents were bound for the incinerator, a fire-breathing hole with a metal door out in the lobby.

Twenty-seven minutes later Albert was really getting into a good rhythm, but he was also feeling that dreaded sense of deep, almost sleepy boredom setting in. Albert wished he had an assistant of some sort. Maybe a boy his age, who would help him build tunnels out of the dead letters, and play Fruitcake Wars with him. Albert had a few acquaintances in school back in the city. But never in all his life had Albert ever had a true best friend.

He wanted that more than anything in the world.

Albert thought of his dad, driving his mail truck around Herman, the cool kind missing a whole door on one side, and wished that was where he was—anywhere but here. He started to nod off, the soft drone of static-filled music in the background, and slammed his forehead on the counter.

That was when the dog walked in.

Its fur was a wiry mess of jet black, but its nose was pink, which struck Albert as a mismatch, like when one of his younger brothers wore swim trunks and a Christmas sweater at the same time. The dog was about the size of a loaf of bread, and shaped like a beagle. Its eyes were the brightest shade of blue Albert had ever seen on an animal.

"Hey, little guy, where'd you come from?"

The dog walked through the back door of the dead letter office like it knew exactly where it was supposed to be. And in its mouth, covered in a dripping glob of dog slobber, was an envelope.

"Are you lost?" Albert asked. "Because if you are, I could sure use the company. I have fruitcake."

Albert didn't have a dog of his own in New York, so when he slowly reached down toward the animal, his fingers trembled a little. But the dog placed its head on Albert's palm, and Albert's nerves settled down, just like that. The dog's fur *looked* wiry and stiff, but it was soft on Albert's fingers in the strangest of ways. Its blue eyes looked right into Albert's brown ones, and that weird pink nose was sniffing the air. One of the dog's eyelids moved.

"Did you just wink at me, or do I need a candy-bar break?"

Albert picked up one of the fruitcakes he'd unwrapped and bit into it. It had the consistency of a brick left over from the Civil War era. Albert felt lucky not to have broken a tooth as he looked down and noticed that the dog had set the slobbery envelope on the floor.

"You're a smart boy, aren't you?" Albert said to the dog. It cocked its head like it was listening, in the way smart dogs do. "You're like a carrier pigeon!"

He took the envelope. It was torn at the corner from the dog's teeth. It was just like any other letter. Rectangular, unmarked, and . . . *wait.* Albert flipped the envelope over. He had to look at it twice to be sure what he was seeing. Scrawled right there, in deep-red cursive, was his very own name.

Albert Flynn.

Had Albert Flynn been any other boy, he might have set the envelope aside and reported the *Case of the Albert Envelope* the moment his father returned from his mail route. But he'd been opening other people's mail for three days. Well, okay, a total of one hour, twenty-seven minutes out of those three days, but still. The idea of a letter for *him* was too delicious to leave unopened.

"Now this," Albert said to the dog, "is cool. Don't you think so?" He hadn't expected the dog to answer, of course, but he still looked to see if it was listening. When he did, he discovered that the dog had pulled the rock-hard fruitcake out of the trash bin and was gnawing on it happily.

"Go right ahead," Albert said. "Make yourself at home."

He focused on the letter. Albert had gotten very good at opening envelopes without tearing the precious contents inside. He picked up a letter opener shaped like a shriveled claw on one end and sliced open the top.

He'd hoped for something strange, because he was very fond of strange things. It would have been a real letdown if he'd discovered a letter from his mom inside, reminding him to brush his teeth and eat his vegetables.

He was not disappointed with what he found.

CHAPTER 2

The Forest Maze

I f there was one thing Albert knew for certain, it was the look of his dad's handwriting.

It was sloppy script, so terrible it looked like a chicken had discovered a pencil and decided to take up writing. So when Albert opened the envelope, he knew at once that the letter inside was from Bob Flynn.

Hey, Kiddo, the letter said. (Or at least, that was what Albert guessed it said. The letters were so wacky he couldn't be 100 percent sure.)

I'm running way behind today on my usual route.
Normally, I wouldn't ask you to do this without me, but
I've got a very important letter that needs delivering.

Albert's face broke into a smile. His dad had never, ever, no matter how many times Albert had begged, *ever* let him deliver actual mail before, let alone do it completely on his own. He looked down at the dog, which was well on its way to eating the entire fruitcake.

"I've been promoted!"

He read on.

> *There's an important letter sealed in this envelope. It's for a guy who does NOT like coming into town. Ever. He's sort of a hermit. When mail comes for him, which is rare, it's always a rush. Follow the map below. Don't worry; you won't be on your own. Farnsworth knows just where to go.*

"Farnsworth?" Albert looked at the dog. The animal scratched his head, opened his mouth, and burped.

"My dad has a dog and I don't even know about it? You gotta be kidding me."

He looked back at the letter and his eyes widened.

At the very bottom, in bold chicken scratch, was a final warning.

> *Do NOT, under any circumstances, read the enclosed letter.*

"Well, that's not fair at all," Albert said to Farnsworth. His fingers itched to open up the letter and see what secrets were inside of it. But Albert had a job to do, and he wanted to do it right.

The bottom of his dad's note had a map. It was made up of little stick images of the forest outside of Herman. (Bob Flynn's artistic abilities were on par with his penmanship.)

"The woods?" Albert said to Farnsworth. Albert *loved* the woods. There was fishing in there, trees to climb, and trails to explore.

The map his dad had drawn was simple. Walk right out of the post office, take Main Street down to the edge of the woods, and walk straight until he passed a tree that looked like a giant slingshot. Fork left there, hop the trout stream, and climb up the hill until he came to his destination, marked with an *X* on the map.

"This Mr. Hermit guy must live in a cabin out in the woods. This just gets better and better!" *Especially if it gets me out of this dead letter office,* Albert said to himself.

He looked at Farnsworth again—the dog was licking his lips, having just finished off the last of the fruitcake.

"You're a big eater for such a little guy," he said. "Good luck digesting that thing."

The little dog thumped his tail on the dusty floor. Albert grabbed the envelope and tucked it safely into the back pocket of his cords. If he left now, he could deliver the letter way before sunset and be back in time for dinner with his dad and Pap. He turned to Farnsworth.

"Okay, wait here. I have to tell Pap."

Albert slid around the maze of piled-up letters, holding his breath so as not to knock them over, and peered out the half-open front window of the back office.

Pap was sitting on the porch of the post office with

two other old men, their balding white heads leaning over a game of Tiles. It was this way every hour of every day. Three old men and a game that looked an awful lot like dominoes that no one ever seemed to win, because, well, it just didn't ever end. Maybe the old men couldn't remember *how* to finish it.

"What's the progress report in there?" Pap asked without looking up from his Tiles.

"A dog came by and visited me," Albert said.

"Wiry hair, pink nose?" Pap asked. Albert nearly fell over backward when he heard the words. Pap always had a way of surprising him. One of the other old guys elbowed Pap in the ribs as he picked up two Tiles with matching symbols.

"Uh . . . yeah," Albert said. "I guess so. And blue eyes. It brought me a letter from Dad. I'm delivering a piece of mail."

"To the woods, eh?"

Farnsworth let out a little whine from behind Albert. Albert sighed. He just wanted to get out of there and deliver the letter. *Why so many questions from Pap?*

"How'd you know? Actually, it doesn't matter. I gotta go!"

"Don't get lost," Pap said.

Albert thought he heard two of the old guys grumble about something, but it was hard to hear what they were saying. Albert shrugged his shoulders and walked to the back door of the old post office, Farnsworth right on his heels.

The main road was just as familiar to Albert as slicing open the top of an envelope. They went a few blocks, passing by a crack in the road that looked like a smile. An old woman on a bike rode past.

"Hello, Virginia!" she said to Albert. "You're looking lovely today."

Luckily she didn't stop, because that would have almost certainly led to a major chat session with someone who thought he was a girl, and that was a conversation he didn't have time for. Albert double-timed it to the edge of the woods and stared into the maze of trees. The wind blew, making the branches of the trees shiver. It almost looked like they were waving Albert in.

Farnsworth raced onto the path, leaping over a small boulder and ducking under a fallen tree in nothing flat.

"Doggy sugar high," Albert surmised, and though he couldn't say exactly why, he had a feeling an adventure was about to begin. "So this is what it feels like to deliver mail. Cool."

Albert followed, breathless, as Farnsworth leaped over tree roots and uneven patches in the ground. It was dangerous work, running through these woods, but Albert was good at this stuff. In gym class, he'd beaten all of his schoolmates in the mile run, and then, right after, he'd climbed the tall rope in the gym in just twenty-four seconds.

Albert kept up a good pace, following Farnsworth's wagging tail through the trees. Every so often, the animal would stop, sniff the ground, and bark. They hadn't crossed paths with the slingshot tree yet, and the dog seemed to understand where he was going, so they kept on.

Farnsworth was small and could slip beneath thorn patches without gaining so much as a scratch, while Albert had to stop and find a way around. It was exciting running through the woods, crashing through little streams that soaked Albert's shoes. He felt like he was Indiana Jones about to stumble onto some hidden cave with gold piled high to the ceiling. It was infinitely better than sorting through dead letters.

They finally passed the first marker on the map Albert's dad had drawn—a tree that did, in fact, look like a giant slingshot without the string, its limbs split into two branches spreading outward. Albert imagined himself shooting massive rocks into the sky, knocking down forest zombies and wildebeests.

Farnsworth barked, reminding Albert of the mission they had. The dog took off again, forking left around the slingshot tree. Albert followed, running down what looked like a worn trail in the ground, as if someone had passed through here many times before. Albert wondered how many times his dad had come down this way to deliver mail. And why, after all this time, hadn't he told Albert there was a person living in the woods?

As he ran, Albert's shoelace got caught on a stray root. "Wait!" He called to Farnsworth to stop, but the dog was fast, and by the time Albert had released himself, the mutt had disappeared into the trees.

"Farnsworth!" Albert yelled, but the dog didn't return. He looked back in the direction from which he'd come, and saw that the ground was thick with leaves and roots crisscrossing one another like a maze. He shivered, but then stood up straight.

"Dad's counting on me to deliver this letter," he said to himself. "I can do this." He looked down at the hand-drawn map again. "The stream is next."

He walked on, swerving around big trees and under branches, until he reached a rise in the trail. He climbed up, grabbing exposed roots and pulling himself along, until he reached a shelf. There he found the stream, like a silver scar in the ground. And sitting patiently, wagging his tail, was Farnsworth.

"There you are," Albert said. He stooped down and placed his hand on the dog's head. Farnsworth licked his hand, turned around, hopped right into the stream, and then across to the other side. Albert followed after him, leaping across the stream. The opposite bank was steep, and by the time he'd scurried up it on all fours just like

Farnsworth, the dog had already raced off again through the trees.

"Wait up!" Albert shouted, and this time, he followed even closer, keeping his eyes on Farnsworth instead of the map. After all, his dad had said the animal knew exactly where to go. He couldn't lose him again, not if he wanted to make it to his destination before sunset. Speaking of destination . . . his dad hadn't said *where* he would end up. Albert guessed it was a house sitting in the woods, with an old man like Pap waiting for him on the front porch. He decided that no matter what, he'd deliver the letter in time, then cut out quick and make it home before it got dark. He couldn't wait to see the look on his dad's face when he told him he'd done the job right, all on his own.

His dad was gone the whole day, delivering mail, and at night, they always ate the same frozen dinners in front of the TV. They talked about fishing and hiking and all the things Albert wished they'd spend their summers doing, but never really did much of. Bob Flynn wasn't remarkable, by any stretch. But he was Albert's *dad.* And that was enough for him to be Albert's favorite person in the world. He never wanted to disappoint him.

After a while, Farnsworth barked again, drawing Albert away from his thoughts. They had almost reached the bottom of the big hill, just like his dad's map said they would.

"You want to race the rest of the way, don't you?" Albert said, as he bent down to scratch behind Farnsworth's velvety ears.

The dog's ears perked up, and he took off in a flash, faster than Albert had ever seen him run before. It was a wild chase, both of them running through the forest as fast as their legs would carry them. Just when Albert was about to pass the little dog, his foot got caught on a thick vine.

Albert's feet went out from under him. He flipped through the air and landed in a cloud of dust on the hard ground. It was *awesome*. He'd felt like he was flying.

"Did you see that?" Albert shouted. He'd expected Farnsworth to be at his side, wagging his little tail.

But Farnsworth was gone, *again*.

It was then that Albert realized just how dark the woods were becoming. He looked up at the sky. It was barely visible through the tops of the trees, but Albert could see the deep-pink-and-orange swirls overhead. Sunset was here, and by the looks of it, it was almost over. How long had he been in the woods? Time passed quickly, Albert realized, without a clock to measure it by.

"So much for delivering this letter before dinner."

Albert called out, hoping for the dog to come running back with a stick in his mouth. He looked down at the map again. The directions ended with the top of the hill, right where he was standing.

Albert spun around, searching for a house, or a tent, or *something* in the woods. But there was nothing. Just trees, trees, and more trees.

A half hour later, with darkness coming on fast, Albert felt like he was trapped inside a maze. He sat with his back up against a tree and really thought about his situation for the first time since he'd left the dead letter office.

He hadn't found the house or the person. He hadn't delivered the letter, and by now, his dad had probably figured out that Albert had failed. But the really troubling thing, the thing that was starting to make him afraid like he hadn't been in a long time, was that he was lost.

The map was no help anymore, Farnsworth was gone, and no matter how hard Albert tried to make sense of the woods, it all just looked the same. Every time he got close to finding his bearings, the ground itself seemed to have changed around him, and Albert was sure he'd walked in a thousand circles.

"What now?" he said to himself. He picked up a rock and tossed it as hard as he could. It landed against a tree trunk with a loud crack that echoed through the woods. Albert wished he had a friend with him right now, someone to help figure this all out. He could feel the letter in his back pocket, just waiting for him to deliver it.

His dad had said not to read it, not under *any* circumstance.

But Albert had made it all this way, followed all the directions right, and now . . . nothing. These were pretty dire circumstances, as far as Albert was concerned. Surely, if his dad knew he was lost, he'd want him to read it for a clue. . . .

Albert pulled the letter out of his pocket.

The writing was barely readable in the fading light. At first, Albert thought there was nothing on the paper at all. But as he tilted it, sure enough, there at the bottom of it, scrawled in his dad's chicken scratch, was one simple message:

> *Albert's time has come.*

The letter slipped out of his fingertips. It was about *him*? Maybe he'd read it wrong. He picked it up again and spent the next thirty seconds reading it over and over until the message sounded like it was screaming inside of his head. *Albert's time has come.*

"My time?" Albert said. "What time?"

He looked in the direction of Herman. Or at least he thought he did. How far into the woods was he?

"Farnsworth?" he called halfheartedly.

He took one more look at the letter, shook his head, and started down the hill for home.

"I give up," he said.

His timing was perfect, for right then, a shadowy figure moved in the trees, coming his way.

CHAPTER 3

The Troll Tree

Whatever was moving in the trees nearby, it wasn't Farnsworth. The figure was much larger than that. A girl, maybe, from the slight build of the shoulders, and the way the figure took such small, delicate steps. Could it be the person he was supposed to deliver the letter to?

"Hey!" Albert shouted. "Hey! Over here!"

Whoever—or whatever—it was, it didn't answer. When Albert took a step forward, hoping to get a closer look, the person or the thing vanished entirely. A twig snapped to Albert's right. He whirled around, and there, in the trees, was *another* figure.

This one was tall and thin, most definitely a boy.

"Hey, you!" Albert yelled. He waved his hands.

He called out twice. But the person or the shadow or whatever it had been vanished again, right in front of Albert's eyes.

There were noises, like the night woods had started to come alive. And one of the noises, way up in the distance, was familiar.

"Farnsworth!"

Albert followed the barking through the trees. He got closer and closer to the sound until he found Farnsworth standing in front of him with the soft light of evening bouncing off his little eyes. It was the most welcome sight Albert had ever seen.

"I forgive you for leaving me," Albert said, as he reached down and placed his hand on the dog's head, "but could you try not to do that again, please? It's getting dark out here. And in case you didn't notice, we're lost."

Albert didn't take his eyes off Farnsworth after that. He was too afraid the little guy would bolt ahead again. So when he finally did look up, what lay before him came as a big surprise. The forest cleared away, like the ground itself was sacred, and there in the middle, an ancient tree stood alone against the night sky. It was the wildest, most peculiar thing Albert had ever seen. The trunk of the tree was as wide as three school buses were long, and so short that if he wanted, Albert could have taken a small leap and been able to skim the leaves with his fingertips. And because he was a boy with a big imagination, he couldn't help but call the tree by a name that seemed fitting.

"A Troll Tree," he said, because it was the most accurate description he could think of. It looked like it belonged in the dark wood of a fairy tale.

Albert stood there for a while staring at the thing he'd named a Troll Tree, with a crooked smile on his face. He'd explored these woods for five summers and counting. How had he not come across this monstrous thing before? It had to have been there all along, and just now, at the age of eleven, he had finally discovered it.

Farnsworth barked, a low, rumbling sound that made Albert jump.

"What is it, boy?"

The dog padded forward and grabbed Albert's shoelace, pulling on it like a chew toy. Farnsworth was dragging him toward the tree, as if it were important. And something in Albert's feet must have agreed, because they carried him along with the dog. Walking toward the tree was like walking toward some sort of bright, beautiful beacon. Albert's chest felt lighter. His fingertips tingled, like they wanted to reach out and touch the solid bark.

They circled and circled and circled the tree, or at least that was how it felt to Albert. Finally, just when Albert's head was starting to spin, Farnsworth raced off, out of Albert's line of vision. Albert walked a little faster, turning the wide corner around the tree.

"Farnsworth? Hey, buddy?"

Albert looked to the woods searching for the dog, and found instead that while he'd been wandering around the tree, the forest had turned to night. Only a hint of sunset remained, far off on the horizon. The trees swayed softly, like ghosts moving noiselessly closer. Albert backed up against the great tree and began sliding along its rough surface. Somehow, having the solid weight of the endless trunk against his back made him feel less afraid. At least nothing could jump out at him from behind and carry him away.

Suddenly, the coarse feel of the bark on his right palm and fingers changed—now it felt smooth, like polished brass—which made Albert pull his hand back like he'd been shocked by an electric fence. *Okay, this is getting seriously weird.* He inched his fingers out once more and felt the cold, slick surface of something very untreelike. There was nothing left to do but turn around.

There, on the side of the trunk where bark should have been, was a smooth wooden door.

Albert took a step back, confused. Was *this* where his dad had wanted him to end up? It was the only thing that resembled a house he'd come across all day. At least it had a door—that was something. But the map hadn't led him here. Nothing had, really, not even Farnsworth.

Albert pulled the letter out of his pocket. It was crumpled now, and whoever was behind the door would surely know Albert had read it, but he didn't care. What he wanted, more than anything, was to get out of the woods.

He took a step forward, swallowed the knot in his throat, and knocked. The sound echoed.

No answer. Albert knocked again, a little harder this time. Maybe the person inside *was* like Pap, and couldn't hear very well. Maybe they'd grown weary of waiting for their letter and gone to bed. Albert noticed a round copper handle on the door. He reached for it and turned it enough to understand that it was not locked, then pulled his hand back.

"I can't just wander into someone's tree house, can I? I'm not even sure that's legal."

He felt the hairs on the back of his neck rise as the wind made the trees groan and sway. His hand went quickly to the door, and this time he turned the knob all the way.

The door swung inward with a long, loud creak, like it hadn't been opened for a million years. Surprised that the door had opened at all, Albert remained outside and peered in. It was darker inside than it was outside, like looking into a bottomless well.

"Hello?" Albert called into the tree house. His voice

echoed back to him, a ripple of sound. He poked his head in just the slightest bit, and called again. "Is anyone there?"

Albert heard something rushing up behind him, and fearing for his life, he ducked inside and slammed the door shut. His breath came in waves as he realized just how dark it was inside the tree, and then things turned considerably worse—something was moving next to his leg.

The thing chasing me was fast enough to get in here, too, he thought, his heart skipping a beat. But then he heard the soft pant of a dog, and reaching down, felt the familiar silky fur.

"Farnsworth!" Albert knelt down in the pitch-black and gave the dog a good scratch. "You scared me half to death. If this relationship is going to work, you need to stop running away. Understand?"

Albert kept scratching under Farnsworth's chin, which helped him feel a little less afraid and a lot less alone. He resolved to go back outside and walk home by the light of the moon. Enough was enough. He could find his way back if he set his mind to it. Albert reached up with one hand—he didn't want to stop scratching Farnsworth—which was when he realized there was no door handle where there should have been one.

"Uh-oh," Albert said. "This is bad. *Really* bad."

He felt all around the door, but it was no use. It was

a door with no handle on the inside, a door made for trapping someone. He turned back to Farnsworth and started scratching him behind the ears, hoping beyond all hope that the dog wouldn't run off again, and that was when Albert screamed for the first time on his adventure. Farnsworth's bright blue eyes had begun to glow like a Bunsen burner. It was like they were heating up, sending a soft glow of blue light into Albert's face. Albert tried to back away, but there really wasn't anywhere to go—the now-bright light confirmed it—there was no door handle to be found.

Albert slowly turned around to face Farnsworth, careful not to make any sudden movements.

"Okay, little doggy . . . That fruitcake must have messed up your wiring, huh?" He bent down slowly, got up the courage to scratch the dog behind the ears again, and when nothing else unusual happened, ran his hand back and forth in front of Farnsworth's eyes.

"Okay, blue light coming from dog's eyes—no big deal, Albert, no big deal."

If he was being honest with himself, a dog with glowing eyes was actually pretty cool. But Albert was also stringing together a series of thoughts that led to a terrible conclusion. What if his dad hadn't really sent the letter and the map? What if the dog was sent by a witch or a warlock or a forest troll? Obviously the dog wasn't normal. Maybe the dog was sent by a witch to find the new kid in town and lure him into the woods. Albert had made every mistake in the book. He'd followed a dog into the wild, hadn't left any instructions about where he'd gone, entered a tree, and closed the door behind him.

Albert looked down at Farnsworth, not sure he could trust the dog as much as he once did. The lights in his eyes were still bright, but they had dimmed a little.

"Looks like your light's going out," Albert said. He scratched behind Farnsworth's ear and his blue eyes brightened like a dimmer switch being turned. The dog turned around, sending beams of blue light down a corridor that ended at a wall of dirt and roots. Albert saw for the first time that he really was inside of a tree. There were twisting, turning roots shooting every which way down the middle of a tunnel that led to the wall.

"Whoa," Albert said.

Farnsworth ran down the tunnel, hopping and ducking as he went, and arrived at the far end, staring back at Albert. It was like looking into two Tonka truck headlights, and the headlights were getting dimmer.

"Man, I wish this dog would sit still," Albert said.

The thought of everything going pitch-dark again got Albert moving in a hurry. As the light from Farnsworth's eyes dimmed more and more, Albert made his way expertly through the tangle of thick roots. More than once he had to climb up toward the ceiling to pass through, or slither through the middle like a snake. And just about the time Farnsworth's pilot light went out, Albert dropped down next to the dog.

He was about to scratch Farnsworth behind the ears again when a sound rang out from his left, where the tunnel turned sharply against the wall of dirt. It was a terrible, shrill squeal, like a door creaking on rusted hinges. Albert's heart stopped, right there in his chest.

A few feet ahead of Albert, where the tunnel finally ended, a ribbon of light escaped from the bottom of a closed door. There were shadows inside, moving back and forth.

Someone else was in the tree.

CHAPTER 4

The Path Hider

Albert had been taught all his life not to open closed doors, especially if he did not know what was behind them.

But he'd already broken that rule once, and given the circumstances, it only made sense to break it a second time. He revved up Farnsworth's eyeballs, a trick he was starting to really get the hang of, and pointed the dog in the direction of the sliver of light. There were no roots to avoid on the short path between him and the door, so he arrived a little faster than maybe he'd wanted.

"Are we doing this?" Albert whispered, looking down at Farnsworth, who was scratching at the door to get in. Albert took a deep breath, recataloged all the terrible decisions that had brought him to this moment, and reminded himself that there was no way out. He starved to death inside of a tree or he forged ahead—those were his options.

Instead of a handle, the door had an outline of a human hand, like it had been carved in, just waiting for someone to press his palm to it. Albert lifted his hand and held it right in front of the handprint. For a second, nothing happened, and Albert let out a breath he hadn't even realized he was holding. But just as he was about to pull his hand away, something changed. There was a hiss, then a click, and a tremble from somewhere inside of the door. Before Albert could react, the door swung open, and a strange orange light shone from within. Whoever had been there before was gone; the space behind the door was empty.

Farnsworth stepped inside and sat down on the floor of an orange platform, wagging his tail like this was any ordinary day, in a very ordinary place. The platform wasn't large. It seemed to have space enough to hold a few people standing side by side, and so Albert stepped on it, too.

"Now what?" Albert asked Farnsworth. The dog barked, and as soon as he did, the platform began to move.

Down and down it went, deeper and deeper under the forest outside of Herman, Wyoming. Wind rushed up into Albert's face, and his ears popped the way they did on the airplane when he'd left New York. There was a very real part of Albert that began to think he was either dreaming a really unusual dream or he was the dumbest boy in the world. Those were the only two ways he could imagine ending up in such an outrageous situation.

The platform slowed down quickly, like an elevator coming to a basement floor. Albert stepped off, and found himself standing in a room crisscrossed with copper pipes that twisted and coiled in all directions. Some of them were as fat around as telephone poles; others were thin like a garden hose, wrapped with wires and cables. Steam hissed out of the pipes, filling the place with a damp heat that made Albert's shirt cling to his skin.

It's like a mechanical forest, Albert thought. He found himself frozen there in front of the platform, unable to move. *Where am I?*

Farnsworth circled around Albert's feet, yipping and hopping like he was home and couldn't wait to show Albert around the place. The dog grabbed ahold of Albert's shoelace again and started tugging.

"All right," Albert whispered, unable to speak too loud. He followed Farnsworth through the maze of pipes, ducking every so often as steam escaped from holes in the copper pipes. Soon the pipes started to spread off to the sides of the walls, leaving an open space large enough for him to move comfortably about. And there, just across the room, stood a man, looking downward into what looked like an open grave.

Albert ducked behind a pipe and hid at a safe distance.

It took him a moment to gather the courage to peek out. The man was tall and thin, almost spiderlike, and on his head was a miner's helmet, the hard kind with a light on top. Wild strands of rusty-orange hair flopped out from the edges of the helmet.

Farnsworth, who looked at Albert like he was crazy for hiding, wagged his tail and took off toward the strange man, barking.

"Hello, Farnsworth," the man said. "Did you bring the package?"

Oh, great, Albert thought. *This really is a warlock, Farnsworth is his dog, and I'm about to be cooked in a stew.*

Farnsworth yipped across the room.

"Is he, now?" the man said to the little dog.

Albert scooted deeper into the shadow of the pipe, but hot water dripped onto his back from one of the pipes overhead and he jumped out into the open. The warlock, or whatever he was, was too busy to notice, though.

"*Move,*" Albert said to himself. "Come on, it's not that hard. You can do it."

The man paced back and forth around the open area, peering down into holes Albert couldn't see the bottom of. Every few seconds he'd stop, reach down with delicate motions as if he was moving pieces on a chessboard, and then slide over to another hole and repeat the process. He mumbled a lot, as if he was trying to coax things to move in certain ways.

"You might as well come out from behind the pipe," he said at length. "Not much sense in hiding." Then he went back to work.

Albert took a deep breath and stepped out from the shadows, moving around a fat pipe the size of a giant's thigh. *So far, so good.*

"You have something for me?" the man asked without turning around.

There was a small part of Albert that thought, *Hey, I'm just delivering mail down here, no big deal.*

Albert pulled the envelope out of his back pocket and unfolded it. He took two more steps forward and set the envelope on the top of a copper pipe.

"I guess I'll be on my way, then." He began backpedaling. "Pleasure meeting you. I can show myself out. Really, it's no problem."

"Could you bring it to me?" the man said, holding his hand in Albert's direction without turning his attention away from whatever weird work he was doing.

Albert picked up the envelope and paced back and forth a few times. What he really wanted to do was leave, but he didn't really know how to make that possible. He marched toward the wizard or the mad scientist or whatever he was, and resolved to deliver the letter, even if it turned out to be the last thing he ever did.

He passed by one of the holes in the ground on his way to the man. It had a round rail that came to about Albert's belly button, and not being able to help himself, he peered over the edge. Inside lay something Albert recognized at once as a miniature version of the forest he'd just come from. There it was: the same wide perfect circle of trees. And from above, he could clearly see the streams he'd crossed with Farnsworth, and the paths he had stumbled through. The Troll Tree stood right in the middle, only this one was the size of Albert's hand. The rail contained an array of buttons and knobs that Albert very much wanted to touch. He reached out his hand, nearly had his finger on a button . . .

"I wouldn't do that if I were you."

Albert nearly jumped out of his underwear. The man was standing right next to him, staring over Albert's shoulder like a vulture. Under the miner's hat, he had two different-colored eyes. One was blue like the sky, the other copper like the pipes around them, and his eyes were carefully observing the small forest inside the hole. The man reached down and turned a knob, crinkled his long, thin nose, and stared into the forest.

"Who are you?" Albert asked. He couldn't help himself.

The man looked at Albert like he was crazy for not knowing.

"I'm the Path Hider, of course," he said. "What do they call you?"

"Uh . . . Albert," Albert said. "Albert Flynn." He held up the letter he'd already opened. "Are you . . . expecting a letter from someone?"

The Path Hider looked at him from the corners of his eyes.

"Maybe."

Albert held out the envelope again and the Path Hider bobbed his head back and forth like an ostrich, examining the envelope every which way. The guy had a really long neck.

"This mail has been opened."

"Yeah, about that," Albert stammered. "It was kind of a tough day. I mean, that's no excuse for opening someone's mail, but—"

The Path Hider snatched the letter with his spidery fingers before Albert could finish.

"You're not that easy to find," Albert said, and then suddenly he couldn't hold back the questions any longer. "Why's my name on that letter? How do you know my dad? How come your dog has headlights for eyes? Where am I? What's going on? What are you *doing*?"

As Albert asked these questions, he watched the Path Hider open the crumpled-up letter. It took him longer than Albert thought was necessary to read four words, but when the Path Hider was done, he looked right at Albert.

"Flynn, you say?"

Albert nodded. "That's me."

The Path Hider rubbed his chin. "Wait here a moment."

Albert watched as the Path Hider stooped down and pressed one of the buttons on the rail, a large one with what looked like a zigzag etched onto its top.

"We must hide the paths," the Path Hider said. "No one can know of your arrival."

Okay, that was one *question answered, at least.* Albert looked down into the hole with an uneasy feeling and watched as the miniature forest began to move, shifting in hundreds of little squares, like Tiles, all around the Troll Tree.

"That's my forest," Albert said, astonished. "That's where I came from."

The man moved from hole to hole—three of them, Albert noted—pressing buttons, shifting versions of other forests that Albert did not recognize. Some had trees without leaves that looked like bare arms stretching to the sky; others had leaves that were orange and red, the way they turned in New York in the fall.

"Are these real forests?" Albert asked. The man looked up from his spot by a hole, a few feet away.

"As real as a graviton's hiss, dear boy." Albert had no

idea what a graviton was. "This way, that way," the Path Hider said.

He waved Albert over. Together, they peered down into a hole Albert hadn't yet seen. The miniature forests inside, Albert saw, were stacked into three levels. Albert recognized each of the forests as the ones from the other, smaller holes.

"Help me shift it, will you?" the Path Hider asked Albert. He was starting to crank a giant wheel, a big, rusty one that groaned and squealed as Albert helped him turn it.

"I hide the paths," the Path Hider said, blinking his different-colored eyes, "so that we can keep our secrets safe."

"What secrets?" Albert asked, but the Path Hider waved him off.

"Later," he said, and pointed back into the hole. "*Watch.*"

Albert looked on as all three levels of forests shifted and switched places, little pieces of them changing and sliding from left to right, up and down, like a game of Tiles.

When the forests settled, the man smiled.

"Coffee break," he said.

Albert was so confused he simply followed the Path Hider to a corner of the room, where there was a stained gray couch. He took a seat beside the Path Hider, in the middle of all the pipes and levers and strange holes. Despite the incredible circumstances he found himself in, he was starting to feel less afraid and more curious.

"What kind of mojo are you cooking up down here?" Albert asked.

"Coffee?" The Path Hider held a thermos out to him.

Albert shook his head no, and then ventured one more question he hoped would lead to an answer.

"Can you at least tell me where I am?"

A pipe hissed over their heads. Steam shot down in between them, blurring the Path Hider for a moment. When it cleared away, Albert saw that the man was smiling at him again.

"You're home, dear boy," he said. "Welcome to the Core."

Albert was as confused as he had ever been in his life. He opened his mouth to speak, but before he could get a word out, Farnsworth barked and ran off toward the platform that had brought them underground.

Albert peered through the steam as the orange platform, which had left while he wasn't paying attention, returned. A boy and a girl were standing on the platform, their shapes very much like the ones Albert had seen in the forest. The girl had a wide grin on her face, while the boy, who had glasses too large for his face, looked startled and scared and lost.

"Ah, here we are." The Path Hider stood up and motioned for Albert to join him as he walked toward the two newcomers. "It seems the rest of your party has arrived."

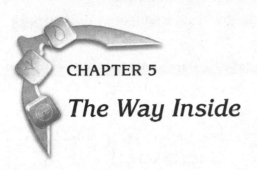

CHAPTER 5

The Way Inside

At first, no one spoke. Unless you counted the way Farnsworth was greeting the newcomers. He ran circles around them, yipping at the top of his little dog lungs.

"Hey, little buddy," the girl said, though she didn't reach down and pet Farnsworth. Instead she looked up at Albert as if he was Farnsworth's owner. "Your dog is excited."

The girl had the wildest, curliest blond ponytail Albert had ever seen, complete with pink streaks. She was wearing jean shorts, a purple T-shirt that said *Falcon Swimming Team*, tall black socks over her skinny legs, and a pair of hiking boots covered in mud.

"Oh, he's not my dog," Albert stammered. "He sort of

led me in here, I guess. But he's not mine."

The Path Hider raised an eyebrow, but he didn't speak.

"Whatever you say, Freckles," the girl said.

Albert started to say his name, but the boy who had arrived with the girl asked a question.

"Hey, so, uh . . . where the heck are we anyway? I've never seen this part of Texas in my life. Must have taken a serious wrong turn on that cow trail."

The boy was a foot taller than Albert, long and thin like a tree branch. He had small almond-shaped eyes behind black-rimmed glasses. A mess of dark hair stuck out from beneath a red baseball hat.

Both the boy and girl stared at Albert like he was supposed to answer their questions.

"There's no time to sit and stare like Hoppers in the moonlight," the Path Hider said, and again, Albert noted that he had no idea what the man was talking about. "I need to get you three on your way, and fast."

"Could you maybe explain what's going on first?" Albert asked. "That kid says he was in Texas a minute ago, but I was walking down a trail in Wyoming, so it seems like this whole situation just got a lot weirder. And I didn't think that was possible."

The tall boy smiled. "I'm with Freckles."

"It's, uh . . . Albert," Albert said. "Albert Flynn."

"I'm Birdie Howell," the girl added. "And I was out in the woods beyond my parents' property. In *Oregon*."

Birdie didn't seem all that bothered by the fact that she was in a room under the earth, filled with pipes and steam and a bunch of people she'd never met before in her life. In fact, she seemed excited, bobbing back and forth on her feet like she couldn't wait to explore.

The tall boy looked unsure, but he smiled again, and held a large hand out to Albert. "Leroy Jones," he said. Albert shook his hand in what he hoped was a reassuring way.

All three of them—Albert, Birdie, and Leroy—stared at the Path Hider as he took his helmet off, revealing a shock of coppery-orange hair.

"It's not my place to do the explaining," he sighed. "And it's too late for turning back. I'm afraid you'll have to keep going."

The Path Hider looked down at the dog. "Farnsworth, you know what to do."

Farnsworth barked, his tail thumping over Albert's ankles, then took off running across the steam-filled room.

"Go on, then." The Path Hider poked Albert with a long, spidery finger. "Follow the leader. He knows the way."

The Path Hider pointed across the room, past the old couch. Albert saw the wide mouth of a tunnel—something he hadn't noticed before through all the steam.

"I'm not so sure about this," Leroy said. He glanced nervously back and forth between Birdie and Albert.

Birdie bobbed on her toes. "That's what makes it so exciting!"

Albert, feeding off of Birdie's energy, found that he wasn't afraid anymore either. He was determined to get to the bottom of whatever was going on. He'd also been wishing for a long time to have a real adventure, and to spend time with kids his own age instead of his younger siblings.

And here it all was.

This was a thousand times better than sorting through dead letters or hopping and blinking across town.

"I tell you what," Albert said, turning to Leroy. "Birdie and I will go first and see what we're dealing with, then you can follow. How about that?"

Leroy shrugged. "Works for me."

"I'm game," Birdie said, fiddling with her ponytail. "We've come this far down the rabbit hole. Might as well see what's down there. Maybe it's treasure, like we won the lotto!"

"Or a three-headed monster," Leroy said, adjusting his baseball cap on his head. "But I guess if we're going to get eaten alive, we might as well do it together."

"Some advice, if I may?" the Path Hider called out to them as they reached the mouth of the tunnel. "Hold on tight and don't lean out the windows. And know that you're not in any danger. Not yet anyway."

He waved good-bye with his long, bony hand and turned away as they entered the shadows. As soon as Albert, Birdie, and Leroy crossed into the tunnel, there was a whooshing sound, like wind. Flames atop copper torches flickered to life on either side of the tunnel walls. The fire was as blue and bright as the sky had been in Herman that morning, while Albert was hopping across town.

"You guys," Birdie said. "I think there's something wrong with these flames."

Birdie reached closer and closer to one of the flames, then flicked it with a finger. Then she put her whole hand into the dancing light.

"The fire's *cold*," she said.

Albert held his hand out to test the blue flames as he walked by. They *were* cold, like he'd just dunked his hand into one of the streams outside of Herman. "That's *awesome*!"

The sound of Farnsworth barking up ahead echoed off the stone walls.

"I guess we should keep going," Leroy said. He produced a yo-yo from his pocket and spun it nervously in his palm. "Let's see where the tunnel leads."

They walked at a downward sloping angle for a long time, going deeper under the earth with each step. Water dripped from the rock walls, and overhead, the pipes and wires were still crisscrossing the ceiling.

Finally, Farnsworth came into view up ahead, his blue eyes lighting the curved walls with an eerie glow. The tunnel had opened up into a small cavern. Just above Farnsworth was a metal bar, thick as Albert's thigh, and hanging from the bar was a large metal gondola with open windows. It reminded Albert of a car he'd once seen on a Ferris wheel.

At the sight of the trio, Farnsworth growled playfully and hopped into the gondola. It swung and creaked on its track, dangling back and forth like a pendant on a chain. On closer viewing, the box-shaped contraption was rusted and ancient.

"A gondola that's about a million years old," Birdie said, walking up beside Albert.

"No way am I getting on that thing," Leroy mused.

"Yeah, I dunno, guys," Albert said.

He didn't want to admit it, but this time, he thought Farnsworth might have inhaled a little too much pipe steam. Birdie was right. The gondola *did* look like it might crumble under their weight. He thought about what the Path Hider had said, and Albert's stomach fluttered at the thought of a ride that would require them to *hold on tight*.

"I don't know about you guys, but I'm tired of standing around," Birdie piped up. She strode forward and hopped right into the gondola beside Farnsworth without a hint of fear on her face. The gondola groaned and swayed back and forth, but it held strong. "You guys coming?"

Okay, Albert thought. *Birdie is either totally fearless or completely insane.*

Albert settled on the former and took his place on the metal bench beside her. Farnsworth hopped onto Albert's lap and wagged his little tail. The dog looked back and forth from Albert to Birdie, light from his eyes bathing them both in a deep blue.

"Leroy?" Albert leaned outside the box. Leroy was standing there, arms crossed, staring at the two of them like they'd just taken a large dose of crazy pills.

"I can't believe I'm doing this," he said, staring at his toes. He took another long look at the rusted old track the gondola hung from. And then, like Albert and Birdie and Farnsworth before him, Leroy stepped inside.

Leroy hardly had time to put his yo-yo in his pocket and settle down on his seat before Farnsworth barked three times fast. There was a sound of a lever being thrown somewhere far behind them. The gondola began to move. It was slow at first, creaking along the prehistoric track overhead.

"Maybe this wasn't such a good idea," Albert said, holding on to the rail until his knuckles turned white as snow.

The gondola rolled along the rails, picking up speed, and soon it was plummeting into the darkness. Albert held Farnsworth close as wind whipped through his hair. Both Birdie and Leroy screamed at the top of their lungs.

Albert couldn't see anything but flashes of blue light from Farnsworth's eyes. The gondola took violent turns left and right, shooting down steep declines and swinging from side to side. Albert's stomach threatened to sprout wings and fly right out of his mouth. He clutched Farnsworth so hard he was afraid the dog might explode.

A second later, the gondola suddenly shot upward through a stone cavern, completing a double loop that left everyone gasping for breath. Then, after a final, gut-wrenching turn, the gondola settled down, slowing to a more leisurely pace as it glided farther under the surface of the earth.

Farnsworth stared in Birdie's direction, bathing her in beams of light. Her ponytail was puffed up like a mass of cotton candy, but she was beaming.

Albert smiled back. "If I'd have known it was going to be like that, I never would have gotten in this thing, but that was actually kind of incredible!"

For the first time, all three of them were laughing. As they caught their breath, they entered a wide space dotted with hundreds of bright blue flames, and gazed up into a stalactite-filled ceiling far overhead.

"Stone fingers!" Leroy yelled, pointing at the long stalactites. "I've seen them in books."

Chunks of glittering diamonds sparkled everywhere,

embedded in the walls, and when Albert got brave enough to poke his head out the window and look down, he was pretty sure the darkness went on forever.

"It's amazing!" Birdie yelled, but just as she said those words, something swooped through the gondola—in one window and out another—right in front of her face. She let out a little shout.

"*Whoa*. Did you guys see that?" Albert asked, spinning in his seat to see where the creature had gone.

"Did something just fly through this gondola?" Leroy asked as the blood drained out of his face. He sank down lower into his seat.

Without warning, the cave filled with black-winged creatures pouring out of holes in the walls. Some were the size of Albert's fist, some almost as big as his head.

"Bats!" Albert screeched.

He'd seen bats before on television and online, but he'd never been in the same space with even one, let alone thousands of them. As the bats flew around in the open air, dipping and diving, Albert's heart hammered in his chest. He felt something land on his shoulder, but didn't have the courage to turn his head and see what it was.

"Uh, Albert?" Leroy said. "Something furry just landed on you."

It was like Leroy's saying it made it real. Albert jumped up and started flailing around. "Get it off!" he yelled.

Leroy assumed a karate pose for a kung-fu kick while

Birdie tried to get a closer look.

Albert calmed down a bit knowing these new friends had his back. *Just bats, Albert. Just bats. It's not like Dracula's coming to eat you . . . hopefully.*

"Can you hear them?" Birdie asked.

Albert took another deep breath and listened. The bats were *singing*. It wasn't a language Albert knew, but it was almost like the bats had human voices, high-pitched and strange.

Farnsworth barked and the singing bat on Albert's shoulder finally flew away, out into the swarm that grew thicker as they went.

Leroy sat back down and turned the brim on his red baseball cap forward again. "I was about to put a move on that thing, big-time."

"*Sure* you were." Birdie giggled, and Leroy's face went red as a cherry.

The bats followed the gondola through the cave, singing their strange song and flapping their furry wings. Albert felt like he was in a trance, unable to move or blink. After a while, Farnsworth's head drooped on Albert's lap and the lights in the dog's eyes went out. They traveled down the track and through the swarm for a time, adrift in a sea of blue flames.

The bats didn't follow when the gondola unexpectedly sped up, and as Farnsworth raised his head and his lights went back on, all three kids felt as though they'd awoken from a dream.

"Never trust a swarm of singing bats. Especially furry ones," Leroy said. "What just happened?"

They rounded a corner into colorful light that made Albert shrink back and shield his eyes.

"Documents, please, ladies and gentlemen," a woman's voice said.

Albert blinked his eyes a few times, letting the lights settle in. The gondola had stopped at some sort of suspended platform. On it sat an uneven metal booth that looked like it could only be held aloft by magic. The sides were made of thin sheets of copper, buckling at random places, and the countertop looked like it was made from the hood of an old car. Behind the platform there were barrels stuck to the walls, as if they were simply floating, full to the brim with lumpy things Albert couldn't quite make out.

A short, stocky woman stood behind the counter. Albert was shocked to see a black snake slithering around her shoulders and neck.

"Documents, please," the woman said again, more impatiently this time. Albert and Birdie stared back at her, unblinking. Leroy dug in his pocket and held out a yo-yo.

"Oh, for Calderon's sake," the woman said. Her snake hissed in a most unfriendly way. "I'd know a fresh set of Keepers anywhere. It's the moon eyes, like you've seen a ghost!"

"We didn't see any ghosts," Birdie piped up from her seat. "But we did see some crazy bats that sang to us back there."

The woman smiled and sat heavily on a metal stool that groaned, as if it was about to crumble beneath her weight.

"Memory Wipers. If you ever leave the Core for good, and probably you will," she said, "the song they sing will make you forget everything you saw and all you did here."

Leroy exhaled and leaned forward, elbows onto his knobby knees.

"I'd like to forget that entire ride. Maybe we've been here before, but we just can't remember it."

The snake woman let out a bark of a laugh. "You clue in fast, for a newbie." She pulled out three rugged backpacks and set them on the counter of the booth.

"One for each of you and you're on your way."

Leroy reached past Albert and grabbed the bags, one at a time, and handed them out.

"What's this stuff for?" Birdie asked as she started to open the top of her pack.

"And what *are* you?" Albert asked. "Some kind of witch or something?"

"I'm Lucinda," the woman said, cackling. "You might say I'm in the supply-and-demand business. Didn't that Path Hider tell you *anything*?"

The snake hissed in response as Lucinda pointed her ring-covered hand at the bags on their laps. "Clothes, boots, essentials, a trinket or two. Everything you'll need."

Albert untied the leather lace that held the pack closed. Inside, there were a pair of boots, a toothbrush and toothpaste, a few pairs of socks. Underwear. Deeper inside the bag he found something more interesting: an egg-shaped compass that wobbled when Albert held it out on his palm.

"That's a lifesaver the first few days inside the Core," Lucinda explained. "In time you'll find your way around the place, but everyone knows the Core's got a tricky mind of its own. It likes to get the newcomers lost. Just say where you want to go, and the Core Compass will show you the way."

Birdie was digging in her bag. She pulled out a silk sack filled with strange metal orbs that fit in the middle of her palm. She held one of them out.

"Ah, yes," Lucinda said. "One of my specialties. Break one of those over someone's head and you'll get a surprise."

Birdie didn't wait for additional explanation. She smashed one on top of Leroy's head like an egg. There was a crack, then a flash of fire, and in an instant, a tiny white bird appeared. Farnsworth wagged his tail at the bird, as if he wanted to play. The little bird chirped, ruffled its feathers, and flew into Birdie's lap.

"It's a Floppywhippet," Lucinda said as she smiled. "It will produce bubble-gum eggs for the next few minutes. Then it will fly away and never be seen again."

Birdie looked a little unsure, but she smiled and stroked the bird's tiny head anyway. It laid a tiny orange egg in her hand and chirped happily, rolling the egg forward with its beak.

"It wants you to eat it," Leroy said.

Albert thought birds were cool enough, but this was getting a little dicey. Then again, the egg did look like candy.

"I'll give you five bucks if you eat one," Albert said to Birdie.

"I'll do it," Leroy said. "I'm starving." He popped an egg into his mouth and began chewing. "It's good! Like sherbet!" The bird cooed and preened.

During the next two minutes the Floppywhippet laid six more eggs in various colors and flavors, and Leroy found a small metal sculpture of a cat in his pack that Lucinda said would give him incredible balance when he rubbed its head.

"But it only works once," she warned. "So use it when you really need it."

The Floppywhippet fluttered away into the darkness.

"I'm gonna miss that little guy," Leroy said as he popped the last gum ball in his mouth. (It was bright yellow and lemon flavored.) "Where are we going?"

"Questions, questions," Lucinda said. She reached over and gave Farnsworth a small blue bone, which he started to gnaw on.

"Helps his eyes glow brighter," Lucinda said. "Now off you go!"

Then Lucinda knocked three times on the side of the gondola, and whispered some strange words that Albert couldn't quite hear or understand. Albert felt the gondola shiver beneath his feet and start to move again.

"Good-bye!" Birdie shouted behind her.

They picked up speed. Soon they passed over a glittering green river, and shortly after, went through a waterfall that soaked the top of the gondola. After they took one last heart-pounding drop down into darkness, their ride came to an end.

Albert turned to look out the window just as the gondola came to a stop across from another floating orange platform. *What is it with these things?* Two rusted metal doors stood behind the platform, embedded in the cave walls.

"Whoa," Leroy said. "Check it out."

Farnsworth was so excited he wriggled out of Albert's grasp and hopped out of the gondola, onto the orange platform. He turned and barked at them as if to say, *What are you waiting for?*

"I guess this is our stop," Albert said, throwing his

backpack over his shoulder. He was about to climb out of the gondola when it started to move again, heading slowly back in the direction from which it came.

"Better move quick!" Leroy said. "I have a feeling the Path Hider would just send us back here again. And I don't think I can handle that ride twice in one day."

All three jumped the narrow expanse that separated the gondola from the platform, and watched as the rickety contraption turned the corner and disappeared.

"Now what?" Birdie asked.

Albert shrugged.

Farnsworth ran to the doors and starting scratching, his bark echoing through the cavern.

The doors started to quake. They opened forward slowly, groaning as if they hadn't moved in years. They stopped halfway open. A shadow emerged, indiscernible at first. Albert took a half step back. This could be a warlock, or a giant, or the witch he'd been wondering about all day.

But when the shadow stepped out into the light of Farnsworth's eyes, Albert felt himself relax.

The figure that came out was one of the most normal-looking people Albert had seen all day.

Unless you counted the miniature blue dragon perched on his shoulder.

CHAPTER 6

The Core

The young man standing before them was tall and lean, with dark brown hair that flipped out just past his ears.

"I've been waiting for you three all day," the young man said with a British accent. "I thought you'd fallen off the trolley."

Leroy glanced at Albert with a worried look on his face. "Apparently people sometimes fall out of the trolley."

"Must have been our lucky day," Albert said.

"I'm thinking we should talk about this later," Birdie said, elbowing Albert in the ribs.

The young man smiled and went on.

"I'm Trey. And you three must be Albert, Leroy, and Birdie."

Trey bowed low to the ground, the little blue dragon on his shoulder somehow managing to hang on.

The dragon was just like Albert had always imagined a dragon would be—with scales and claws and wings—only it was the size of a parrot. The tiny beast turned toward Trey, opened its mouth, and sent a blue flame into the side of Trey's head.

"Cold, just like the flames you've seen so far," Trey said.

"I used to want a pony or a unicorn," Birdie said. "Now I just want one of those."

"Alfin usually stays in Cedarfell with some of the other creatures," Trey said, sensing their curiosity about the dragon. "But I thought you'd like to see her. And she does enjoy getting out once in a great while."

Leroy took a step closer to Albert. "Can we trust this guy?" he whispered into Albert's ear.

They looked down from Trey to Farnsworth, who was sitting at Trey's feet, wagging his little tail. Farnsworth hadn't done them any harm so far. In fact, he'd led Albert to the coolest place he'd ever been in his entire life. The dog had a taste for adventure, as far as Albert was concerned.

"Farnsworth seems to like him," Albert answered, with a shrug.

Alfin suddenly took flight and disappeared through the half-open door, from which a warm glow was spilling. Trey looked down at the three of them (except for Leroy, who nearly matched his height).

"What you're about to see is Balance Keeper business. It stays here."

"What's a Balance Keeper?" Birdie asked.

Trey had a mischievous look in his eye as he answered.

"*You're* a Balance Keeper. So are Albert and Leroy. You just don't know it yet."

Albert was more confused than he had been in the Path Hider's tree. What the heck *was* a Balance Keeper? And how did Trey know their names?

"What if we want to leave?" Leroy asked, swallowing the lump in his throat. "What then?"

Trey lowered his chin in Leroy's direction.

"One thing I can promise you right now," Trey answered. "You're definitely not going to want to leave."

With that, Trey reached over to the door, slipped his hand through the crack, and pulled it wide open.

Albert had lived in the country with his dad and the city with his mom, so he'd known what it was like to bounce between two very different worlds. But now he'd entered a third kind of world, and as the doors opened wide, Albert felt his jaw drop.

It was like he'd stepped into the world of a fantasy video game.

The room—*no, the cave*—was as tall as it was wide, and as Albert stared up at the massive iron chandelier that hung from the ceiling, he began to feel impossibly small.

It wasn't just the hugeness of the cave that surprised him. It was the fact that it was full of *people*. Hundreds of them. They were normal looking, not dressed in warlock cloaks or miner's hats, but in average clothes like shorts and T-shirts, though some of the shirts did have special markings. They all seemed to be wearing boots identical to the ones in Albert's pack.

People were crisscrossing the floor in all directions like ants single-mindedly fulfilling their tasks. Some of them carried round maps. Some wore hard hats and had grease stains on their faces. A boy with a broom moved past, sweeping up dust on the cave floor. A group of kids ran by, laughing and chasing one another.

Albert knew he would never forget what happened next: The whole place went so still and quiet Albert could hear his own breathing. Everyone stopped and stared at Albert and his new friends. And then, after getting a good look at the new recruits, they all went back to whatever it was they were doing.

"Do I have bed head or something?" Albert asked, matting his hair down in case it was poking out in seven different directions.

"Well at least it's not full of cyclopses and monsters," Leroy said. He wiped off his glasses, as if to make sure what he was seeing in the cave was really there. "I was worried about that."

"Me too," Birdie said, glancing up at Leroy. "And I hate cyclopses. Like, for real."

As Albert watched, he noticed that some of the people wore necklaces, thick, black cords on which hung white Tiles with black symbols. They looked like the very same Tiles that Pap and the porch buddies played with outside the post office. *Odd,* Albert thought, *but not entirely surprising, now that I think about it.*

He tried to watch specific people, but everyone walked in different directions, some disappearing down smaller, dimly lit tunnels that vanished into darkness.

Leroy nudged Albert. "I want one of *those,*" he said, and pointed to a boy holding a giant three-pronged fork with blue goo oozing from its tips. "What *is* this place?"

Trey followed Leroy's gaze out into the chaos, a sly look on his face.

"You've arrived in the Main Chamber of the Core," he said, stepping past Albert, Leroy, and Birdie with his hands spread wide. "You're many miles under the surface of the earth."

"It's so . . . ," Albert started, but he couldn't find the words to describe how incredible it all was.

"The Core tends to leave new arrivals speechless," Trey said. "You're not the first."

A boy with floppy blond hair and a silver-gray T-shirt ran past. A silver bird with long, curly feathers that stretched to the floor sat on his shoulder.

"Newbies!" the boy shouted, as he gave Albert a high five. "Sweet!"

The boy crossed over an old, stone bridge that arched to a high point in the middle, like the tip of a triangle. A glittering silver stream ran beneath it. Albert scanned the room. The streams jutted outward in different directions from a massive iron wheel that spun slowly in the very middle of the cave floor. The streams ran toward three doors, under which they seemed to disappear. Each of the doors had its own unique symbol embedded into it—like a symbol on a Tile, but these were far larger, far more ornate, as if they had been carved long ago by someone with very skilled hands.

"The water is one of the many things you'll love about the Core," Trey said, noticing Albert's eyes growing wide at the sight of two boys diving into the depths of a shimmering pool. Trey pointed out the three doors, right where each meandering stream ended and disappeared into the cave walls. "You'll learn about what lies behind them, soon enough."

The same wide pipes they'd seen in the Path Hider's room were scattered like vines across the walls and ceiling. Buttons and wheels and strange knobs were all over the walls.

Trey started to lead Albert and his friends through the Core. Suddenly, some sort of giant creature ran past. Birdie let out a little shriek.

It was an oversized black cat, and at the sound of Birdie's voice, the creature turned. It stared at her with three yellow eyes the size of Ping-Pong balls. It started to purr, the sound so loud it reminded Albert of a motorcycle starting up in the city.

"He's Professor Asante's companion creature," Trey said. "Best not to touch him, or look into his eyes for too long. Cats can be unpredictable."

There was, it seemed, an endless array of fantastical things in the Core.

"What's that?" Albert heard himself ask, pointing at a strange cloud of blue dust that erupted when a girl threw something small and silver across the cave.

"Are those monkeys hanging from the ceiling, or something else?" Leroy asked.

"Is that a *talking* frog?" Birdie asked from Albert's right.

Trey shook his head and smiled.

"All your questions will be answered in due time," he said, herding the three of them along like lost children. He looked toward the high ceiling as if it might tell him the time. "It would be best not to show up late for your introduction. First impressions are only made once."

Albert fell in step with the rest of them and thought about what a strange day he'd had. The Core had been here all this time, with all these people, right under *Herman* . . . and Albert had never known about it. Judging

by the looks on Leroy's and Birdie's faces, they hadn't
either. It was like discovering a hidden treasure in the
attic of your own house—always there, but not quite
visible unless you really *looked*.

"This way, this way." Trey's voice pulled Albert back
to attention.

They headed down a long, barely lit tunnel, away
from the noise of the people rushing about. Farnsworth
appeared again, running past Albert's untied shoelace,
and stopped before a closed door.

"Now listen carefully," Trey said, bending down to
scratch behind Farnsworth's ears. The dog's eyes lit up as
he barked happily. "When you go in, show some respect.
The Professor is always busy. But he's set aside time just
for you."

"Who's the Professor?" Leroy asked, fixing his baseball
cap just so on top of his head.

Trey thought a moment before answering. "You might
say he's my boss. You'll be learning quite a lot from him."

Oh, great, Albert thought. *It's summer, and we're about to
have professors?*

Trey turned away from them and knocked lightly on
the door. Then he opened it just enough to slip inside,
and left them standing in the tunnel alone.

"Still think we made the right choice?" Leroy asked
as the door closed behind Trey. Farnsworth yipped up at
them, as if he'd understood the question.

"Farnsworth thinks the place is all right," Birdie said, and reached down to pet the dog's soft fur. The dog thumped his tail and licked Birdie's hand. "At first I wasn't so sure. A place like this shouldn't exist. But I'm totally glad it does."

"And now we're all here," Leroy mused, smiling at her as he touched one of the cool, blue flames on the wall beside them. "It's like magic."

Birdie nodded. "Do you guys *believe* in magic? I didn't think I did, until today."

Albert nodded, and pointed at Farnsworth's glowing eyes. "If that's not magic, if this whole *place* isn't magic, then I don't know what is."

The door creaked open in front of them, and they all whirled around. Trey poked his head out.

"The Professor will see you now."

One by one they filed through the door, Farnsworth right on Albert's heels.

Albert had seen a lot of strange things today. He'd even felt like he was floating inside of a dream. But what lay behind the door took his breath away all over again.

Across the room, a glowing blue waterfall tumbled out of an impossibly high ceiling, water pooling on the cave floor. Bright yellow-and-purple birds danced around the waterfall, singing a lively song that made Albert wish he'd worked a little harder in choir class.

"Whoa," Leroy said, or at least, that's what Albert

thought he said. The sound of the rumbling water was so loud he couldn't really be sure. Albert followed Farnsworth, Leroy, and Birdie across a raised pathway, closer to the waterfall, where a fine mist landed on Albert's freckled nose.

The pathway led behind the waterfall and Farnsworth darted ahead, running off to greet whoever—or *whatever*—lay hidden behind a series of curved walls. Albert's heart started to beat faster, like the times when he'd seen scary movies. He felt like something awful would jump out from behind each corner he passed.

It wasn't the boogeyman around the corner, though.

Behind an ancient oak desk sat a man in a shimmering green jacket. He was scribbling something on a long piece of parchment paper.

The man looked up, set the pen down, and smiled.

Albert gulped. "Dad?"

CHAPTER 7

Professor Bob Flynn

As far as Albert was concerned, Bob Flynn had always been an average, vanilla-variety dad. Bob spent eight hours a day delivering mail. On weekends he read books and fought a losing battle with Pap for the best recliner in the house. Did it get more average than that?

Bob Flynn could *not* be spending his days in the Core, miles under the surface of the earth, in a place that shouldn't even exist.

Yet here he was, standing behind a desk, staring at Albert with a look of satisfaction on his face.

"Dad?" Albert asked for the second time, because even though his dad was standing right in front of him, Albert just couldn't believe it was true.

"I knew you'd make it," Professor Flynn said, looking right at Albert.

They were nearly identical versions of each other—Professor Flynn the larger, Albert the smaller—down to the three large freckles on each of their noses.

"Mr. Jones, Miss Howell," Albert's dad said, clearly pleased to see them, too. He waved them all over to his desk, where three chairs sat open and waiting. "Have a seat. I'm sure you're all exhausted. Getting down here the first time is quite an experience, but you'll get used to it."

For a moment, Albert wondered if all of this was a strange vision from eating that bite of stale fruitcake back at the Herman Post Office, but he took his place in the middle chair, Leroy and Birdie on either side of him. Trey stepped into the office, too.

"I delivered the letter," Albert said, once they were all settled.

Farnsworth barked and looked up at Albert as if he was owed something.

"Farnsworth helped," Albert added. "And by the way, did you know this dog has flashlight eyes?"

His dad's laughter echoed off the stone walls. The sound only drove it home further that there was a *lot* about his dad Albert didn't know.

"I had no doubt you'd deliver that letter to the Path Hider," Albert's dad said. "And yes, I know about

Farnsworth. He's a Canis Luminatis. A rare breed."

He glanced up at Trey, who was dutifully standing beside the desk. Alfin had returned to his shoulder.

"There are those who didn't think you'd get the job done," Albert's dad continued. "But I knew you would. You're a Flynn. You were made for this."

Trey's face reddened with embarrassment, as if *he* had been one of the naysayers.

"You *all* did well by arriving at the Path Hider's tree," Professor Flynn said, glancing at each one of them in turn. "The Path Hider's location is the only way into the Core—it's the train station, if you will. You came from different places, some farther than others, but once you reached the Path Hider, you were at the outer gate of the Core. From there, it's twelve miles down and a mile to the east. Very few people know about this place, and the ones who do keep it a secret. You should already feel proud to be here."

Albert *did* feel proud, but he was still having trouble believing the man in the green jacket was his dad. All this time, he'd thought his dad was *Bob Flynn, Postman*. And now he was *Bob Flynn* . . . Well, Albert didn't know what his dad was.

Albert's face must have given away his thoughts, because his dad piped up.

"Yes, Albert. It's been hard to keep it a secret all these years." He smiled at the three of them. "But it was necessary. A Balance Keeper should never discover the Core until it is his or her time."

"We keep hearing about Balance Keepers. But what *is* a Balance Keeper?" Leroy asked, leaning forward and placing his pointy elbows on Professor Flynn's desk. "And is *my* dad here?"

"Yeah, what about *my* parents?" Birdie chimed in.

Professor Flynn raised an eyebrow. "I'm glad you asked. Leroy, it was your father who was a Balance Keeper, long ago. He and I were in the same unit. He chose to go back home after many noble years of service here."

Leroy leaned in even farther. "So he knows I'm here?"

"Oh yes," Professor Flynn answered. "If you ever reach the status of professor—and that's a very, very big *if*—then you never forget, even if you leave and don't come back. A Core professor never loses the memory of his or her experience here. Not so with everyone else. The Memory Wipers take care of that. Your father, Leroy, was a professor, but he won't be joining you."

Then he turned to Birdie. "Miss Howell, your grandmother was the Balance Keeper in your family. Your grandmother was quite a woman—very brave and strong willed—though she had a quick punch when her temper flared up."

"I hardly knew her." Birdie nodded. "But my mom always said I was a lot like her. Won't my mom be looking for me?"

"Your mother, as well, had the Balance Keeper gene, but she chose to stay on the surface and live a normal life, as some do," Professor Flynn answered. "She knows exactly where you are."

"I guess that's why she was the one who suggested I go into the woods and find some big, ugly tree," Birdie said, running her hands through her ponytail.

Professor Flynn nodded and shifted in his chair. As he did so, Albert caught a glimpse of a white Tile on a black, corded necklace hanging around his neck, like those he'd seen people wearing in the Main Chamber. But his dad cleared his throat and shifted again, and the Tile disappeared under his green coat.

"In the Core," Professor Flynn began, "you three will become a team. You will function as a training unit and learn all the skills you need. This training will take time and perseverance. You must commit yourselves entirely to the task."

"To *what* task?" Albert asked. "You do realize how confusing this all is, don't you?"

Professor Flynn nodded knowingly. "We find that it's best not to say too much at the outset. Trust me, it would only confuse you more. You'll learn best by doing, not by listening. You were all chosen for very important, secret work. And it won't be long before you understand the Core the way all the other units do."

Professor Flynn paused and looked at the three

gawking faces before him, and then he continued on.

"That said, here are the basics: you will be trained in the fine art of entering hidden underground Realms and fixing problems—here we call them Imbalances— in order to keep the people on the surface of the planet safe. It's dangerous work, but if you take your training seriously, you'll be fine. Maybe even champions."

"What kind of Imbalances?" Leroy asked. "Like, the way a scale doesn't balance if you put more weight on one side than the other?" He was chewing on his thumbnail, unable to look away from Professor Flynn.

Albert's dad smiled like he'd just overheard a secret. "In a way, yes. We clean up problems that plague the ecosystems in the Realms. The Core, *here*, leads us to these Realms. The Core is the gateway."

"Those three doors in the Main Chamber," Birdie said. She raised an eyebrow at Professor Flynn. "Are those the gateways to the Realms you're talking about?"

"Smart girl," Professor Flynn said. Birdie smiled smugly.

Suddenly, Professor Flynn waved over Trey, who had been standing in the shadows in silence, and whispered something into his ear. Albert very much wanted to know every word that passed between them. Here was his dad, a leader in some secret society, and Albert had never known. And here was this guy he didn't even know, in on his dad's secrets. Who was Trey anyway? A

Balance Keeper, too? What about all those people in the Main Chamber? He'd seen hundreds of them, all ages, when they first entered the Core. Surely not *all* those people, especially the old dude with the floor-length beard, could restore Balance in the Realms. Albert spoke up the second Trey returned to the shadows.

"So, is everyone in here one of these . . . *Balance Keeper* people?"

"We all work as one family, to keep it all running," Albert's dad said. "There are cooks, creature caretakers, Core mechanics, professors, launderers, medical teams, and communication teams to monitor the world above."

"But Balance Keepers are, like, the totally elite, right?" Birdie asked, her blue eyes wide.

Albert's dad nodded. "Balance Keepers are the entire reason for the Core. You give us all a reason to keep it running, and keep it safe." He stopped for a moment, looking all three of them over. Albert sat as still as stone.

"Without the Balance Keepers to ensure the Realms stay Balanced," his dad said, his eyes landing on Albert, "the entire world could come to a dire end."

His words sparked a thought in Albert's mind. Just this morning he'd heard something on the radio about a plume of ash heading toward New York City.

"The ash clouds back home," Albert said. "This place has something to do with that, doesn't it?"

Professor Flynn nodded his head. "It's why we brought

you here, at this moment in time. It seems one of our Realms may be heading toward Imbalance."

Albert thought of his family back in the city. He thought of the ash covering the streets, piling up so high it covered all the cabs.

"Is New York going to be destroyed?"

Professor Flynn smiled comfortingly, which both surprised Albert and settled his stomach all at once.

"No. That's why we have Balance Keepers, like you. That's why we train, for when things like this happen."

"So this Realm . . . the Imbalanced one . . . is right under New York?" Birdie asked, crossing her arms.

"The Realms shift places. They could be in any place under the earth at any time. However, when a Realm becomes Imbalanced, it freezes in place. Right now, the Calderon Realm is stopped under New York, yes, and it will stay there, wreaking havoc on the city, until Balance is restored. And of course," Professor Flynn added, shrugging his broad shoulders, "if it isn't solved, the problem will simply continue to grow, expanding from New York to nearby places, and so on."

"I think I'm gonna be sick," Leroy whined. Albert gave him an encouraging thumbs-up.

Professor Flynn turned back to the group. "You were each born with the blood of a Balance Keeper. You have the power to go into these hidden Realms, but this power must be unlocked. That will take time and practice.

"You three will live inside the Core and train for every situation that could come up in the three Realms. Once you've trained in all three, you'll have the chance to become First Unit Balance Keepers, officially in charge of keeping a specific Realm in Balance. But first things first—this term you'll just train for Calderon, which just happens to be the Realm I oversee." Professor Flynn winked at Albert.

"Trey is my Apprentice; he will do everything he can to help you along."

"Wait a sec," Leroy said. "Back up. We're supposed to stay here? Like, overnight?"

"How long?" Birdie asked, right after.

"You mean . . . no more boring dinners alone with Pap?" Albert asked, desperate for his dad to say *yes*.

Professor Flynn nodded.

"You will remain here for the duration of the summer. You will live in the Core—you'll eat, sleep, and train. The Core will be your home. That is, if you choose to stay. A Balance Keeper must make the choice on his or her own."

Birdie grinned. She looked back toward the waterfall, then directly at Professor Flynn. "I *love* it."

"If we stay, what happens next?" Leroy asked. He still looked a little unsure.

Albert looked at his dad, too. He was just as curious as Leroy was.

"Every Balance Keeper is given a Tile," Professor Flynn said. He pulled out the Tile Albert had caught a glimpse of so they could really see it. The black symbol on the Tile was a strange cone-like shape, almost like a megaphone. And although Albert had no idea what its significance was, there was something about the Tile that carried the ancient weight of importance.

All three of them leaned in to get a better look.

"A Tile will give you skills and powers you cannot possess in the world above. How does that sound?"

"Like . . . I could get real-life ninja powers?" Leroy asked excitedly. "Because I'm telling you, I'm destined to be a ninja."

"I want to punch a hole through a wall!" Birdie clapped her hands together.

"Wait a second, Dad. *You* have a *power*?" Albert asked, desperate to know what secret thing his dad could do. What if he was like a superhero? "What is it?"

Professor Flynn smiled sheepishly. "I can speak the language of the Core creatures."

"That is *ah*-mazing." Birdie clapped her hands again.

I never took Dad for an animal guy, but that's pretty sweet.

"I'm in." Albert nodded. "*So* in."

Leroy turned to Birdie and they nodded at each other.

"So am I," they said together.

Albert looked at both Leroy and Birdie and saw how excited they were. This wasn't just about him. This was about all *three* of them, together.

For once in his life, Albert was going to have real *friends*. The three of them were going to be a team. His dad was going to spend time with him, and teach him how to do amazing things.

And that, above everything else, made Albert happier than spending an entire summer in Herman, Wyoming.

CHAPTER 8

The Waterfall of Fate

Professor Flynn took them swiftly back in the direction from which they'd come, until they arrived at the waterfall.

"Let the other professors know we're proceeding as planned," Professor Flynn said to Trey in a hushed tone. "And prepare the rooms. We should be ready within the hour."

Trey turned to Albert and his friends and nodded with a look of encouragement, then disappeared into the shadows with Alfin riding along on his shoulder.

To the left of the waterfall, sitting against a flat, gray wall, there was a circle of darker stone that rose up like a pedestal. The top was a couple of feet across.

"This is the Libryam," Professor Flynn said, looking

at Albert. "Go ahead, step up on the platform. I want to show you something."

Albert hesitated. What if the platform suddenly rose into the air and banged his head into the ceiling? There had been so many surprises throughout the long day, he didn't know what to think.

"Nothing is going to happen, trust me," Professor Flynn said.

So Albert stepped on the stone surface of the platform. He felt it move ever so slightly.

"Plenty of time remaining, of course," Professor Flynn said. "The Libryam measures how long you can stay in the Core before you must leave. The longer you stay, the closer to the bottom the platform will sink. It's like a scale, only this scale tells us how many days you have left."

"And how many is that for Albert?" Birdie asked.

"Same as for you and Leroy. You all arrived today. You have approximately seventy-four days left."

"Seventy-four days? That's it?" Albert wanted more. He'd only been here a few hours, and already he never wanted to leave this place. Back home was *school*. And studying really wasn't Albert's thing—it was boring and he'd always been just mediocre at it. Back home, too, he didn't have any friends. He'd already had more fun with Birdie and Leroy in a few hours than he had all year in New York.

"What happens if we stay too long?" Leroy asked. His eyes widened. "Do we disintegrate?"

Professor Flynn laughed. "After a certain point you can never go back to the surface. Stay in the Core too long, and you're here forever. Trey is like that; he chose to stay. Some do; some don't. Some are born here. They can never leave. But if you leave at least once every seventy-five days, you can keep going back and forth. Stay away too long and the Memory Wipers' lasting effects will make you forget you ever came here—unless you're a professor, like me."

"And my dad," Leroy said proudly.

"And your dad, yes. Professors don't forget. Not ever. Understand?"

They all nodded as Professor Flynn turned to the waterfall.

"Your Tile will come from the Waterfall of Fate," Professor Flynn explained, pointing into the churning water before them. "Your power in the Core is destined; it has been chosen. You need only discover what it is."

They quickly determined that Birdie was the oldest— by a total of three months and seven days—and she was elected to go first. Leroy came in a close second, and Albert, to his dismay, was the youngest by six months.

"You're all eleven," Albert's dad said. "The perfect age to become Balance Keepers."

"Why's that?" Birdie asked.

Professor Flynn smiled. "Because at this age, you're always ready for adventure."

Albert smiled. He thought about how he'd simply run into the woods following a random blue-eyed dog earlier in the day. "Totally."

"All right," Professor Flynn said, waving the three over with his hands. His green jacket sparkled, picking up the light from the waterfall behind his shoulder. "This is simple, really. Birdie, go ahead and get into the water."

"You got it!" Birdie said. She rubbed her hands together and nodded, then smiled. She kicked off her shoes and stepped forward. The water was shallow, little waves of it lapping at her toes as she waded in.

"It's warm," Birdie called over her shoulder. She waded farther in, until she stood in the water up to her waist.

"Now what?" Birdie called out. She looked like she couldn't wait to dive all the way in.

"Swim to the bottom, beneath the waterfall. It's not as deep as it looks," Professor Flynn yelled back. "You'll see a lot of Tiles down there, but don't just grab the first one you find. It should feel as if the Tile is choosing you, not the other way around."

Birdie took a good look at the length of the waterfall and the way it crashed into the pool.

"Here goes nothing."

She dove in and disappeared beneath the waters.

On the surface, Albert watched, waiting for Birdie to come up. At first, he wasn't concerned. She was wearing a swim-team shirt, right? But then a full minute passed.

"She's been down there a long time," Albert said to his dad. He kicked off his shoes. Leroy followed suit, both of them ready to dive in and save their new friend, but Professor Flynn held out a hand to stop them.

"Patience," he said. His face was as smooth as stone. "All part of the process."

"Dad, she could drown!" Albert felt like time was frozen. But his dad simply shook his head, and pointed at the pool beneath the waterfall.

"Look."

Finally, there was a splash, and Birdie's head surfaced. There was a huge smile on her face.

"You have no idea how amazing that was!" she screamed as she swam back to the shore. "I felt like I didn't even need to breathe under there! I could have stayed underwater there forever!"

Birdie walked out of the waterfall pool and held her Tile out to Professor Flynn.

The Tile was white with a black symbol on it, just like all the others Albert had seen, only this one had the shape of a water droplet.

"What's it mean?" Birdie asked. Her clothing and hair dripped into a wide puddle around her feet.

"A water symbol," Professor Flynn said, tilting the Tile

every which way. He smiled, and patted Birdie on the back. "I started to wonder, when you didn't come up for air. You've been given the ability to stay underwater for a long time, Birdie. Or rather, *not* breathe when you're submerged. And you'll have special skills underwater, too, though I can't say for sure what they will be. How did it feel?"

"It felt like I was a mermaid," Birdie said, awestruck. "Like, I could totally beat a dolphin in an underwater race!"

"Fascinating," Professor Flynn replied. He seemed to be logging the information for future reference.

"It's probably the best Tile there is, if you ask me," Birdie said, wringing out her ponytail.

"But you don't even *know* what the other Tiles are," Leroy mentioned.

Albert wondered if Birdie might sprout fins and jump back in the water, never to be seen or heard from again.

"That is pretty sweet, though, I guess." Leroy nudged Birdie, then handed his glasses and baseball cap to Albert. He didn't look scared, for once. "All right. My turn. Let's do this! Megapowers, here I come!"

Albert watched as his new buddy walked in and disappeared beneath the surface of the water. Leroy didn't take nearly as much time as Birdie had.

In just twenty-seven seconds, he surfaced, a white Tile held in his hands.

"Definitely not mermaid powers!" Leroy said, gasping for air as he got out of the water and held his Tile out to Professor Flynn. "Please tell me I just acquired mad ninja skills!"

"Ah," Professor Flynn said, when he inspected the symbol. Leroy's had the shape of a thin tree with three twisting, curling branches. "This is a Synapse Tile."

"Come again?" Leroy said as all the excitement drained out of his face.

"Very rare and powerful. It gives you a photographic memory and increased reasoning skills, among other mental abilities, Mr. Jones. A Tile I've seen before, but not often. Congratulations."

Leroy's shoulders sank. "You gotta be kidding me right now."

He took his place next to Birdie, looking very much like he'd like to go back into the water for another try.

It was Albert's turn next. He felt as nervous as a dog about to take a visit to the vet. He didn't want to get some stupid, useless power, like speed walking or eating really fast. Albert wanted to fly like Superman or shoot fire from his fingertips like the character Fuego in his favorite video game.

"Go on," his dad said, placing his hand on Albert's shoulder. "There's nothing to worry about."

Albert handed Leroy's stuff back and stepped forward into the water.

"I just swim under and scoop one up?" he asked.

"Let it choose *you*," Albert's dad called back over the roar of the waterfall.

Albert was a good swimmer. He loved it almost as much as he loved exploring the woods outside of Herman, so when he took a deep breath and sank beneath the surface, it was as natural as riding a bike. He could feel the pounding of the waterfall over his body, and some strange sensation that he was getting lighter, like he'd felt when he'd found the Troll Tree.

Albert stretched his arms out, then his fingers, reaching for a Tile on the bottom of the pool. At first he felt only smooth stone, no Tiles. He swam left and right, feeling for a Tile. There had to be hundreds under here, right? But nothing came up. He surfaced, took a gulp of air, and went back under.

Finally, as he began to feel like he would never find a Tile, Albert's fingers closed over something warm and solid. There was a shock that ran through his body, making him feel hot and cold all at once.

Albert readied himself for the power. Maybe he'd fly right out of the lake! But as soon as the sensation had come, it fizzled away.

He surfaced, gasping for air, and held his Tile up.

Albert made his way over to the edge of the water. He was about to hand his Tile over to his dad when he realized something. His Tile wasn't like the others.

Instead of pure white, with a black symbol, it was exactly the opposite: a shiny black Tile with a white symbol on one side. The symbol was a perfect circle. In the middle of the circle was a horizontal line, with a triangle hanging off each end.

"Um . . . Is it supposed to be this color?" Albert asked. He held it up, waiting for his dad to tell him that he'd gotten some incredible power. Mind reading. Mind *control.* Flying. All three!

Professor Flynn stared at Albert with an emotionless expression. He strode forward slowly, and plucked the Tile from Albert's outstretched palm.

"What's it mean?" Albert asked. "It's something cool, right? I can feel it!"

"Why is his Tile different?" Leroy asked, furrowing his brow. "I saw at least seven hundred thirty-six Tiles at the bottom of the pool. None of them were black."

"I guess your photographic memory has kicked in," Birdie said to Leroy. Then she leaned forward, trying to get a good look at Albert's Tile. "It looks like a scale, doesn't it?"

"I don't . . ." Professor Flynn flipped the Tile round and round. His face was blank. Empty. "I've never seen the black Tile before, but I have heard legend of its existence."

"*The* black Tile?" Albert asked. "You mean there's only one?"

Professor Flynn paced back and forth, chewing on his bottom lip.

"I'm sorry, Albert. I don't know what powers it brings with it. You'll have to discover that for yourself. You're a Balance Keeper now. You'll unlock its mysteries; I have no doubt."

But Albert saw a shadow cast over his dad's face, as if he worried about the black Tile and what it might foreshadow.

Trey arrived from wherever he'd gone. He looked inquisitively at the black Tile like the rest of them. He seemed not to know what to make of it, so he turned to Professor Flynn.

"The accommodations are ready for them now."

Professor Flynn stared out at the waterfall, a crease lining his forehead. He kept turning the Tile round and round in his hand, lost in thought.

"Sir?" Trey said. "I said their quarters are ready. Sir?"

Professor Flynn's face cleared, his eyes lighting back up. He handed the Tile back to Albert.

Albert felt like he'd gone trick-or-treating on Halloween and gotten an apple instead of a fistful of candy. It was downright disappointing. His shoulders sank. "So I got . . . nothing?"

"Don't worry about it," Leroy said, nudging Albert. "Someone's gonna know what your Tile means. You'll see."

"Yeah, you'll probably be, like, the coolest Balance Keeper ever, Albert," Birdie chimed in. "I mean, besides me, of course."

Albert wasn't so sure, but he nodded anyway.

"Use these to hold your Tiles," Trey said, handing them each a strong black cord. "And keep your Tile always around your neck; never take it off. Your Tile provides special abilities for you and you alone, but you must keep it with you to feel its power helping you in the Core. Do you understand?"

Everyone nodded, and Albert, Birdie, and Leroy busied themselves stringing the cords through the holes in their Tiles.

"They are part of you now," Professor Flynn said as they worked. "And no one can ever use their power but you."

Albert was aware of his dad watching closely as he placed the Tile around his neck. He knew what his dad was wondering, because Albert was wondering it, too.

What could it mean?

CHAPTER 9

Cedarfell and Treefare

arnsworth was waiting when they left the Waterfall of Fate. As soon as he saw them, he turned and led the way, the light from his blue eyes flickering against the dark walls.

"That little dog likes to play follow-the-leader," Trey said. "And he's always the leader."

"I think he's cute," Birdie said.

Farnsworth wagged his tail as if he understood he was being talked about.

He led them across the Main Chamber of the Core, over the triangle bridge, and through a winding route of tunnels that Albert wasn't sure he'd be able to remember. "Down that tunnel is the Library. That's the place to be. Loads of action, and if you find the need to get in touch with home, you can always use the Phone Booth."

Albert smiled at that. He'd be able to check in on his mom at some point.

A group of men in hard hats passed by them, holding blueprints on long, copper scrolls.

"Maintenance men," Trey noted. "There are lots of odd jobs in the Core: cleanup duty, the cooking staff, the nurses in the Infirmary. Loads more. We all work together to run this place."

The tunnels twisted and turned, this way and that way, until Albert felt like his brain had just gone on a roller-coaster ride. "I'm definitely going to get lost in this place."

Leroy grinned and slapped Albert on the back. "Two left turns, a right turn, duck and walk for thirty-seven seconds, stand up, and go right past the giant statue of some old wart-faced dude."

"I'm sticking with you from now on," Albert said to Leroy. "That Synapse Tile is really working."

"Yeah, just don't do something embarrassing around Leroy," Birdie said. "He'll never let you forget it!" Birdie punched Leroy in the shoulder and suddenly they were all hitting one another playfully as they made their way down the hallway.

There were torches everywhere, casting a pale blue glow throughout the Core as they walked. Every so often, the tunnels would open wide into mouths of space, as if they were yawning. There were statues of strange creatures—a rabbit with four antlers on its head, a monkey with six arms. The strangest of these statues had the body of a round man and the face of a toad.

"Frog man makes me nervous," Leroy said as they passed by.

"Wait until you meet him in person," Trey replied, staring up at the strange statue. "He's a crafty one. Hard to predict."

"You mean that thing is for real?" Albert asked, glancing around as if a living, croaking version of the statue might jump out from a hiding place in the shadows.

Trey didn't answer as they moved on, passing a room full of long rows of tables. A man no taller than Albert's thigh stood near an old oak desk at the front, polishing a glowing, silver sword.

"That's Professor Bigglesby." Trey nodded into the room. "A dwarf born and raised in the Core over one hundred fifty years ago. He's still an exceptional fighter. One day you'll learn a lot from him."

The old Professor turned in their direction and locked his eyes on Albert's black Tile. His head tilted sideways briefly, but he belied no emotion as Albert slipped past the open door.

The encounter gave Albert pause—somehow he didn't think he should trust Professor Bigglesby.

Trey led them up a steep incline in one of the tunnels,

where a glowing, purple moss clung to the low ceiling, flickering like fire. "You'd be smart not to touch that," he warned as Leroy reached out. It was too late. Leroy's hand glided along the softness as if it was doing him no harm, but then he pulled his hand away. His fingers expanded like balloons.

"Whoa," Leroy said. His face turned a sickly shade of green.

"That can't be good," Birdie added, staring at his fingers as they swelled to the size of tennis balls.

Trey kept walking through the maze of tunnels, but called over his shoulder, "Give it a good shake; usually does the trick."

Birdie snorted as Leroy shook his hand and his fingers deflated as fast as they had *in*flated.

They all laughed and rounded a corner, coming upon an old wooden door. It had the same glowing-hand imprint as the one that had let Albert into the Path Hider's domain.

"Albert and Leroy, you'll stay here," Trey said as he leaned against the door. "In Cedarfell."

"What's inside?" Albert asked.

"So many questions." Trey sighed. "New recruits are exhausting."

They stood, looking at the door to Cedarfell, and a new voice broke the silence.

"I see Miss Howell has arrived."

They turned to see who the strange, musical voice belonged to. It was a very tall woman, so tall she had to stoop in order to fit inside the tunnel. Her eyes were a cool blue, and her pale arms were covered in tattoos of Tile symbols. Looking down, Albert saw she wore sandals and that she only had four toes on each foot.

"Um, yes, that's me," Birdie said, taking a step back so she could get a better look at the strange woman. "I'm Birdie Howell."

"This is Professor Asante," Trey said. "She will escort you to where you'll sleep."

"Not that you'll have much time for lounging around Treefare," Professor Asante said.

"Treefare?" Birdie asked, but the professor said nothing.

Trey turned back to Albert and Leroy.

"Classes start tomorrow morning at the sixth chime. Follow everyone else; they'll show you the way."

Trey turned and headed back down the steep tunnel.

"Should we carry on, then, Birdie?" Professor Asante asked.

Birdie looked at Albert and Leroy. "Meet me by the rivers tomorrow?"

"Of course," Albert called after her, as she followed Professor Asante down the tunnel. "Good luck!"

"Well, here we go," Albert said.

Albert turned and placed his hand into the imprint

on the door. It swung open without a sound. Farnsworth scurried between his ankles and disappeared inside.

At first glance, Albert thought that maybe Trey had led them to the wrong place. This couldn't be a dormitory. It looked like the forest outside of Herman, except there were strange, bright red birds flying overhead, their color changing to orange and back every so often, and when he looked at the ceiling, there were brass pipes spitting steam. Something crashed in front of his feet and he jumped back.

It was an acorn the size of his head.

"Holy mega acorn!" Leroy screamed.

"Careful with those; they'll knock you out cold if they hit you just right," a voice said to Albert's left. He turned, and through the trees came the same boy he'd seen earlier, the one with the light-blond hair. On closer inspection, he was wearing a long-sleeve gray T-shirt with the word *Fury* on it. "First day's always the strangest. I saw you with your Apprentice earlier. You're the Flynn boy, aren't you? Got the same freckles as your dad."

"Uh, yeah," Albert said. "Is this the dormitory?"

"It's way better than the girls' dorms, if you ask me," the boy said. "I'm Jack. Second Term Balance Keeper, at your service. Come on, I'll show you guys the tents."

They followed Jack through the maze of trees until they came upon a campsite. But it was *way* cooler than any place Albert had ever camped. Big, white tents sat on the forest floor in between the trees. Some of the larger tents actually stood with trees poking right out of their middle, like the tents were built *around* the trees.

"So, I guess you two will be roomies," Jack said. He stopped before one of the tents.

Albert poked his head inside. "This is how camping should be. Leroy, look at this place!"

A lantern lit the inside, shedding light on two wooden beds that looked so comfortable Albert wanted to dive right in and burrow beneath the covers. Farnsworth was sitting right on top of one of the pillows, his blue eyes blinding. Beside him, a blue, long-sleeved shirt was folded neatly on top of the covers. Albert stepped inside and scooped up the shirt. It had the word *Hydra* on it. Albert slipped out of his old T-shirt and pulled the Hydra one over his head.

"Team Hydra," Leroy said, smiling at Albert. "It's a pretty sweet name. Has something to do with water, I think."

"Come on out, guys," Jack said from the door. "You can settle in later. Right now we're breaking open acorns!"

There were so many other boys in Cedarfell; Albert couldn't keep up as Jack introduced Leroy and Albert to all of them:

There was Peter, who wore a silver Fury team shirt like Jack's. Jack and Peter had another teammate, Venzee, a girl who dormed in Treefare with Birdie. They were

Second Term Balance Keepers.

Then there was Stan, who wore a green Sapphire shirt. His teammates were Robin and Henna, who also dormed in Treefare. Stan walked around like he owned Cedarfell, but then again, he was a Third Term Balance Keeper, so Albert supposed he had a right to act like he'd been there longer than most.

Heffe and Philip both wore red Terra team shirts. Winter was also their teammate. They were in their third term, too.

There was a boy with a big oil stain smudged across his face who worked in some place called the Steam Room. An older boy sat beside him, a big, fat, golden key around his neck. He worked in the Mailroom, the sort of place Albert definitely didn't want any part of.

Lastly, Jack pointed out a cluster of three boys, sharing an acorn together. Slink, Mo, and Hoyt wore orange Argon team shirts. They were tossing acorn shells across the dorm, seeing who could throw the farthest. They apparently didn't care that throwing the farthest sometimes meant throwing *into* someone else's tent.

Albert elbowed Jack. "Those guys third terms?"

"Nah," Jack replied. "Second terms, but they act like they own the place."

As they sat around a campfire someone had made, a large rabbit with antlers—like the statue they had seen—hopped by. It looked at them inquisitively, and then hopped away.

"Big antlers on that Jackalope," Jack said.

Leroy and Albert looked at each other and shrugged. They were getting used to seeing oddities like very large rabbits with antlers.

Someone smashed open a giant acorn, and they passed it around, drinking a strange, milky liquid that tasted like fizzy cream soda.

"You're the Flynn kid, right?" Albert turned and saw that it was one of the Argon boys—Hoyt, he thought.

He looked Albert up and down, a big fat sneer on his face.

"That's right," Albert said, feeling suddenly uncomfortable being the center of attention. *My dad must have been telling people about my arrival. I've never been noticed this much before! I'm not sure how I feel about this. . . .*

Hoyt paused a moment, looking at Albert as though he might be a threat.

"You're not so special."

"Whatever you say," Albert said, trying to keep his cool.

"What's up with this guy?" Leroy whispered into Albert's ear.

"I grew up here, and I've never seen a Tile like yours," Hoyt said, wiping milky fizz from his face as he passed the Acorn to Slink. "Your professor dad give it to you? Some kind of advantage?"

"My dad treats me like everyone else," Albert said, feeling the heat rise in his neck. "I picked this Tile myself, just like you picked yours."

"What's your power?"

Albert shifted in his seat nervously.

"I don't know. But I'm going to find out." Albert looked down at his black Tile and felt ashamed to have it hanging from his neck.

"You hear that, boys?" Hoyt said to the others. "Flynn's a dud!"

Some of them laughed nervously; a couple smiled. Slink and Mo nodded encouragingly at Hoyt. Obviously, they were a gang of three everyone else feared.

"Don't worry about Hoyt," Jack leaned in and whispered. "He's just jealous your Tile looks cooler than his does. And he's a Pure. They always have attitude."

Albert could guess what a Pure was without having to ask: someone who was born in the Core and had never seen the outside world.

"You got something to say, Jack?" Hoyt asked. "'Cause you know my Tile gives me some extra speed. You won't be able to outrun me if you start mouthing off."

"Nope, nothing at all, Hoyt. Just welcoming our new recruits."

Hoyt shook his head.

"Flameouts, more like it."

This produced a new round of awkward smiles from

everyone but Slink and Mo.

Leroy stood up unexpectedly and crossed the expanse between him and Hoyt.

"We don't mess around in Texas, and my buddy Albert here is from New York City. I think you'll find we can carry ourselves just fine."

After he got over his shock at Leroy's sudden bravado, Albert felt a wave of pride and joined him. Hoyt, Slink, and Mo got up, and suddenly Albert and Leroy were toe-to-toe with the three bullies.

"We'll see how confident you are when you start basic training," Hoyt said with a sneer on his face. "Only the best make it into the Realms, boys. And somehow, I'm not feeling too worried."

Leroy and Albert slowly backed up, returning to their seats. They both understood there would be nothing to gain from having a brawl on the first day. Albert didn't know what skills a Second Term Balance Keeper had, but if Hoyt was born here, surely he'd be some serious competition. Albert clutched his Tile and promised to himself that he'd figure it out, and soon.

"Thanks for standing up to that jerk," Albert said to Leroy when things quieted down.

"We're teammates." Leroy shrugged. "We've gotta stick together."

"I guess we do," said Albert. He could tell Leroy really meant it.

They sat at the fireside for the next hour, learning as much about the Core as they could. Classes would start the next day, as well as real training, which would be a chance for Albert to figure out what his power was. Jack told them that the professors were the greatest and strongest of all Balance Keepers. There was a woman the size of a small tree who'd teach them about Core creatures.

"We met her in the tunnels," Albert said. "Professor Asante, right?"

"That's her!" Peter said. "And Professor Hagglesworth's eyes change color depending on his mood. It's pretty cool, but a little scary."

As the fire grew warmer, Albert very nearly fell asleep. The strange birds overhead had begun to sing a slow song, which reminded him of a soft summer day. His eyelids were just about to slip closed when the room around him erupted into noise. Ten chimes, so loud they rumbled his bones.

"Lights out, boys!" Stan yelled. He had a crooked tooth and a strange, deep voice.

"Finally." Leroy yawned as everyone headed for their tents. "I'm going to pass out the second my head hits the pillow."

Albert nodded as they slipped through the flap of their tent. He turned, ready to tie the flaps together with the leather cords that dangled from each side.

Across the trees, he could see Hoyt and his two pals looking in his direction, but Albert still felt a huge smile spread across his face. He had a friend, maybe more than one, for the first time in his life, and a magical dog that was waiting for him to crawl into bed. He was someplace miles under the surface of the earth, and down here, his dad was a really cool, powerful dude.

He couldn't wait to see what else the Core had in store for him.

CHAPTER 10

The Training Pit

When he awoke the next morning, Albert didn't hear any honking cars or the blaring of the TV. There was no little sister batting his face with her stuffed unicorn; no Mom telling him to get busy with homework or chores. Instead Albert heard the sound of birds in the trees, and watched as whatever light source Cedarfell was lit by grew brighter against the ceiling of the cloth tent.

"Man, I thought you'd never wake up," Leroy said, poking his head through the entry of the tent. Farnsworth followed him in, a big rib bone dangling from his tiny mouth.

Leroy had a plate so full of food it reminded Albert of the piles of mail in the dead letter office.

"How big is your stomach?" Albert asked, seeing the mounds of pancakes covered in powdered sugar, scrambled eggs, and some delicious-looking sausage that was making Albert's mouth water.

"Enormous, I guess." Leroy shrugged. "This is my second plate." He folded a whole pancake in half and shoved it into his mouth.

Albert laughed and slipped outside the tent, where he found a long wooden table completely covered in piles of food. He rushed forward, filled a plate *almost* as full as Leroy's, and stuffed his face like he was a homeless dog that hadn't eaten in days.

By the time all the boys had eaten, the table was only half-empty. Hoyt and his cronies stood by their tent, looking surly and secretive as ever. When Hoyt noticed Albert watching, he pointed at his blue shirt.

"Ready for the Competitions today, Flynn? You and your team are up against mine. I hope you're prepared for pain!"

Albert's heart sank.

"No worries," Leroy said, slapping Albert on the back. "We got this. And besides, we have Birdie on our team. Her confidence sort of scares me."

There was still powdered sugar caked on Leroy's face, so it was a little hard to take him seriously as he added: "I bet your Tile gives you superstrength or something. You'll see."

Overhead, the chimes started to sound. Six times, loud enough to shake the floor beneath Albert's feet. An acorn plummeted from a nearby tree and broke open beside Leroy. He scooped it up and chugged down the sweet liquid pouring out.

"You ready, Hydra?" Jack asked, motioning for Albert and Leroy to follow. "First day's always the hardest, but you'll get the hang of it. You'll go to the Simulator every day. The classroom hours are only a few times a week, but don't worry, they're not as boring as they sound."

They left Cedarfell behind and set out into the halls of the Core. It seemed as if the tunnels they took were twisting different directions than they had the previous night, and before Leroy and Albert knew what had happened, all the other boys had scattered down different tunnels. Albert reached into his pocket and pulled out his Core Compass.

"Main Chamber of the Core," Albert said.

The arrow inside the compass spun on his palm, pointing ahead.

"We don't need that thing for this," Leroy said. "I got this place wired."

And it was true; Leroy had memorized how they'd gotten to Cedarfell. Even Albert's Core Compass couldn't compete with Leroy's mad mental skills.

"Guys! Over here!" Birdie waved from the center of one of the bridges as Albert and Leroy arrived in the

Main Chamber. Farnsworth barked and ran for her, his little tail wagging like a propeller.

"Treefare is *sooo* amazing," Birdie said when Albert and Leroy joined her. "It's like being inside of a magic forest. There's this fog on the ground that makes it warm for our feet, and big tents and great food and—"

Trey's miniature blue dragon, Alfin, came soaring across the Lobby, and Birdie stopped short. Alfin landed on Albert's shoulder, as weightless as a feather.

"Hey, little guy," Albert said, nervous it might bite him in the ear. "How's it going?"

The dragon leaned forward and spoke in a papery, soft voice. Albert jumped at the sound. *You gotta be kidding me. This thing talks?*

"Follow me, Albert-human," it said. "Alfin is a *girl*, not a boy. I must deliver the Albert-package and friends to Trey-master."

Alfin took flight, doing a somersault in midair before zipping off into the nearest tunnel.

Albert, Birdie, and Leroy took chase, struggling to keep up as they followed Alfin down the tunnel. Instead of twisting and curving in every direction, the tunnel led them straight down, deeper and deeper into the Core. The air grew cooler. Goose bumps rose on Albert's arms.

"Do you think Alfin is taking us to our first training day?" Birdie asked. Her pink-and-blond ponytail swayed across the tops of her shoulders. "Venzee, one of the girls in Cedarfell, said the simulations are intense."

"That's what we heard, too," Leroy said. "Just look out for Hoyt. The guy's got a target on Albert's back."

When they'd run so far down the tunnel that Albert was starting to wonder if it would ever end, they came upon Trey. Alfin sat on his shoulder, looking very proud of herself for delivering the Albert-package.

"Ah, I see you three found your uniforms," Trey said, smiling at them as Albert, Leroy, and Birdie stopped before him. They were standing before a copper-colored door set in the stone wall. "Did you enjoy your new quarters?"

"Cedarfell is excellent," Leroy said. "Especially the food."

"Treefare is even better," Birdie added.

"You've never even *been* to Cedarfell," Leroy protested.

"Yeah, but I've been to Treefare, and I'm telling you, it's better!" Birdie crossed her arms and stuck out her hip. Albert, realizing these two were probably going to be bickering like this a lot, got in the middle of them.

"They're both really cool, okay, guys?"

Birdie huffed, and Leroy's face reddened, just a bit. He straightened his glasses.

Trey smiled and nodded at Albert.

"Training starts at once. This way, quickly, quickly."

He turned and pulled a lever embedded in the stone

wall. Steam began to pour out around the edges of the copper door.

When the door opened and they'd passed through, Albert's eyes went as wide as the moon. Standing before them was a cave larger than *any* he'd seen so far. It went up, up, up, into the ceiling, past where the light from Farnsworth's eyes could reach. Waterfalls cascaded down from several openings in the rocky walls, glittering like the water was full of falling stars.

There was a winding stone bridge that sloped back and forth from one side of the cave to the other, crisscrossing until it stopped high in the air over Albert's head. At the end of the path was a floating orange platform, casting off a faint glow.

Leroy gulped. "That bridge doesn't have any railings."

"I must warn you to tread carefully," Trey said, nodding. "Let's carry on, shall we?"

"I want to go first!" Birdie said. "Farnsworth, lead the way!"

Farnsworth yipped and ran onto the path, his blue beams cutting through steam that poured out from different places. They walked higher and higher. Every so often, Albert stopped and looked down. Heights didn't scare him at all. Instead, they made him feel alive, like he was king of the world, looking down into darkness. The path led them through the middle of two waterfalls, one on each side, parted like curtains. Birdie ran her fingers through the water.

By the time they made it to the orange platform at the very top, Albert was very nearly out of breath—they all were—but he smiled as he looked over the edge. The path looked like a tangled spiderweb from above.

"Oh man, that was a rush," Albert said.

"It's *beautiful* up here." Birdie sighed. "I just adore this place."

"I'll never understand you two." Leroy came up behind Albert. His face was as green as fresh broccoli. He leaned his head against the cool cave wall. "I counted three thousand seven hundred eighty-nine ways to fall and die back there. Why couldn't my Tile have given me flying powers? This mental situation is giving me an anxiety attack."

Just then, the platform began to move, floating upward so fast that the sweat Albert had worked up in the climb quickly evaporated even before the platform had stopped at another copper-colored entry. It couldn't be called a door, not really. It was more like a porthole cover, complete with a spinning wheel in the center.

"Are you ready?" Trey asked, turning to the trio. He had a look of wonder on his face, like even though he'd been through the entrance a thousand times, he still couldn't wait to go back inside and see what was behind it.

"Let's do this," Albert said.

Trey spun the wheel and then pushed the copper porthole cover open.

"Welcome to the Pit." Trey beamed, moving aside so Albert, Leroy, and Birdie could look down.

The Pit was exactly like its name: a colossal circular space that sank far into the ground. Around the top there was a ring of seats where a small scattering of people sat, waiting for the action to start.

It occurred to Albert that what stood before him was a lot like the video games he'd played all his life—except that this time he wasn't going to be hiding behind a controller. He was going to *be* the character in the game. The thought made his heart beat fast.

The Pit was a chasm as deep as the one they'd just come from, but instead of waterfalls, there were vine-like cables hanging from the ceiling, and instead of a winding pathway, there were rings of blue fire floating every few feet. There were also a few of the familiar orange platforms, and a black bubble that bounced off the walls like a giant balloon, knocking a boy off course as he tried to swing from cable to cable. It was Hoyt, Albert realized, and his teammates were down there with him. One of the guys, Slink, climbed up a cable with effortless grace, then swung from it, flipped through a ring of blue fire, and grabbed on to another cable. The third boy, Mo, was busy trying to kick the black bubble away from Hoyt.

"Professor Flynn already told you you'll be training for

Calderon this term," Trey began. "What you see before you is a simulation of some of the things you might encounter if the Calderon Realm goes out of Balance." Trey pointed down below. "The cables represent vines. The bubble represents a King Firefly, but here we call it the Melatrix. And the fire is self-explanatory."

Leroy readjusted his baseball cap on his head. "How much fire is in the Calderon Realm?"

"I bet you there's lava, too! I bet I could probably swim in it!" Birdie said.

Leroy whined, and Albert patted him on the back.

"Well, usually, there isn't much fire," Trey said. "But there are many Calderon creatures that breathe fire, and we've seen that get out of hand on various occasions, depending on what's causing the Imbalance in the Realm."

"Great," Leroy said, rolling his eyes. "Just great."

"And are the King Fireflies always big bullies like that?" Birdie asked, a look of concern on her face. "The fireflies back in Oregon can be a little annoying, but that Melatrix just about took off that boy's head."

"Professor Flynn will get to that in a moment," Trey replied.

"When do we start?" Albert asked. He wanted to begin now, dive in and finally do something dangerous. More importantly, he wanted to test out his Tile.

"In a few minutes. Professor Flynn and the Calderon

First Unit should be arriving any moment to show you how everything works."

"My *dad* is going to teach us how to navigate this thing?" Albert asked. "No way."

Just then, Professor Flynn walked down a steep flight of stairs from the viewing area. He was wearing his usual green professor's coat, the fabric sparkling like polished emeralds, and there were three people behind him. When he arrived next to Albert and the rest, he didn't waste any time on formalities.

"You are the Hydra training unit, who will train for the Calderon Realm this term," Professor Flynn began. He moved aside and introduced the three people standing behind him. "This is the Calderon First Unit: Grey, Aria, and Terran. Grey here is the Core's best weapons handler, Aria is a talented Wind Tamer, and Terran is Professor Asante's granddaughter. Terran and I share the same power. These three earned their spot as Calderon First Unit after successfully completing training for all three Realms. And if I remember correctly, they earned more points in these simulations than any training unit had earned in decades. Am I right?"

"Yes, sir," the three teammates said together.

More than any other team in decades? Geez, Albert thought. *No pressure or anything . . .*

Professor Flynn continued. "Normally, since you're the First Term Calderon training unit, you would get some attention from these three. Unfortunately, we've had some recent . . . abnormalities in the Calderon Realm that Grey, Aria, and Terran have been investigating, specifically that the King Fireflies have been acting uncharacteristically antagonistic. Their strange behavior could be a sign of a greater Imbalance in the Realm, and if that's the case, the world above might be in danger. So the First Unit might be busy while you train, but I did want you to meet them."

Grey stepped forward, pushing back a mop of black hair on his head. He had obviously been named for his eyes, for they were the brightest shade of gray Albert had ever seen. He looked positively wolfish.

"Don't let the Pit scare you," Grey said. "You're going to get banged up; that's normal. Just stay focused; don't let your attention drift. The best competitors are those who stay alert and miss nothing. Above all, give it everything you've got. The Pit will make you pay if you're lazy."

"Don't let *Grey* scare you," Aria said, nudging him on the shoulder with a rueful smile. She had fiery red hair and stood almost as tall as Leroy. "We're just happy to have a training unit to impart our wisdom to. You three will do well; I'm sure of it."

"And don't forget," Terran added, tightening her dark ponytail in a very Birdie-like way, "you've got an entire world of secrets to uncover down here. Have some fun, Hydra!"

They all watched as the First Unit left the same way Albert and his friends had just come. Albert was excited to have met them, even if it had been too brief. They all walked with their heads held high, and just knowing that the three of them had actually been *inside* of a Realm made Albert want to be just like them. One day, maybe he, too, would be walking past a team in training, heading into a Realm to save the world. His dad's voice broke him out of his daydreaming.

"What you learn in the simulations will carry over into what you might face in the Realms. The simulations are different depending on the day, since the Realms themselves are constantly evolving. As soon as a course is completed, it will morph into another set of obstacles. Your challenge today is to reach the top of the Pit." Professor Flynn pointed to the very top of the ceiling overhead, where a silver bell hung from a looming stalactite.

"That's it?" Birdie exclaimed. "Sounds easy to me. Can't we add in some fire?"

"Or maybe we could do something nice and calm, like . . . read some books, or something?" Leroy groaned.

Albert glanced back and forth between his two friends, struck by how different they were.

Professor Flynn chose to ignore the comments and went on. "Beat the obstacles; ring the bell. Normally your team would be competing head-on against another

team at the same time—Argon and Ecco are the second-
and third-term teams training in Calderon with you—
but the first day is for getting the hang of things, so you'll
compete separately. The goal right now is to learn to start
functioning as a team and getting the job done quickly.
Those are of the utmost importance."

Work together; complete the task quickly. Got it, Albert
thought.

"That said," Professor Flynn continued, "today your
score will be tallied against Argon's. You'll see both
teams' points on our Pit Leaderboard."

Professor Flynn held out his hand, motioning for the
trio to look down into the Pit. There, on the side of the
rounded walls, was a glowing leaderboard. It looked
sort of like the kind that Albert saw when he watched
football games on TV, but instead of numbers, there were
blue balls of flames tallying the score. The left side was
Argon—Hoyt, Slink, and Mo. As the three boys in the Pit
got closer to the top, another blue ball of flames appeared,
stacking itself on top of the others. More points for Hoyt
and his cronies.

"We're going to beat these punks," Birdie said. She
cracked her knuckles and leaned forward, as if she
couldn't wait to climb into the Pit and prove herself.

Professor Flynn continued. "Between Hydra and
Argon, whichever team has the most points at the end
of the day will win a prize. Yours and the eight other

training units' scores are also tallied on the Main Leaderboard, which Trey maintains. If the need arises, whichever team has the most points *might* be called upon to enter a Realm behind the First Unit."

There was a clang just as he finished speaking. Albert looked up, guessing where the sound had come from. Sure enough, Hoyt was at the top, hanging one-handed from a cable with a giant sneer on his face. His teammates hooted and hollered along with the small gathering that sat watching around the top of the Pit. A moment later, the entire simulation went still. The cables hung slack, the blue flames fizzled away, and the Melatrix popped with a shower of sparks. The members of Argon started making their way to one of the orange platforms.

"Under seven minutes," Trey shouted over the cheers. "That's brilliant, boys! Absolutely brilliant!"

Albert groaned. "Seven minutes? How is that even possible?"

"The chances of that are pretty high, actually, if you do everything the right way," Leroy said.

"*Not now*, whiz kid," Birdie said, silencing him.

The orange platform carried Team Argon up and out of the Pit, and suddenly Albert, Leroy, and Birdie were face-to-face with Hoyt and his team.

"Careful down there, Hydra," Hoyt said as he walked by. "With that useless Tile Flynn's got, you three will probably be down there all day. You'll probably set a new record for longest Pit time *ever.*"

"Don't listen to him, guys," Albert said. He boarded the platform beside his teammates. Trey blew a whistle, and the platform started down into the depths of the Pit. When they reached the bottom, they found that while the floor looked like normal cave ground, it had a bouncy feeling, like a trampoline.

Albert tried a cannonball, just to test it out. Sure enough, when he landed on the floor, he bounced up a few feet before settling back down again.

Man! This is going to be fun! A sound caught his attention and he looked up.

Professor Flynn glided down to them in a rusted metal cage. He spoke into what looked like a curled animal horn, and it magnified his voice throughout the Pit like a microphone.

"All right, team. The rules are simple. There *are* no rules." Professor Flynn had a strange gleam in his eye. It made him look ten years younger.

"As I said before, today's simulation goal is simple. One of you has to reach the top and hit the bell. If you do it in less than seven minutes, you win leaderboard for the day. Be prepared for me to intervene in the challenges. Sometimes these alterations may seem drastic, but they're designed to help you think on your feet. We're training to save the entire *world* here, team! Do your best."

Just the mention of saving the planet made Albert's

stomach buzz with excitement. He was *dying* to start and see what it was all about.

"What's the prize for the winner each day?" Birdie asked, looking up at Professor Flynn.

"Copper Medallions," Professor Flynn answered, speaking into the giant horn. "So you can purchase Realm items from the Core Canteen."

Albert noticed Hoyt's smug face looking down at them from above; Hoyt was already assuming his team would win the Medallions for the day. Albert was desperate to prove him wrong.

"Everyone ready now? Let's begin." Professor Flynn must have pressed a button—the cage rose halfway to the top of the Pit.

"Wait!" Albert yelled upward. "How do we even know what to do?"

"Just go with it!" Professor Flynn yelled back. "Learn by *doing*. Trey? Ready the Pit!"

Overhead, Trey busied himself setting features in the simulation on a control panel Albert and his friends couldn't see from where they stood. Then Trey blew a silver whistle and the Pit came to life.

The black cables began to shake like writhing snakes. The circles of blue flame ignited, hovering high in the air over Albert, Leroy, and Birdie. The Melatrix appeared, as big as a recliner, bouncing back and forth from the Pit walls like it was eager to shove them off their course.

"What do we do?" Leroy asked. He looked to Albert for an answer.

Albert shrugged. "I guess we dive in, like my dad said."

He took a step forward, to where one of the cables trembled in front of him. When he reached out and wrapped his fingers around the cable, it seemed to get angry, shaking harder like it wanted Albert to let go. But Albert started to climb it anyway, one hand over the other. Beside him, Birdie and Leroy began the climb on writhing cables, too. At first, they seemed to make good time. It was hard work, but not nearly as hard as it would have been up in the rest of the world above. For some reason, Albert felt like he weighed five pounds instead of eighty-seven. If he wanted to, he probably could've let go and bounced all the way back to Herman.

"I feel light as air!" Albert called out.

Leroy, whose face was covered in a sheen of sweat, called out from a nearby cable. "I think I ate too many pancakes this morning, because I do *not* feel light as air, Albert!"

"Me either!" Birdie cried out, though that didn't stop her.

She climbed past Albert and Leroy in a flash, almost as fast as Hoyt had done.

Birdie was nearly halfway to the silver bell at the top when the Melatrix came rising out of the depths of the Pit. It was heading straight toward her.

"Look out!" Albert shouted. His grip loosened on the cable and he slid down a few feet as he tried to kick the Melatrix, but it was too quick as it passed. The Melatrix avoided his feet like it had a mind of its own. It shot past Albert and increased its speed. Then it hit Birdie right in the back with a loud *smack!* Her hands weren't strong enough to hold on. She screamed, and Albert and Leroy watched, helpless from their cables, as Birdie tumbled through the air toward the ground.

When her body crashed into the floor, it seemed to suck her in for a moment, like the ground was inhaling. When it spit her back out, Birdie shot upward, and managed to grab ahold of Leroy's cable.

"That was awesome!" She grinned. But when Hoyt and his team started laughing, Birdie's face grew bright red.

"Don't worry about them, Birdie," Leroy said. "Just do what you've been doing."

"Nice try at the deflection, Albert," Professor Flynn spoke from his platform. "But the Melatrix represents a crazed King Firefly, and here's a hint: Kings are no fools. You have to trick them. Another thing—always prepare for the worst. A surprise attack could come at any moment!"

"Let's try this again," Albert said. He climbed higher, looking upward at the silver bell. "Leroy! What's the best way to reach the top?"

"Well, you're on the cable with the least amount of danger right now!" Leroy said. He looked shocked that he'd known the answer, but it had to be his Tile, working its magic as he looked all around the Pit.

"Okay! Here goes nothing!" Albert said. He wanted to win *so* badly that he almost didn't see Professor Flynn move his cage forward so fast that it sliced through Albert's cable. The cable instantly went slack, and Albert was falling toward the floor.

"Jump!" people screamed from overhead, cheering him on.

It was like instinct. Albert felt his hands take over on their own, like something was telling them what to do. He let go of his useless cable without thinking. His eyes closed, and for some reason, he pictured Spider-Man, swinging from his web over New York City. Albert felt like he needed to stretch his arms a little to the left, so he did. That's when he felt something skim his fingertips. He opened his eyes and closed his hands around a cable just in time.

"Well done!" Professor Flynn said. "Quick reflexes, Albert! Very impressive!"

Albert was shocked. It was like something inside of him *knew* what to do. Was it the power of his Tile?

"That was wicked!" Leroy shouted from across the Pit.

The Melatrix was at Leroy's back, trying to knock him from his spot on the cable. Albert turned just in time to see Birdie scurry up from below, wiggle off one of her boots, and launch it at the Melatrix.

"Get away from my teammate!" she warned. The second the shoe hit the Melatrix, the Melatrix bounced away and started floating in circles around them, like it was a shark trying to think of another way to come at them. Albert couldn't help but laugh at her ferocity.

"A surprise attack!" Professor Flynn shouted. "That's the spirit, Birdie! That's how it's done!"

Birdie cheered as Leroy started to climb higher. Farnsworth yipped from the sidelines and snapped at the Melatrix as it bounced by. Albert looked around for what to do next. If Leroy was climbing, he should do his best to keep the Melatrix away from him.

If he could just get to that next vine, he could smack the Melatrix off course. But to get to the next vine, Albert would have to swing through a ring of fire. It hovered a few feet above him between two cables, a big, wide mouth of blue flames. His arms were exhausted. His hands were burning from gripping the cables so tight, but he readied himself to swing.

"Yes, Albert! Try the fire!" Professor Flynn ordered.

Albert knew he couldn't just swing from one cable to the next—who was to say these blue flames were cold like the rest had been so far?

"Rock back and forth!" Birdie said from below. She'd managed to swing from one cable to another. Albert watched Leroy fall behind her. His foot hit Birdie's hands on the way down, and they both crashed into the Pit floor together.

The two of them started arguing like Albert's siblings, forgetting the simulation around them for a moment.

Albert was on his own. *Come on, Tile,* he thought. *Work some magic for me here!*

He started swinging the cable like Birdie had advised, back and forth, until he had some good momentum going. When he felt like he was ready to go for it, he swung backward one more time, away from the blue ring.

On the forward swing, he let go, stretching his body like Superman, so he could squeeze through the center of the ring untouched.

He was almost there, almost about to sail through when, *SMACK!*

The Melatrix hit him square in the face.

Albert tumbled through the air and landed on the floor of the Pit. He could hear Hoyt's team laughing and jeering at him from above.

The floor sucked Albert down and then spit him back out. He tried to grab a cable on the bounce back up, but his hands were too sweaty. He fell again and bounced back up, and by now, Leroy had scurried up a vine. He grabbed ahold of Albert's arm as he flew upward.

They hung from a cable like two monkeys on a tree branch.

"Thanks, dude," Albert said.

"No problem," Leroy groaned. "Now grab on. My arm's about to pull out of its socket."

In the next hour, Leroy and the Melatrix went head-to-head seven times (Leroy lost six), Birdie got a bloody nose from Leroy's foot slipping on a cable and kicking her in the face, and Albert caught his shirt on fire from the blue flames, which turned out to not be cool after all. The possible-Tile-magic-event didn't happen for Albert. Instead, things got increasingly worse.

The entire Argon team finally left, shaking their heads. In fact, it seemed everyone who had been watching grew tired of their mistakes and went off to do other things in the Core.

Just when Albert was about to die from embarrassment, Trey blew his silver whistle, and the Pit shut itself down. The cables went slack, the Melatrix popped again, and the fire rings went out.

As the trio slid from their cables down to the spongy floor, Albert saw Farnsworth's eye lanterns go out. Even *he* was disheartened from the mess they'd made of the day.

"That was horrible," Leroy said, collapsing onto his back on the Pit floor. "That Melatrix had a serious problem with me."

"My nose hurts," Birdie groaned from his right. (It came out like, "By dose hurzz.")

"Useless Tile." Albert sighed.

Professor Flynn motored down to them in his floating cage. He pulled to a stop and parked just above Albert's head.

"Don't let today's obstacles get you down," he said. "Everyone messes up a few times on their first day. Tomorrow, you'll be ten times better. And the challenge really begins once Argon gets in there with you."

At the mention of Hoyt's team, the three of them groaned. Leroy muttered something about his mom's homemade spaghetti.

"Get to your feet and brush yourselves off," Professor Flynn said. "Trey will escort you to Lake Hall for some lunch. Core food will make everything better, especially the pecan pastries. I love those in particular." Then he reached into his pocket, pulled out three Medallions, and turned to Trey. "I hesitate to even give these to Argon, since they didn't find it suitable to stay and support their new Balance Keeper comrades, but they did win them. Make sure they get them."

"Yes, sir," Trey said, and pocketed the Medallions.

Then Professor Flynn pressed a button on his cage and moved up and away, leaving Albert, Birdie, and Leroy to lie in their misery.

"That was . . . ," Albert started.

"Totally *not* Medallion-worthy," Birdie finished for him.

"Food," Leroy whimpered. "I . . . need . . . food."

Trey blew his whistle. Their orange platform sank down to greet them. As they stumbled on and soared away to the top of the Pit, Albert couldn't keep his mind off one thing.

For a moment there, it seemed like his Tile had done something for him. It was like it took over and made him a Core master for a few seconds, and then it had fizzled out.

And if he could figure out *how* to access that power, and exactly *what* that power was, his team might have a chance.

CHAPTER 11

Lake Hall

Trey led the trio through the tunnels and out into the Main Chamber.

"Don't worry too much," he said. "Like Professor Flynn said, it gets easier."

"It better," Albert said. "Or we're in big trouble."

"Everyone's first day is tough. But I assure you, once you three learn to work as a team, the magic will begin to happen."

"Let's hope so," Albert said.

Leroy and Birdie were so exhausted, they hardly spoke a word. Even Farnsworth looked tired, the glow of his eyes faded to a soft and sleepy sky blue. They parted ways to get cleaned up in Treefare and Cedarfell, and hoped food would improve their moods.

Birdie and Trey were waiting for Leroy and Albert outside Cedarfell when they reappeared a half hour later. Birdie's ponytail had its usual curl back, and there was a big smile on her face.

"Everyone back to normal?" Trey asked. They all nodded their heads and followed him through the tunnel, Farnsworth and Alfin leading the way.

Lake Hall was a five-minute walk through the Core. They marched down a set of winding stone steps that looked like they belonged in a dungeon. At the bottom of the stairs a wide, brightly lit cave opened up before them. The first thing Albert noticed was a glass window that spanned one side of the cave. Magma flowed behind the glass in swirls of blazing orange and red.

"Is that . . . ," Birdie started to ask, with her mouth hanging open.

"Magma from the earth's core," Trey said, matter-of-factly. "Scientists don't have their information about the Core *all* wrong. We just let them find what we want them to. The Path Hider is clever when it comes to dealing with those in the world above. Not to worry. The glass hasn't shattered or melted in a thousand years."

He led them down a final couple of steps to the ground level of the cave, where a huge lake spread out before them. There were numerous floating docks on the surface of the water, each with a circular table sitting on top. The other Balance Keepers, in their colorful team shirts, sat at high-backed chairs around the tables, talking and laughing. The Core workers sat at other tables, chattering away like old friends. Some of them were adults; some were children even younger than Albert. The most ornate table, a carved wooden one off to the right, held the four Professors and their Apprentices. To the far left, there was a dock without a table. Instead, golden bowls lined its edges. Some of the companion creatures, now including Farnsworth and Alfin, were there slurping food from their bowls. Trey talked as he led the trio to the edge of the lake.

"Take a turtle and go to your table. It's the one closest to the window and the stage, with some of the other young Balance Keepers."

"Aw, man, I was hoping we'd get to swim across." Birdie sighed.

But Albert had something else on his mind. "Wait a second. . . . Did you just say, *Take a turtle*?"

Leroy chimed in. "Did you just say, *Closest to the window*? Where the lava might bust through?"

Trey nodded. "We can't have you all wet while you eat, can we? And Leroy, stop worrying. You'll be fine."

Trey bent down to the water and touched it with his fingertip. Several bumps appeared on the surface of the water, moving toward them. As Albert looked closer, he realized they were four turtles the size of small boulders, with glittering green shells.

Trey stepped onto the first turtle to arrive, and it bobbed softly on the water's surface. Its head turned sideways and an ancient eye blinked at Trey. Albert, Birdie, and Leroy followed suit, and before they knew it, the turtles were swimming, taking them to their tables. The ride was surprisingly smooth, like standing on a sliding walkway at an airport.

"Turtles, I am a fan. You're excellent swimmers," Birdie said as hers reached the dock. She hopped off and the turtle dove, disappearing into the deep.

When Albert and Leroy arrived, they took their places at the last empty chairs of the table. There were fifteen other kids sitting with them, eight boys and seven girls. Hoyt and his two teammates were among the group. It seemed like Albert couldn't get away from these guys.

"Yo, Flynn. I thought you'd still be in the Pit trying to make it through the easiest simulation *ever.*"

"Cool it, Hoyt," someone said behind Albert. He turned around, and was surprised to see Aria, the First Unit girl. Grey and Terran arrived beside her on their turtles. The three of them stepped off onto the floating dock and took their seats beside Albert, Birdie, and Leroy. The First Unit was sitting with *them*? Albert felt a wave of pride.

Aria rolled her eyes at Hoyt again, who was still snickering across the table.

"You're just jealous because Albert doesn't have a pea brain, like you," Birdie said, a look of sheer determination on her face. Hoyt's face went as red as a candied apple.

"He's not a Pure," Hoyt shot back. "None of them are. If I were the First Unit, I wouldn't be so keen on having these duds as my trainees."

"I'd watch what you say about us, Hoyt," Grey quipped, not missing a beat. "In the end, we're all in this together. And don't forget that Aria, Terran, and I report directly to Professor Flynn."

"And if you don't watch it, I'll tell Greymark to pay you a visit," Terran said. She pointed at the companion dock, where a massive gray wolf with yellow eyes gnawed on a bone the size of Hoyt's entire body.

"Whatever," Hoyt mumbled.

Albert and Leroy exchanged satisfied glances.

This is as good as it gets, Albert thought. *The First Unit, standing up for me and my team? I'm starting to really like this place.*

Hoyt and his boys shook their heads and went into their own private conversation. They were on the far side of the large table, so Albert and his friends could speak quietly and not be heard.

"Thanks," Albert said to Terran and Grey. Then he leaned past Birdie to shake Aria's hand. She had skin like a china doll, and her eyes were as green as emeralds.

"Hoyt has a crush on Aria," Terran explained. "He saw her win the Pit Races last year and hasn't stopped teasing-slash-flirting with her since."

"I'd like to show him one of my ninja moves. Or two. Or three," Leroy said, bunching up his fists.

Aria burst into laughter. "You're funny. What's your name again?"

"I'm uh . . . uh . . ." Leroy looked like he was about to melt into a puddle right there in his chair.

"His name's Leroy Jones," Albert said for him. He gave Leroy an encouraging nod. "He'll be fine once we feed him, right, Leroy?"

"Yeah," Leroy said, and mumbled something about his mom's spaghetti back home.

"We *are* excited to have you as our trainees, by the way," Terran piped up. "We used to be Hydra, you know, before we became the Calderon First Unit."

"The team names rotate," Grey added. "When a team has completed all three terms of training and graduated to First Unit status, a new team of First Terms gets the name. It's kind of weird you're Hydra now, actually. I still feel like the name is part of me."

"It's like we've inherited your legacy," Birdie said. "That's encouraging! We might be even *better* someday!"

"Ha." Grey chuckled. "We'll see about that. You've got some work to do after today's Competition, but I've got a good feeling about you three."

Albert smiled. Maybe there was hope for them yet, though if he didn't get some food in his stomach soon . . .

There was a rustling noise overhead, and Albert

looked up. The air was suddenly full of white birds that sparkled like diamonds. Their wings spanned ten feet or more, and they held baskets in their talons.

"I hope those things aren't delivering babies," Leroy said.

"Not babies, silly," Aria said. "Food! And they're called Whimzies."

"Whimzies," Birdie said, watching the birds circle closer. She grinned.

One of the Whimzies swooped down and dropped an oval basket in the middle of the table. Albert could smell cheeseburgers, and BBQ, and spaghetti with meatballs. Another Whimzie swooped down and left a second basket. It was full to the brim with desserts in every color of the rainbow.

Smaller birds came, swooping down to leave white plates before each person. Then, most magically of all, bottles full of bright pink juice appeared beside each plate, as if they'd just popped right out of the table.

"Try the Core Juice," Grey said, removing the cap and taking a sip. "You never know what you're going to get, but it's usually good. Looks like I got berry blast."

Albert took a big gulp of his juice. "Cherry cola," he said with a big grin.

"Mine's fizzy coconut!" Leroy said.

They both looked at Birdie, who hadn't said a word. She sighed, took a sip of her pink juice, and nodded.

"Water," she said. "Filtered. That is *totally* lame."

"I always get water, too," Terran groaned. "Sometimes I miss getting to drink Cokes from back home."

"At least it's healthy," Aria said, gulping down more of her berry blast.

The boys laughed. They all filled their plates with food from the baskets, and spent the next hour talking about everything that had happened to them so far.

Albert learned that breakfast and a late lunch (or was it dinner?) were the only meals of the day. In the Core, food filled you up for longer periods of time.

"Your body will adjust in a few days," Grey explained. "Until then, eat more than usual. It has to last you, and you'll need your strength for the Pit if you're going to beat the other teams."

Leroy was shoveling food into his mouth at record speed.

Albert glanced over at Hoyt. He was jabbering on about old simulations his team had defeated. Albert saw that he was sporting a new necklace with a second Tile. The second Tile was red, not white, with a silver triangle that glowed purple in the center. Albert heard him say he'd purchased it with the Medallion Argon had won.

"It will give me more energy if I touch it," Hoyt said, when he saw Albert looking. "Not that I need more energy to pulverize *your* team."

Albert wanted to stand up and yell in Hoyt's face, but

he knew Aria, Terran, and Grey were watching, and that that wasn't the mature thing to do. Here he was, sitting with the *First Unit*, chatting like they were old friends! Albert held his chin up as he looked at Hoyt.

"The best team will win in the end," Albert said. Hoyt just laughed, and went back to bragging about the Pit. Albert turned back to his friends.

"You can get more Tiles?" Birdie was asking Terran.

"They only work once," Terran explained. "But yeah, you can buy them at the Canteen."

When everyone had moved on to dessert, one of the professors took the stage in front of the giant lava window. Albert hadn't seen this guy yet, but the second he saw the man's eyes, he knew it was the one Jack had talked about in the dorm.

"That's Professor Hagglesworth," Grey said to Albert, Leroy, and Birdie. "He's got weird eyes like your companion Farnsworth."

Professor Hagglesworth was of average height and build. He had peppery-gray hair, thick glasses on his nose, and eyes that shone a dim purple. He spoke into a MegaHorn like the kind Professor Flynn had used in the Pit.

"Is this thing on?" He tapped the tip of the horn and a high-pitched static noise exploded throughout the room.

Everyone covered their ears. Farnsworth howled like a coyote, and some sort of monkey with blue fur launched a banana at Professor Hagglesworth's face. He dodged the banana as if he'd done it a thousand times before.

"Professor Asante is otherwise detained and won't be doing the introductions. You're stuck with me, I'm afraid. I see everyone has made themselves at home." His eyes changed to yellow, the color of daisies. "Today is the first official day of the summer, and all of our Balance Keepers have arrived. Everyone, let's welcome our newest recruits!"

He pulled out a crumpled list from his pocket and started to call out the names, one Realm at a time.

There were three new Balance Keepers training for each of the three Realms: Belltroll, Ponderay, and Calderon. Everyone clapped politely for the first two trios of recruits, while Professor Hagglesworth announced the Tiles they had received. There was a girl in Ponderay who could touch fire without being harmed. Albert wished for half a second she was in Hydra—that sure would be a useful power in Calderon. There was a boy in Belltroll who could talk to animals, a girl in Belltroll who could see through solid objects, and a boy in Ponderay who, apparently, could control the climate within a hundred feet in any direction. There were a couple of others, too, but that was all Albert could remember—he didn't have Leroy's Synapse Tile.

So many awesome powers, Albert thought, *and I still have no idea what mine is. I've got to figure this thing out, and soon.*

Finally, Professor Hagglesworth got to the Calderon Realm.

"Team Hydra consists of Albert Flynn, Birdie Howell, and Leroy Jones," the Professor said. "Don't be shy. Stand up!"

The three of them stood and everyone clapped.

"Go Hydra!" Grey, Aria, and Terran yelled together.

Professor Hagglesworth waited for the noise to die down. Then he spoke again.

"Birdie has been gifted with a Water Tile!"

Birdie did a little under the sea dance, loving the attention, as everyone cheered and her tablemates clapped her on the back.

"Leroy has been gifted with a Synapse Tile, very rare!"

The noise around the room erupted. Leroy took off his hat and did a quick bow. A blond girl at the workers' table blew a kiss toward Leroy, and his face turned red all over again. He pushed his glasses farther up his nose and turned away.

"And last but not least," Professor Hagglesworth said, "we have Professor Flynn's son, Albert Flynn. He has been gifted with . . . what did you say it was, Professor Flynn?"

Albert wanted to sink down into his chair and put his head in his hands. Professor Flynn crossed the stage and whispered something into Professor Hagglesworth's ear.

"A Tile of unknown origin?" Professor Hagglesworth

seemed to take this news with a mix of concern and curiosity. "I guess we have a mystery on our hands with you, Albert. Time will tell!"

Instead of cheers, Albert heard whispers rise from all around, and felt everyone's eyes on his back. They were craning to get a good look at his Tile. All he wanted to do was rip it off and toss it into the water for the turtles to snack on. He quickly slipped it inside his shirt, then sat down in his chair and forced himself to look brave. Why did he have to get the dud? Why couldn't it have been someone else?

Across the table, Hoyt was laughing his pig-faced head off.

"No worries, Albert." Leroy lowered his voice. "They're just jealous, all of them."

"Leroy's right," Birdie whispered. She gave Albert a big grin. "I'm sure of it."

"Keep your head up, Flynn." Grey nodded to Albert. "A good Balance Keeper always stays positive."

The way they were smiling at him, nodding their heads in encouragement, made Albert feel a little better. He took a deep breath and turned back to listen to the announcements.

"As you all know, tomorrow begins the first official day of Competition."

The dining hall erupted into cheers. Albert, Leroy, and Birdie joined in. Across the pool, the companion creatures began to howl and hiss and chirp and blow fire. Farnsworth's eyes lit up like they'd just been plugged into a light socket.

"Now, now, calm down, calm down," Professor Hagglesworth said, his eyes changing to a calming blue. "I must remind you all. This year we have a new Apprentice: Mr. Trey Link, who will be assisting Professor Flynn. He went through several grueling rounds of competition to earn this coveted spot."

Trey stood up from his table across the water, and the cheering started all over again. He looked as proud as ever. Almost all of the girls in the room watched Trey with googly eyes. Albert couldn't help but be a little jealous at the way his dad looked up at Trey, like he was the son Albert could only dream of being. Albert wondered how many years his dad and Trey had spent together in the Core, training and bonding inside of the *real* Realms.

Terran put a hand on Albert's shoulder. "He's proud of you, Albert. He talks about you all the time, you know. He's been waiting for you to come here for years."

"Thanks." Albert sighed. "I just want to figure out my Tile."

"We'll do some research and figure it out," Leroy joined in. "Someone here is bound to know something! You'll see." They turned back to Professor Hagglesworth.

"You're a lively bunch this year," the Professor

continued. "Don't let the news I'm about to tell you dampen your spirits."

Professor Flynn rose to his feet, his towering presence hard to ignore. "Let me tell them, if you please."

Hagglesworth's eyes turned red as fire for an instant, then dialed back to a more calm shade of orange.

"As you wish. It is *your* Realm, after all."

Clearly, Professor Hagglesworth didn't like Albert's dad.

"Professor Hagglesworth wanted to have the Calderon Realm, but your dad beat him to it," Grey explained to Albert. "They're not exactly best friends."

Albert didn't know a person in the world that didn't like Bob Flynn. Apparently there were power struggles at play inside the Core that Albert knew nothing about.

He watched as his dad shared the news:

"It has come to our attention that Calderon is in more trouble than we'd expected."

The room buzzed with whispers.

Professor Flynn smiled comfortingly, the way he used to do when Albert was little and skinned his knee. "Remember, this is what we train for. It's what we prepare for. And it still may not be as bad as we think."

Albert remembered the ash clouds in New York City. He found Trey in the crowd, but his expression was a mask of calm. Grey and Aria sat still as statues, not giving away a hint of concern.

"We will continue to keep a close eye on Calderon, and Belltroll and Ponderay, too. But Balance Keepers, remember as you train: you may be called on to serve at any time. Work hard; be ready."

"We've got to get our act together," Leroy muttered beside Albert.

"Now, dinner is done!" Professor Flynn shouted. "Tomorrow marks the start of classroom hours for *all* students, not just Balance Keepers."

Everyone groaned together.

Professor Flynn smiled. "Oh, come on, now. After dinner is free time. Now the *real* fun begins!"

The room erupted into hoots and hollers, and everyone started doing some strange clap in unison. Albert tried to keep up.

Leroy, remembering this was the last meal of the day, stuffed his pockets with rolls.

As they rode their turtles across the water and started the long walk back to the dorms, Albert couldn't keep his mind from wondering: With a Tile like his, would he ever be of any use?

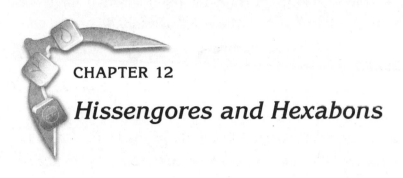

CHAPTER 12

Hissengores and Hexabons

"I don't know about you guys," Birdie said, "but I'm ready to kick some butt in the simulation today."

"Aren't we all?" Leroy sighed. It was the next morning, and the three of them met up at the same bridge again. They had regular class before Pit training.

"So, where *is* our first class?" Birdie asked. She was holding up a circular map of the Core that Ellery, Birdie's Second Term roommate in Treefare, had loaned her. Albert looked over Birdie's shoulder. No matter which way she turned the map, Albert only got more confused.

"I wish we didn't have to go sit in a boring class," Albert groaned. "This is summer. Not summer *school*."

"I'm looking forward to a little reading and stuff. Less dangerous for a change," Leroy said.

"How can you think about reading when we could be training in the Pit? The Pit is awesome!" Birdie said, giggling. The two of them went at it again, arguing like siblings.

Farnsworth howled, as if his dog ears couldn't take it anymore. Albert got in between his friends. "Come on, guys, cut it out! We should get to class right now anyway. Do either of you know *what* our first class is?" He'd been so exhausted last night that he hadn't bothered to look at the schedule.

"It's Core History, with that little dwarf guy," Birdie said. "I was hoping to get my hands on some sort of sword or shield or something, but Ellery said this class is totally lame."

"Hey, I like lame. Lame is safe," Leroy said. He motioned for Albert and Birdie to follow him down a dimly lit tunnel. "Come on. We passed Bigglesby's room yesterday. I remember where it is."

The three of them set off, Leroy and Farnsworth in the lead.

At the end of a winding tunnel, Professor Bigglesby's door stood ajar. Students were filing in slowly, taking their places in chairs before a large stage. There was a teetering pile of books that reminded Albert of the post office back in Herman. He grabbed one and scanned the room for an open place to sit.

"Hey! Flynn, over here!" someone yelled from the

back. It was a small boy with black hair and bright, tiger-orange eyes.

"Who in Calderon is *that*?" Leroy asked. Farnsworth scurried away and greeted the strange boy, licking him all over his face.

Albert shrugged, but he and his friends went to see the boy anyway. They sat down beside him, Albert the closest. "Um . . . hi?"

"Hey. I'm Petra. I know all about you, Albert Flynn. I know all about *everyone* in the Core." The boy looked at Birdie and Leroy. "And you must be his friends. I've heard all about you, too. Sorry your first day didn't go so well."

"Who are you again?" Leroy asked, leaning past Albert to get a good look at Petra. "What Realm did you say you're training for?"

Petra's face fell for a second, but his smile came right back. "I'm not a Balance Keeper or anything. Just a regular Core kid, born and raised."

"So you're, like, a Pure?" Birdie asked. "Cool!"

Petra nodded. "Not all of the Pures get to be Balance Keepers. Some of us are destined for different things. I'm on cleanup duty with my mom, at night. Sometimes Professor Bigglesby lets me clean the weapons!"

"Hey, that's pretty cool, too," Albert said. He imagined Petra brandishing a massive spear ten times his body size, and held back a laugh. The kid seemed pretty interested in everything around him. Petra probably knew loads of secrets about the Core.

"So, do you have any dirt on Hoyt?" Albert asked. "He's a Pure, too, right?"

"Yeah," Petra said. "That's something else you should know—just because I'm a Pure doesn't mean I'm a fan of Hoyt. I'll be rooting for Hydra in the Competitions; you can count on it."

"Hey, thanks, dude," Albert said. It looked like he had yet another friend in the Core already.

"I think class is starting." Birdie clapped her hands.

The room hushed down as Professor Bigglesby waddled into the room. He was as short as a yardstick, but the sword he carried at his side was the same one Albert noticed the other day. It was at least twice his size, and had to weigh far more. The blade dragged behind Professor Bigglesby on the floor.

"Good morning, students. As you might have guessed from my sword, this term we will master a variety of weapons."

"Yes!" Albert gave Birdie a fist bump. Leroy let out a little whimper.

"But today," Professor Bigglesby continued, "we brush up on the exciting topic of Core History! Please turn to page three-fifty-six in your textbooks."

Everyone groaned, except Leroy, who pulled out

his book with a fat grin. "Now that's more like it," he whispered.

At the front of the class, Hoyt shouted out a complaint. But Professor Bigglesby carried on as if he hadn't heard anyone at all. He turned on some sort of ancient, windup projector, and began to show old photographs of the Core. It turned out that the Core had been there for thousands of years.

Albert didn't really like school that much. He couldn't stand studying, his grades weren't that impressive, and most of the time he got in trouble for not paying attention to his teacher. He couldn't even count on his fingers the number of disciplinary letters that had been sent home to his mom.

Compared to school back home, though, this class wasn't so bad. At least he got to see historical pictures of everything. In the back of a picture that showed the building of the triangle bridges, Albert thought he saw two familiar, glowing eyes.

"Hey! That's our dog!" Albert whispered to his friends. Farnsworth's eyes lit up at the sight of his photograph. His tail thumped against Albert's boots.

Leroy flipped through to a new page in his textbook. "The Canis Luminatis can live up to one thousand years. Farnsworth is probably still a puppy!"

They followed along as Professor Bigglesby talked all

about Core History. Albert sat dumbfounded as he learned that the ancient Greeks had discovered the entrance to the Core centuries ago.

Professor Bigglesby went on. There was some pretty cool stuff going on here, but soon Albert felt his eyelids drooping. He wished he were back in his bed in Cedarfell, listening to the birds chirp as he fell asleep.

That's when the alarm bell went off.

It was loud and awful sounding, like a cat screeching after being sprayed by water.

"Something's wrong in one of the Realms!" Petra squeaked.

He stood up and ran across the room to Professor Bigglesby's side.

Everyone looked like they were about to panic. Students stood up, ready to rush from the room. Hoyt turned around and gave Albert an awful look. *Scared?* he mouthed.

No, Albert mouthed back, but he felt like his heart was going to leap right out of his chest.

Farnsworth howled and ran from the room. Leroy was mumbling something about feeling sick, Birdie was running her fingers nervously through her ponytail, and one girl at the front of the room was actually crying.

After a few moments of chaos, the bell shut off, and the room fell into complete and total silence. Professor Bigglesby raised his tiny arms into the air. "Only a drill, students, only a drill. But I daresay the real one is coming. Better be ready when it does."

His eyes seemed to stare at each student in the room until they landed right on Albert's black Tile. His brow furrowed. For a second, he looked almost . . . afraid.

"The Balance Keepers must be especially prepared for such a time. That's enough for today. Class is dismissed."

As the room cleared, Albert and his friends hung back. Petra came to see them off, a worried look on his face.

"You three should train extra hard," he said, pacing nervously. "If you hear that alarm again, you have to be ready. It will mean bad news. *Very* bad news."

"Well, I guess that's perfect timing for us to go and practice, then," Albert said.

He looked at the giant, round clock on Professor Bigglesby's desk. It was almost time for the first head-to-head Competition. At least they knew they wouldn't have to face Argon today. They'd be up against the other Calderon training unit, the Third Termers called Ecco. The thought helped clear some of Albert's dread from the alarm. In fact, he found he had a spring in his step. Today was his day; he could feel it.

When Team Hydra reached the copper door to the Pit ten minutes later and opened it, the Pit looked like an entirely new place. There were no cables or rings of fire, and the black Melatrix wasn't bouncing around, waiting to pulverize Leroy. Instead, there were floating orange ledges scattered around. At the very top, on both sides opposite each other, sat two large metal buckets. And where there had once been bouncy ground at the bottom, there was now a sea of blue.

"Oh yeah." Birdie smiled, looking down at the water. "This is good news, you guys! My Tile can help us win!" She held it up to her mouth and planted a big kiss on the water-droplet symbol.

"I wonder what those buckets are up there for," Leroy mused aloud.

They walked along the ledge to the other side of the Pit, where Trey and Professor Flynn sat waiting. There was already a huge crowd of Core workers gathered to watch the action. Petra was among them. He gave Albert, Leroy, and Birdie a big thumbs-up.

"You've arrived early," Professor Flynn said, smiling at Albert. "I like the dedication."

"We wanted to scope out the scene before the other team got here," Albert said to his dad.

"About that," Professor Flynn started. "James from the Ecco team had an unfortunate run-in with a Jackalope last night, so we've rejiggered the schedule. You'll be up against Argon again today." Albert, Leroy, and Birdie exchanged defeated glances.

There goes my good feeling, Albert thought.

"But not to worry! Today's challenge is a good one.

Especially for you, Birdie." He pointed down at the water. "A little hint for you three, if I may? Watch your back. You never know what might come after you."

Before Albert could ask what his dad was getting at, the door of the Pit opened and Hoyt and his team walked in. Leroy groaned.

"Don't let them see us sweat," Birdie whispered. "I'm going to pulverize them!"

"*We're* going to pulverize them," Albert reminded her. "We have to work as a team, remember?"

"That's not how it works on the swim team," she said.

"But if we work together, we can win," Leroy added.

"Fine," Birdie said. "But if you two boys slow me down . . ."

Leroy rolled his eyes. "Girls," he whispered to Albert.

Professor Flynn had everyone line up around the edge of the Pit while Trey explained the challenge.

"As you saw yesterday, you'll need mental and physical skills to navigate the Realms. In Calderon, you're going to come across some pretty scary stuff. There are a lot of high obstacles you're going to have to scale. Sometimes, you won't be able to figure out a clear way to reach the top, and you might have to problem solve."

"Ooooo, Synapse Tile time!" Leroy said, elbowing Albert.

Professor Flynn spoke up. "Grey, Aria, and Terran have also recently reported that they suspect the source of the current Imbalance in the Calderon Realm is a problem in the large body of water there, so we thought we'd give you some swimming to do today."

"Told you my Tile would come in handy!" Birdie whispered to Albert.

"Today's challenge will help you hone those mental and physical skills, but even more important, your teamwork skills, which you started to work on yesterday. There's a reason we send Balance Keepers into the Realms in teams: the more you work together, the more successful—and safe—you'll be. So, today's challenge is this: Go to the bottom of the lake, find the tokens that spell out a secret word, then place the tokens in the buckets. Grab as many tokens as you want while you're assembling the word, but once you have your word, only two tokens may be placed in the buckets at a time, and only two tokens can be carried by any one player at a time. Whichever team completes the challenge first wins."

"That's it?" Albert asked. It seemed easy enough. The secret word might be a little tricky, but together, his team could figure it out.

"That's it," Trey said, but he had a mysterious gleam in his eye.

Trey blew his silver whistle, and two platforms with diving boards appeared, one on each side of the Pit. Albert, Leroy, and Birdie took the one to their left, and Hoyt, Slink, and Mo took the right. As the diving boards began moving down deeper into the Pit, Albert thought of how badly he wanted to win. He grabbed the Tile around his neck.

"Let's hope this Tile does something today," he said, to no one in particular.

The platforms stopped a few feet above the water and Professor Flynn called down to them.

"Are both teams ready?"

"Ready!" all six Balance Keepers shouted at once. Leroy took a deep breath. Birdie rocked back and forth on her heels. Albert cracked his knuckles.

"BEGIN!" Trey shouted. He blew his whistle, and the Pit came to life.

All the ledges overhead began to move, up and down, left and right. And *fast.* The other team didn't waste any time. Slink dove headfirst toward the water. Mo sat down on the edge of the floating platform and waited for Slink to come back up.

"Figure out the secret word! I'll wait for you up top!" Hoyt shouted to his team. When he saw Team Hydra looking at him, he grimaced. "See you later, newbs!" Then he bent his knees, took a *big* leap, and landed on the next platform up like it was no more difficult than playing hopscotch.

"That was ridiculous!" Leroy screamed. "He just jumped up five feet, four inches without even breaking a sweat!"

Albert looked up at the platform. It did seem a little high from where he was standing now, but if Hoyt could do it, he figured he could, too. He thought again of how he'd jumped across Herman, Wyoming. He'd thought that was adventure, but this—*this*—was adventure. He wasn't about to let a little leap stop him now.

"Birdie." Albert turned to her. "Get underwater. Start looking at the tokens and see if you can figure out what the secret word is."

Birdie nodded and dove into the water with a loud *splash!*

"Leroy, can you stay here and wait for Birdie? When she brings those tokens up, start laying them out. Try to figure out the secret word."

"Ten-four, big buddy," Leroy said, tipping the bill of his baseball cap. "What are you going to do?"

Albert stood on the very edge of the platform and looked up. "I'm going to do what Hoyt just did. I don't know his plan, but he must have a reason for going up there." Leroy nodded, then turned his attention to Birdie.

Albert bent his knees, took a deep breath, and jumped.

He got his upper body on the platform overhead, but his feet were still dangling down below. He let go and landed back on the diving board, nearly bouncing Leroy off into the water below.

"Uh, Albert? That wasn't exactly a leap. More like a bunny hop," Leroy said behind him.

"Thanks for clearing that up," Albert said. He gritted his teeth and tried again. This time he got most of his body on, then pulled his legs up. *Not bad, but not as easy as I thought it would be.*

Birdie surfaced and placed a handful of tokens on the platform. Some were as small as quarters, while others were the size of her entire hand. They were all different shapes, with different colors on them. Albert thought he spotted the tip of the letter *E*, but he couldn't be sure.

He tried another leap to the next platform. Again, he had to pull himself up.

"They're puzzle pieces!" Birdie said. "There's hundreds of them down there! I don't know which ones to grab!"

"Get as many as you can," Leroy said. "And hurry!"

Another attempt at a jump. Another lame pulling himself up. Was Hoyt really that much stronger than him?

Slink's head popped up across from Birdie's. He appeared to have at least two pieces.

It's just a jump, Albert thought. *A big jump. You can do it.*

"We're already ten steps ahead of you!" Hoyt yelled from overhead. He was hopping from platform to platform, landing on them with an effortless grace that made Albert's stomach drop. Now he was just showing off. "Quit now, before you guys embarrass yourselves!"

Albert reluctantly watched Hoyt, studying the way he moved with such power and grace. He sighed. He had to hand it to the guy—he was good, even at the things his Speed Tile didn't help with.

Birdie surfaced with more tokens, and Leroy started piecing them together. There was a snap and a letter *I* appeared. "*Yes!* We're doing it!" Leroy shouted.

It was like that little victory was just the encouragement Albert needed. He took a deep breath.

I can do this. He thought about the time he jumped for hours on his cousin's trampoline in California, how he felt like he could leap to the moon if he wanted. *I wish I could just jump like I did that day . . . maybe even higher than Hoyt.*

Out of nowhere, there was a buzzing feeling in his legs, like they couldn't wait to move. Albert bent his knees, gritted his teeth, and jumped with all his might.

He shot into the air like he'd bounced off a springboard. He almost didn't land on a platform, but as one of them floated to the left, he came down on the edge and threw his weight forward so as not to fall. He collapsed, gasping for air. *Maybe he* was *as strong as Hoyt. . . .*

"Very nice, Albert!" Professor Flynn shouted into his MegaHorn. "Way to add a little fire to the Competition!"

"Go, Albert!" Petra screamed from the audience. Everyone cheered, and Farnsworth, somewhere in their midst, let out an encouraging howl.

Across from Albert, Hoyt's jaw hung open. Albert tried it again.

Come on, Albert. Leap! He imagined monkeys at the zoo, leaping from tree to tree like it was as easy as breathing.

When the platform he was on passed another one moving upward, Albert jumped and landed right in the center.

"Yes!" he shouted. *Now I'm doing it!*

Below, he could hear Leroy hooting and hollering, cheering him on, and he thought he saw Birdie surface again with more tokens.

"Hydra is making progress!" Professor Flynn said. "As soon as they spell out their word, they can start taking their tokens up to the buckets."

Albert watched from above as Birdie and Leroy struggled to spell out the secret word. Across from them, Slink and Mo were having trouble, too.

"It's just you and me, Flynn!" Hoyt bounced past Albert, and suddenly, Albert realized: this was about *teamwork*. He'd said it himself to Birdie earlier. They wouldn't win if Albert wasn't down there with them, making their entire unit whole. It was just like Hoyt to miss that point. Albert leaped down and landed on the platform next to Leroy and Birdie.

"Are the words going to be the same?" Leroy was asking Birdie.

"Fill me in!" Albert said to his teammates.

"We're trying, but so far no luck!" Birdie groaned. "Thanks for coming back to help, by the way."

Birdie turned and dove back under the water. Albert followed after her, taking a deep breath before he submerged. The water wasn't salty, so he could open his eyes for a few seconds and see what was below. Hundreds of tokens sat on the bottom of the pool, piled on top of one another. Across from where Birdie swam, Albert could see Slink sifting through the tokens. The kid was swimming torpedo fast.

His breath was running out, so Albert surfaced.

"I think Slink has a Water Tile like Birdie's!" Albert said to Leroy.

"Thanks for the uplifting news, buddy!"

Birdie surfaced again, two tokens in her hand. She looked like an angry, wet cat. "I can't figure it out, you guys! It's, like, a total maze down there!"

Albert bobbed up and down in the water. "I'll do whatever I need to do to help; just tell me what to do!"

"Just . . . figure it out! I don't know, but we're running out of time!" Birdie said. She dove back under, and Albert wished so badly he could follow, but there was no way he could hold his breath that long. What he wouldn't give to have a Water Tile like Birdie's, with that cool droplet symbol on it. . . .

All at once, Albert felt impossibly light. The Tile around his neck seemed to buzz with life, and he just *knew* what to do.

He dove under the water, took a breath of air, and . . .

What?

Somehow, Albert was doing what Birdie could do. It was like he had a Water Tile. There was no time for questions. Albert dove, following Birdie to the bottom of the pool. She looked shocked when she saw him, but he shook his head and pointed at the bottom of the pool. Together, they grabbed as many tokens as possible. With two people instead of one, they might have a fighting chance.

As soon as they surfaced, hands full of tokens, Leroy started rummaging through the new finds.

"Wait a minute, I think there's something here!" Leroy said.

Albert climbed out of the water and onto the platform beside Leroy. What had just happened to him? Was that his Tile, finally working its magic? What he'd done should have been impossible.

"What was that?" Birdie asked Albert. "How did you swim down so far? You couldn't do it earlier. . . ." She had a look of complete shock on her face.

"I don't know," Albert said. "Let's figure it out later!"

"I've got it!" Leroy shouted.

He started dishing out commands to Albert and Birdie. In seconds, they'd fit six specific pieces together and finally discovered their secret word.

"It spells *HISSENGORE*!" Leroy shouted. Then he turned to Albert and Birdie. "You guys aren't going to like this."

Birdie's eyes widened nervously. "What's a Hissengore, Leroy?"

"Let's just say it hisses a lot and hope we don't actually see one."

Slink and Mo had their six tokens together, too, or Albert guessed they did, when they all shouted, "HEXABON!" in unison.

CRACK!

Albert's head snapped up toward the sound. Overhead, the side of the Pit wall opened up, and out shot two creatures in a blur: one green, one brown.

"Oh no!" Slink cried from the right, just as a brown monkey with six arms dove down onto him, screeching like a banshee. "I hate Hexabons!"

"What on earth is a *Hexabon*?" Birdie squealed, involuntarily edging back on their platform.

"Hexabon—a six-armed primate that longs for human contact . . ." Leroy spewed the definition out, then looked embarrassed and shocked. "I read it in class the other day, okay?"

Albert turned just in time to see a bottle-green snake, several feet longer than Birdie was tall, wrap itself around Leroy. It was hissing and burping little puffs of green smoke into Leroy's face.

"Um, you guys, this snake has some *serious* bad breath." Leroy forced out a laugh, but he looked like he might pass out any second.

Albert didn't know what to do. Smelly breath didn't seem very threatening, but he guessed that if they were in Calderon, the real Hissengores would do a lot more than just breathe on them. He had to help Leroy. He scrambled forward and kicked the Hissengore's scaly side.

"I hate snakes!" Birdie whined, but she started kicking anyway. Across from them, a Hexabon seemed to be attacking Slink by hugging him and licking his face.

"Forget about me!" Leroy said. "Get the tokens up there. Albert, start jumping, *now*!" He was punching the Hissengore over and over, but the snake didn't seem to care. It was laughing at him, burping even more, until Leroy's knees buckled.

Birdie grabbed the first two tokens, yanked them apart, and shoved them into Albert's hands.

"You have to go! Jump!"

Albert gave Leroy a nod, tightened his grip on the tokens, and bent his knees. *Come on, Albert, time to fly like Superman!*

He rocketed into the air like he'd just been flung from a slingshot, and landed square on his feet on a platform. *That swim must have loosened me up,* Albert thought. Hoyt bounced past, nearly kicking Albert in the face. Albert dodged him, but his grip on the tokens loosened, and they tumbled out of his hands and back down to the bottom.

The crowd groaned overhead, and Farnsworth let out a disappointed howl.

"Albert!" Birdie yelled from below. "Get back down here!"

She was trying to jump up to a platform, but Albert could see she wasn't going to get far.

Albert leaped but overshot the distance and landed right in the water. *Epic fail,* Albert thought.

"Sayonara, loser!" Hoyt yelled when Albert surfaced. Now it was clear he was using his Speed Tile powers, too. He leaped up four platforms in three seconds!

"Albert!" Birdie screamed. "Get out of the water!"

Birdie pushed the two tokens into Albert's hands again as he emerged onto the platform. "Take these to the top; I'll be right behind you with two more."

While Leroy wrestled with the Hissengore, Albert took a leap. He landed, and was about to jump to another, when Hoyt slammed into him in midair.

"Not so fast, Flynn!" Hoyt said. He leaped, using Albert's head as a springboard, and dropped two tokens into the bucket. Albert crashed hard back onto the platform, his legs all wobbly like Jell-O.

"Let's go, Hydra!" Petra screamed from the crowd.

There was a *ding,* and another Hexabon appeared out of a hole in the wall on Hoyt's side. It leaped at him, and they crashed all the way down to the water in a big six-armed-monkey embrace.

"There's going to be another Hissengore once we put our tokens in!" Albert yelled down to Birdie.

She hadn't managed to leap to a new platform. If he was being honest with himself, he didn't know how *he* was jumping so high, but he didn't really care, so long as he was keeping up with Hoyt.

"I'll wait for you here!" Birdie said. "You put the tokens in the bucket!"

"Got it!" Albert yelled. He jumped from level to level, barely missing getting pummeled in the face by a moving platform, and slam-dunked the first two tokens into the bucket.

"He shoots, he scores!" Albert screamed, fist pumping the air.

The second Hissengore appeared almost instantly. It was lightning fast and wrapped itself around Birdie's ankles, tugging her downward.

"Throw the tokens!" Albert yelled.

She launched them upward, but Albert watched in horror as a moving platform knocked them down. The second two tokens clattered to a stop on another platform that swung over to Hoyt's side of the Pit.

Albert passed Hoyt leaping up from the bottom with two tokens in his hands as he leaped down to retrieve the fallen tokens. His muscles were getting tired—he didn't know how much longer he'd be able to keep this up. As if to rub that in, he heard the clatter of Hoyt dropping Argon's tokens in.

Albert did some quick math. Now Argon had only

two more to go before they'd win. Another Hexabon appeared, but Mo turned to look at it, screeched some sort of monkey command, and the creature stopped in its tracks. Then it started dancing. *Huh. Apparently Mo's Tile allows him to talk to animals.* Albert filed that info away for future use, then jumped to the top and dunked Hydra's second two tokens in. Moments later, a third Hissengore appeared below.

Meanwhile, Hoyt had hopped down to the bottom and grabbed his team's last two tokens.

"Albert, do something!" Birdie yelled.

Albert saw the Hissengore burp a cloud of green into her face. She nearly rolled off the side of the platform.

Not far from Birdie, Leroy had managed to get out of the first Hissengore's grasp, but now the third Hissengore surged forward. Leroy hopped out of the way with a screech.

The sound cleared Albert's head—he *did* have to do something before his friends suffocated on Hissengore burps.

Albert leaped down from his platform and landed on another. It started to move upward again, so he jumped to the right, landing on the next-lowest one, then down a few more.

Leroy was just below him now. Leroy picked up the last two tokens and threw them sidearm toward Albert. He leaped into the open air and caught them in mid-dive.

Out of the corner of his eye, Albert saw Hoyt pull away from the iron grip of a Hexabon just in time to catch the last two tokens Mo threw in his general direction.

"Albert, *go!*" Birdie screamed.

"Go!" the crowd screamed along with her.

Albert needed more energy. He thought of his cousin's trampoline again. *This is just like that,* Albert told himself. He leaped onto a platform going left. Hoyt went right, and when their platforms moved, they passed in midair. Albert was about to jump when he was slammed from behind. It was Mo!

"I don't think so, Flynn," Mo hissed in his ear.

Albert tried to wiggle out from under his assailant, but Mo was both heavy *and* strong.

Not now! Albert begged. *We're so close!*

Albert gathered all the strength he had, thinking of those pro wrestlers he liked to watch on TV. Suddenly, he felt like he could lift a truck if he wanted to. *Whoa.* Albert launched Mo right off of his back like the kid was made of popcorn.

Hoyt had stopped to watch Mo, but was still a couple of platforms above Albert, and using his Speed Tile, too. Albert didn't know how it was possible Hydra could win now, but he felt a surge of adrenaline so he readied himself to leap anyway. *Come on, just jump like those Jackalope things in Cedarfell,* he thought. He pushed off and found he could now jump between platforms like it was no effort at all. Two platforms from the top, Albert was level with Hoyt. He leaped with all his might. To his surprise, he soared right past the final platform and on toward the bucket. Hoyt had just landed on his final platform and pushed off. They were mirror images of each other, both of them reaching, stretching for their buckets. Albert was *so* close. . . .

But he wasn't close enough. Hoyt tossed his tokens in a millisecond before Albert.

There was a clang from overhead.

"Argon wins by a hair!" Trey shouted.

"*Yes!*" Hoyt screamed. "You'll never beat me!"

Albert landed on the highest platform with a *thunk*. *I had no idea I could jump that high . . . not that it matters now.*

The simulation stopped. The Hissengores and Hexabons disappeared back into the walls of the Pit, and Slink and Mo cheered their heads off from down below.

The platform Albert was on sank slowly to the bottom of the Pit, where Leroy and Birdie stood waiting. He dropped the final two tokens into the water and watched them sink to the bottom, disappearing into darkness.

"We should have won," Albert said, slumped over at the shoulders. "We were *so* close. I'm sorry, guys. It's my fault we lost."

"Nah, it's nobody's fault," Leroy said. He straightened his baseball cap on his head, which was dripping water off the bill. It was crushed and lopsided, and smelled like

Hissengore burps. His glasses were fogged over.

"We would have won if it weren't for their foul play," Birdie said. She pulled the elastic band out of her ponytail and let her wet curls fall loose around her face. "I saw what Mo did to you, Albert. He tackled you. That wasn't fair."

Albert wiped sweat from his forehead. "But my dad said there are no rules; only winners and losers."

"Still," Leroy joined in, "that was messed up. They play dirty. We wouldn't have done that."

Their platform started moving up, carting them to the top of the Pit.

Across the way, Argon was busy celebrating. Trey gave them each a Medallion for the Core Canteen.

"It should have been us with those Medallions," Albert sighed.

"Next time," Leroy said.

"Yeah, next time," Birdie agreed. "We did great today. We're getting better. We worked as a team—my water skills and Leroy's mental skills got those tokens together. I guess we'll have to work on our physical skills, but Albert, you shouldn't have been able to do half the things you did. Going underwater for so long, leaping so easily, throwing Mo off your shoulders. What came over you?"

Albert didn't answer, because Albert didn't know.

When they arrived at the exit of the Pit, Hoyt held up his Medallion.

"Normally I'd use this to buy something to help me beat another team. But I'm competing against you three again tomorrow, so . . . I won't need it." He tossed the Medallion over his head like it was worthless. It bounced off the rock wall and landed on a platform.

"It was a close battle and you know it, Hoyt," Albert said.

"Whatever, Flynn. Beginner's luck, that's all it was."

But Hoyt's face had reddened, just in the slightest.

As Hoyt and his cronies left, Albert went back for the discarded Medallion and thought an excellent thought.

Hydra was getting into Hoyt's head.

CHAPTER 13

The Cave of Souls

Late lunch was even later than usual, and Hoyt was in rare form. He spent the entire meal going over the events in the Pit, playing it up so it looked like Albert, Leroy, and Birdie had barely stood a chance.

"He's always this way," Ellery said to the trio. "Don't let him get to you. He's just a bigheaded Pure."

"Aren't *you* a Pure?" Albert asked tentatively.

"Well, yeah. But I'm the *pure* kind of Pure. Hoyt's, like, *stained* or something."

"I want to punch him all the way into one of the Realms," Birdie said.

"He's not worth it," Leroy said. "And besides, we know better. We were good today."

Still, even Leroy wasn't eating like usual, and Albert

could barely eat the slice of pizza he'd chosen. Birdie spent the entire time clenching her fists, glaring at Hoyt like she was about to dive across the table and tackle him.

"Remember what we said," Albert whispered to her. "Don't let him get to us."

Birdie unclenched her fists. She dove into her pasta instead.

Man, do I feel sorry for that pasta, Albert thought. But he couldn't blame Birdie either—they should have won that simulation. He forced himself to eat his pizza, thinking what he wouldn't give up if it meant they could beat Argon in tomorrow's Competition.

That night, Albert woke up to a pair of bright blue lights shining in his face.

"Farnsworth!" Albert whispered, patting him on the head. "What are you doing up?"

When the dog's eyes faded, Albert was shocked to see a familiar sight: Farnsworth had an envelope in his mouth, just like a few days before in Herman.

"What's this?" Albert asked. He took the envelope and saw that his name was on the front, written in his dad's familiar handwriting. Albert ripped open the top and read the message:

> *Meet me in the Observatorium. And be sneaky—you're not supposed to be out of your dorm! Farnsworth knows the way.*

Albert hadn't heard of the Observatorium yet. Whatever it was, it sounded supercool, and Albert smiled as he thought about a night of sneaking around the Core.

Leroy was still sound asleep, snoring louder than a lawn mower, so Albert and Farnsworth snuck out on their own, leaving the trees of Cedarfell behind.

In the tunnels, Farnsworth took the lead, his eyes lighting the way. It was scary for Albert, being the only person out there alone after hours. The statues in the tunnels looked like they might burst to life and steal Albert away. A painting on a wall of an old man with a Tile around his neck looked like it was watching Albert, and every so often, Albert would get a feeling he was being followed. He kept turning around, but no one was ever there. He shivered. *Just keep moving.* Darkness gave him the creeps.

Halfway to the main entrance of the Core, the sound of footsteps caught Albert's attention. They were coming his way.

"Hide, Farnsworth!" he whispered. The dog's eyes dimmed to blue embers, and Albert and Farnsworth sank into the shadows as Professor Asante, the giant woman covered in tattoos, walked past. She had a book in her hands, and though she was distracted, Albert knew if he'd moved an inch, he would have been caught.

"That was close." Albert sighed as soon as Professor Asante turned a corner. "Come on, buddy, let's go."

Farnsworth took off at once, leading Albert to the main entrance of the Core. The giant black cat was sleeping by the entrance to Calderon, its purr so loud it rattled the ground beneath Albert's feet. They slipped past the creature, Albert walking on tiptoes, and disappeared down another dark tunnel.

After what felt like forever, Farnsworth stopped in front of a wooden door with a copper handle. The word *Observatorium* was embedded in the door, carved in curling script.

"You sure know your way around this place. Is this where my dad is, buddy?"

Farnsworth wagged his tail playfully.

"All right, then. In we go."

Albert turned the handle on the door. It opened with a loud *creeeeak*. He winced, hoping no one was around to hear it. They slipped inside, and the old door swung shut behind them.

Inside, blue flames on torches lined an old, dusty stairwell. Albert followed Farnsworth down the steps. It was strangely cold here, and as they got closer to the end, Albert felt his heart racing wildly.

At the bottom of the stairs stood another door. This one was larger, made of thick metal. Albert took a deep breath, pulled hard to open the door, and peered inside.

The room was massive, a giant cave that seemed to

go on forever. When Albert looked up, he sighed with wonder.

Stars.

Or, maybe not—they were still underground, after all. In any case, there were thousands and thousands of little balls of flaming light swimming across the ceiling of the cave. They twinkled and danced. They changed colors every few seconds, and they moved in strange patterns, as if wind was blowing them across the cave's ceiling. When Albert stepped inside the room, he felt like he was in a holy place. The light from the flames made the room dance with colors and shapes, like Albert was standing inside a kaleidoscope.

"You made it!"

Albert whirled around. Across the room, his dad was sitting on a large, rounded rock, waving to him. At the sight of Bob Flynn, Farnsworth raced ahead, barking happily. The sound echoed all over the cave.

"What is this place?" Albert asked his dad. He crossed the cave floor and sat down next to him.

"This is the Observatorium," his dad said. "But it's more commonly known as the Cave of Souls. When a Balance Keeper enters the Core, his flame is born. Even though most of our kind will leave here eventually, their flame will always stay lit. It's a tribute to the heroes that devote their lives to keeping the Core and the Earth safe."

"You mean there's a flame up there for me? And one for you?" Albert wished he could reach up and pluck his flame out of the sky.

"Somewhere up there, yes." His dad nodded. "And one for Pap, and his mother, her father, and so on. Our family has been here for centuries, seventeen Balance Keepers in all." He looked at Albert. "Speaking of which, you're finally here, a Flynn Balance Keeper, number eighteen. What do you think, kiddo?" Albert's face lit up with a grin.

"I think it's amazing," he said. Then he admitted something to his dad he realized he hadn't even admitted to himself yet. "I think I never want to leave."

His dad laughed. Farnsworth thumped his little tail. "I know the feeling, Albert. It's a pretty neat place, though it does take some getting used to. I still remember my first day in the Core. I was so distracted by everything, I fell right into one of the rivers."

Albert laughed, imagining his dad as a boy, stumbling into the water. Albert was surprised he didn't do that himself. "Hey, it could be worse. You could've flopped at the simulations, like me."

His dad patted him on the shoulder. "You've done fine, Albert. Over time that will become a distant memory. You'll learn fast, just like I did. I'm sure of it."

Albert saw his dad's eyes fall to his Tile.

"You did some really great stuff today. I was pleasantly surprised."

"That wasn't me," Albert said. He thought about it a little more. "I mean, it *was* me. But it was like . . . my Tile helped me do those things. Do you think that's possible?"

"I think the Core reveals an endless supply of mysteries," Professor Flynn said.

It was the kind of answer that Albert's dad liked to give when he didn't understand something, a way to shrug away the question.

"You said it's some sort of legendary Tile, right?" Albert pressed. "Well, today I could swim like Birdie, and I tossed Mo off my back like it was nothing. What if it can maybe . . . do more than one set of things?"

"That's impossible," his dad said. "Every Tile can harness a single set of powers. That is all."

"But what if mine *could* do multiple types of things?" Albert asked. "You know . . . like if I had two Tiles in one or something?"

His dad frowned. "Albert . . ." For a second, it looked like he was going to say something important. Instead, he just sighed and shook his head. "I've been looking into it, reading books, discussing with the other professors. I'm afraid you'll have to discover the answer on your own."

Another classic Dad answer. Albert nodded and looked up at the flames above. They were moving in a giant spiral now, changing from blue to yellow to red. It was mesmerizing, and it made Albert realize how tired he was. He felt his eyelids drooping.

His dad shifted a bit on the rock. "Albert, there's something else I need to tell you."

Albert gave himself a little shake to wake back up.

"Your mom doesn't know about this place. She never can. Neither can your brothers or sister."

"What? Why not?" Now Albert was wide-awake.

"Knowledge of the Core, when placed in the mind of someone who is not destined to come here, can do horrible things."

"But Birdie's mom knows about the Core," Albert said.

"It's because the blood of a Balance Keeper is in her veins. She chose not to come. Some people choose a different life."

"But Mom would never tell anyone," Albert said. "I was thinking maybe I could bring her down here someday, show her what the Core's all about."

"The Path Hider wouldn't allow that to happen, Albert. He'd keep the way inside hidden, until you eventually gave up."

"That's not fair," Albert said. "Mom should get to see this place, too."

"She isn't destined," Albert's dad said. "The Core is the world's greatest secret. Every Balance Keeper is sworn to protect it. Do you understand? I know it's hard, but you must promise never to tell her, or anyone else on the surface."

Albert looked back to the flames. All those generations protecting the world above, and the world didn't even know it. It didn't seem right. Suddenly he thought about the ash clouds again, in New York City. "Do you think Mom is okay?"

"Yes, I do. There is a team of people down here, the Monitors, who watch the world above. If she were in serious danger, I would be in Calderon with Grey and Aria and Terran around the clock, working to fix the problem."

"You can still go in the Realms?"

Albert's dad nodded. "I can still go in, if it gets bad enough, but the Realms aren't as easy for older guys like me. It tires us out more quickly, has negative effects on our bodies. We don't know why. We only know that is the way of the Realms, and we must respect it so we don't harm ourselves."

Albert thought of his dad as a young boy, running around in the Core, entering the Realms, helping to fix Imbalances. It was strange to picture.

"You can speak to your mom, you know, if that makes you feel better."

"The Phone Booth!" Albert remembered Trey saying something about it earlier.

"So you've heard about it already." Albert's dad

laughed. "But Albert—I need to hear you promise you won't say anything about the Core, for everyone's safety."

Albert fidgeted. Keeping the secret from his siblings would be fine, but from his *mom*?

His dad shifted on the rock again. "You know, Albert, it's strange, having you here. I've been waiting for years. I suspected you'd gotten the Balance Keeper gene when I caught you at the top of the stairs just a few days after you'd learned to crawl. You were always a great adventurer."

"How did you know for sure that I would be a Balance Keeper?" Albert asked.

"The Path Hider has dreams; he sees faces and names. He came to me the moment he discovered you were destined. You were maybe five years old. Then it was just a matter of waiting until you were the right age."

Albert smiled at that. All those summers he had sorted mail, his dad had known he was destined for something special. It made him feel significant, part of something bigger than himself. Instantly, he knew he could protect the Core's secrets.

"I promise I won't tell anyone, Dad. I couldn't. Not if I'm going to be a professor like you someday."

He felt his dad's hand on his shoulder. "That's the spirit, Albert. You'll be the greatest Balance Keeper I've ever known. I can feel it!"

"Thanks, Dad," Albert said. He felt the weight of his

Tile around his neck. He was more determined than ever to harness its power, and discover for real what it could do. He was going to succeed here, if it took everything in him to do it.

"Someday, when you're ready, I'll get to show you my Realm," his dad said. "You're going to love it."

"I can't wait!" Albert replied, thinking about the adventures they would have together. He would get some one-on-one time with his dad and be something great. Did it get any better than this?

The next morning was Saturday—the only day off in the Core. Albert met Birdie and Leroy in the Main Chamber.

"It's totally humiliating," Birdie was saying to Leroy, as Albert approached. "Hoyt's out of control."

"He's just a bully," Leroy said. "The best thing we can do is ignore him."

"No, the best thing we can do is kick him in his smug little face," Birdie growled.

"What happened?" Albert asked.

"Hoyt got a little creative last night, apparently." She sighed, and pointed at Leroy's Hydra shirt. Someone had taken a pen to it and written the word *stinks* right below *Hydra*.

Albert gritted his teeth. "Did you do anything about it?"

Birdie nodded. "I told Leroy I wanted to give the guy

a piece of my mind. A piece of my *fist*, actually, but . . ."

"It will only make it worse," Leroy said. "I've dealt with lots of bullies before. Back home." He looked down at his toes, embarrassed. Albert couldn't imagine anyone wanting to pick on a guy as nice as Leroy.

Hoyt's bullying had just been with words until now. This was something different. He was crossing the line. Albert forced himself to stay calm. "Tomorrow we'll prove Hoyt wrong about us."

They walked farther into the Main Chamber. There were some kids playing diving games in the river. Core Creators, the adults who made all sorts of goodies that could be purchased in the Core Canteen, were letting other kids test out some sort of new paper airplane that shot little balls of fire. An orange-and-black CoreFish swam past in the river, letting everyone take rides on its back. There was a lot to do here, but Albert had heard the Library was the place to be in the off-hours, so they moved on.

The Library was three stories high, with rows and rows of dusty, old books. A rocky tower stood in the center, where kids and adults climbed up and down, challenging one another to reach different platforms first. Off to the left, there were two zip lines where some of the Balance Keepers were lined up to race one another. Albert waved to the Ecco boy, James, and was pleased to see that he looked like he had recovered from his run-in with the

Jackalope. Maybe that meant they'd go up against Ecco instead of Argon in the next simulation.

"I'm calculating fifty-seven things to do, in this room alone," Leroy said. He wandered off toward the rows of bookshelves, but Albert's mind was still on his conversation with his dad from last night.

"Come on." He waved Birdie along with him, across the library.

The Core Phone Booth was nothing more than a hole carved into the wall. An antique device hung in the corner, larger than Albert's torso. "What happened to cell phones?" Albert asked.

"I saw this in a museum once. It's, like, an original phone," Birdie said.

Albert pulled the Medallion Hoyt had thrown away out of his pocket and pressed it into a little slot in the cave wall, right beside the copper phone.

"Hold this to your ear," Birdie said. She helped Albert figure out the weird phone, and that was when he heard a voice speaking to him.

"Recipient of your message, please?"

Albert recognized the voice. The Path Hider.

"Hey! It's me, Albert," Albert said. "Um . . . What's up?"

There was static on the other end of the line, then the cranking of gears. Albert imagined the Path Hider down in his room of pipes and gears, hiding the paths to the

Core. "Who is this?"

"I delivered you a letter a few days ago, remember? Albert Flynn?"

"Ah, the sneaky boy who opened my envelope," the Path Hider said. It sounded like he was talking into a tin can. "Never mind that. Who would you like to call? Your Medallion gets you three minutes."

"My mom, in New York City."

Albert thought he heard the hiss of steam on the other end of the line, then the cranking of more gears. He gave the Path Hider the number.

"Just a moment," the Path Hider said.

In seconds, the phone started ringing.

Albert's mom answered. "Hello?"

"Mom! It's me! Are you okay?" Albert was so happy to hear her voice.

"Hey! Everything's . . . fine. Just fine. How's my champ doing out there in Herman?" his mom asked.

Albert smiled. "I'm great, Mom. Herm—it's great here." It didn't feel right to flat-out lie.

"Are you taking showers? Brushing your teeth twice a day?"

"Oh yeah, of course I am," Albert said, glad that Birdie couldn't hear how embarrassing the call was becoming. "Listen, Mom, I heard about the ash falling. Are you guys okay?"

In the background, Albert's little half sister was singing

at the top of her lungs. She sounded like a squawking bird that had just had its tail feathers plucked out.

"It's a little gloomy, if you want to know the truth," Albert's mom said. "They say it will clear away as soon as we get some wind coming through the city. I'm sure it's not a big deal. Just enjoy yourself—especially that clean air—and I'll let your dad know if things get too smoggy over here."

Albert could tell his mom was trying not to worry him. She had a way of making things seem better than they really were, for his sake.

Now Albert's little brother started wailing in the background.

"I have to go, honey. Make sure you're wearing clean clothes, and eating all your vegetables. Tell your father hello for me, and be sure to make your bed. . . ."

Her voice cut off suddenly.

"Please insert another Medallion," the Path Hider's voice chimed in.

"But I don't have another," Albert said. He looked at Birdie, who just shrugged.

Albert hung up the phone. "Looks like New York's okay, for now."

"Come on," Birdie said. "Let's go check out the Core Canteen, even though you just spent our only Medallion. We can dream a little. I love shopping!"

Birdie pointed to the corner of the library, where there

was a small room carved into the cave wall. There were shelves inside, lined with all sorts of things you'd expect to see at a camp store and more: glass jars full of colorful candy, T-shirts, ropes, knives, hats, compasses, and fancy backpacks. There were colored eggs with who-knew-what inside, necklaces for holding Tiles, and strange tools that were designed especially for the Core and the Realms. And there were whole sections of the packed little store that were devoted to each of the teams. Albert and Birdie made a beeline straight for the Hydra section.

Lucinda was standing behind the counter, her black snake still slithering across her shoulders. It hissed when it saw Birdie and Albert coming.

"I see you've made it past the first few days in one piece," Lucinda said, then leaned closer. "How are you holding up?"

"We're getting our butts kicked, if you want to know the truth," Birdie said.

"Is that true, now?" Lucinda said. "Medallions are the only coin of the Realm," she said. "You better start winning."

Birdie had her eye on a blue wristband that doubled as a light source. It had the word *Hydra* written on it in white letters, and a sign said the wristband would light the way through the darkest corridors in the Core. Albert was looking at a baseball cap for Leroy that said *Hydra* across the front. He was also licking his lips as he looked at all that colorful candy.

Lucinda frowned. "Oh, goodness. Stop drooling. Here." She reached into a leather pouch at her waist, and produced a Medallion.

"Have you been to the back corner of the Library yet? That's where everyone plays Tiles," Lucinda said. "But you have to put up a Medallion to play. If you win a game of Tiles, you walk away with two Medallions: yours and theirs. And with Medallions you can buy things—snacks, sodas, better packs, custom boots, Hydra gear—whatever you need, Lucinda has it."

Birdie reached for the Medallion, but Lucinda pulled it back.

"You two are lucky I have a soft spot for underdogs, but I charge interest. It'll cost you two Medallions."

Albert and Birdie looked at each other and nodded. Who knew how long it would take them to win a simulation? This might be their only chance to get some Hydra gear and candy.

"We'll take that deal," Birdie said.

Lucinda dropped the Medallion into Birdie's hand. "The Tiles room is on the far wall over there, behind the pillar all those goofballs are climbing on. There are some Tile masters in that group, some real sharks. Watch your back."

They found Leroy and dragged him into the Tile room, which had enough space to fit about twenty people or so, kids and adults. The Tiles stations were stone pedestals with flat tops about two feet square, and all but one of them were occupied by people playing Tiles. Albert recognized the game as the very same one Pap played with his porch buddies.

Ellery and Jack had a game going, and waved them over. Albert, Leroy, and Birdie watched as Ellery and Jack concentrated like they were in the middle of a serious chess match for a good five minutes.

Finally, during one of Jack's turns, Ellery spoke.

"So, you found your way to the Tiles Competitions," Ellery said. "It's like a way of life down here."

Now it was her turn again. Ellery leaned forward, moved a Tile across the board, and stacked it on top of another one. It was kind of like dominoes, but the Tiles were stacked into levels of five. It looked confusing. Albert had never been any good at Tiles when Pap tried to teach him. There was a lot of memorizing symbols and logic involved. It just jumbled his brain and frustrated him.

He'd never thought Pap's information would be useful.

"I know this game." Birdie smiled. "It's like mah-jongg. I *always* lose. Albert, are you any good?"

"Define *good*." Albert laughed. "Because sure, I'm good, if losing to your grandpa *every single time you play* is your definition of *good*."

Birdie just rolled her eyes. Leroy, on the other hand,

observed with great curiosity, saying nothing as the game unfolded.

With one more triumphant move, Ellery won and the game was over. She leaned forward and took both Medallions from the center of the board.

"Aw, man," Jack said, scratching his head as if he was still thinking of moves he should have made. He ran his arm across the tabletop and pushed all the Tiles that had stacked up into a rectangular opening on one side of the playing surface, then stood up and walked over to where Albert was standing.

Ellery held up the two Medallions in victory and got up out of her seat, too. "See you guys later! I'm going shopping!"

Jack's Fury team partner, Peter, settled down in Jack's old spot. He had a mega black eye.

"Stupid Belltroll raptors," he said. "They pack a mean punch. All right, who's playing me?"

Leroy scooted forward. "I've never played, but I'll give it a try." Albert was a little surprised at Leroy's enthusiasm, but he supposed that if he had a Synapse Tile, he might be inclined toward stuff like this, too.

Birdie placed their one Medallion on the center of the tabletop, and Peter did the same. A new rack of Tiles rose on both sides, one in front of each player, and the match commenced.

At first, Leroy wasn't doing so well. Albert watched,

holding his breath. Peter's stacks were twice as high as Leroy's. For a second, Albert wondered if maybe this was a big mistake. They were going to be in debt to Lucinda if they didn't win!

But then, halfway through the game, Leroy smiled. "Time to bring on the heat!" He stacked Tiles on top of one another, strategizing like a whiz. Albert was amazed. Leroy played like Einstein.

"Go, Leroy!" Birdie clapped her hands.

"I feel like I'm actually *good* at something for once!" Leroy grinned.

. When the match was over, Peter groaned and shook Leroy's hand.

"Nice game. You're a pro at this, Leroy." Peter headed for the door.

"Did you guys see that?" Leroy asked his pals. "I just . . . crushed him. I don't think I've ever done as well at any kind of game in my whole life." He looked really proud of himself.

"You were incredible, man!" Albert said, nodding his head. "And we won another Medallion!" Birdie clapped her hands again. She held the Medallion up so that it glittered in the light of the blue flames on the walls.

"Who's next?" Albert called out. "Our man Leroy is new at Tiles, but he thinks he's all that."

Players came running to beat the new kid. By the time the next hour had passed, word had spread throughout the Core about Leroy the Tiles whiz. The room was packed with people watching. Farnsworth arrived from his day-long nap and barked with excitement. Petra wasn't far behind. Grey, Aria, and Terran even came to cheer Leroy on, though Albert noticed that they were looking a little worse for wear these days—Grey had a nasty snakebite on one hand, Aria's hair was singed on one side, and Terran looked like she'd lost half an eyebrow. Still, they were as enthusiastic about Hydra as ever.

"This guy's in *our* Realm!" Grey clapped Leroy on the back.

"Just wait—someday he'll be a part of the First Unit!" Aria said, her green eyes glittering.

Leroy beamed. Albert watched, cheering his friend on as Leroy won nine matches in a row, and even came close to beating Carissa, who wasn't only the Belltroll Apprentice, but also a Tiles champion.

As the last game of the night came to a close, Albert wondered: *What would it be like to play Tiles like Leroy, and be really, really brilliant at something like this?* He leaned forward, chewing on his thumbnail, trying to make sense of the game. He looked at Leroy's Tile dangling from his neck, and wished he could understand the secret of how his own Tile worked.

As Leroy picked up a Tile and moved to place it across the board, Albert's eyes went blurry. He rubbed them, confused for a second. *Oh man, I hope I don't need glasses.*

But when he opened his eyes, the blurriness was gone. For just a few seconds, as Albert looked at the Tiles board, he saw *everything*. All the chances to win by picking up a Tile, replacing it with another, moving one left, another right.

Then, just as suddenly as the knowledge had come, it went away. The game was as confusing as it had been moments before.

"Birdie," Albert whispered. "I think something weird just happened."

"Yeah!" She nodded, still watching the game. "Leroy is owning *everyone* at this. That's what's weird!"

Albert shook his head. Leroy placed the final Tile, and the room erupted into cheers. Soon people started filing out, taking the fun into the main part of the Library. Albert stood alone—he couldn't seem to shake the feeling that what had just happened was significant.

"Albert?" Birdie and Leroy were waiting for him, huge grins plastered on their faces. Birdie had a handful of Medallions that glittered like stars. "Come on. We're going shopping!"

Leroy beamed. His face fell when he looked a little closer at Albert. "You all right, man?"

Albert shook it off. "Yeah, I'm okay. I guess." He smiled weakly and followed his friends out of the room.

CHAPTER 14

The Copper Peak

The next time Albert saw the Pit, it had been transformed into the most dangerous-looking course yet. A jagged copper mountain stretched all the way from the floor to the ceiling, filling the center of the simulation. It was shaped like a volcano, narrower as it rose, and slick along its sides. Barrels hung precariously from swinging cables, surrounding the copper formation.

That wasn't the only thing different, though. The observation deck was packed; it looked like the entire Core was in the stands.

"Team Hydra!" Professor Flynn said into his MegaHorn. "Welcome. I'll explain the crowd in a minute, but for now, you should know that there are real dangers here, more than in the past two simulations." He was more serious than usual. "The First Unit reported last night that there is indeed a very serious Imbalance in the Calderon Realm."

Albert felt his stomach drop all the way to his toes. *A serious Imbalance? That means if something goes wrong, a training team might have to enter the Realm!*

He wasn't sure if that made him excited or scared. Maybe a little bit of both.

"Looks like they'll be calling on Argon in no time, boys," Hoyt called out, as he and his team came in late.

"That won't happen if you're tardy again, Mr. Jackson," Professor Flynn scolded.

Albert and his friends stifled their laughs. He couldn't help but notice that a good portion of the crowd was laughing, too.

Professor Flynn spoke again. "Quiet, please, everyone. I called you here today because I have some information to share about the situation in Calderon. I thought today's Competition would be a good place to illustrate what we're up against, because it's important for our training units to know what they may be getting into.

"The barrels you see here are a crude representation of the many flying creatures in Calderon, including King Fireflies. As mentioned last week, the current Imbalance in Calderon has affected these creatures in unexpected ways."

Professor Flynn nodded to Trey, and Trey blew his silver whistle. The barrels began spinning around the copper mountain like swings at an amusement park. Each barrel was held aloft by four cables. Some of the cables snapped forward and back, lurching the barrels off-balance. As if that wasn't alarming enough, the barrels began shooting fireballs. Albert felt himself swallow hard. Things had just gotten a lot more serious.

"Grey, Aria, and Terran report that the King Fireflies, usually gentle creatures, have gone berserk. They are flying erratically and spitting fire." Professor Flynn took a moment to compose himself. "I am sad to report that much of the Realm has been burned to a crisp."

There were some gasps from the crowd. Birdie grabbed Albert's hand.

"The fires set by the King Fireflies are the source of the ash clouds on the surface of the earth, of course," Professor Flynn continued. "The question is, what is causing the King Fireflies to behave this way?

"Our Core Historians have determined that there has been one other instance of King Fireflies going mad in the history of the Realms, centuries ago. Our records from that occurrence show that a stagnant Sea Inspire was to blame.

"As many of you know, the Sea Inspire is the underground lake beneath Calderon Peak. It's the King Fireflies' source of nutrition, like nectar is to butterflies.

"But the Sea Inspire's nutritional qualities depend on the water cycling through four underground tunnels below Calderon Peak, a process that essentially filters the water."

"Like the pump in my aquarium back home?" someone to Albert's right said. It was Slink. *No way. Slink has pet fish?* Albert never would have guessed that in a million years. Hoyt gave Slink a quick kick in the boot and Slink hung his head.

"Exactly, Mr. Parker. If the water doesn't cycle through, bacteria can grow."

"That's lame," Mo said. "Why's this such a big deal? Toss some chlorine in there and we're done."

"Not so fast. You're a Second Term Balance Keeper, Mr. Haxel. You should know why it's not that easy." Professor Flynn looked at Mo with a raised eyebrow, daring him to answer.

Mo mumbled something under his breath that Albert couldn't hear.

"Speak up, Mr. Haxel. You have a pretty large audience, after all."

Mo took a deep breath and spoke in a loud voice. "The Realm always provides the Means."

Huh? Albert thought.

"I've seen that somewhere!" Birdie said, louder than she intended to, Albert guessed.

"It's in the Main Chamber," Leroy said, "carved in the

stone above the entrances to the three Realms."

"That's right, Mr. Jones. Good memory." Professor Flynn winked. "The Realms are natural systems—different from the nature we know on the surface, yes, but natural nonetheless. That means that while the Realms sometimes naturally fall out of Balance, they also provide the Means to Restore Balance again."

"Wait a second," Albert said. "I thought it was *our* job to restore Balance." If the Realms could fix themselves, was all this training for nothing?

"Ah—providing the Means to Restore Balance is quite different from actually *using* those Means to Restore Balance, Albert. *That's* what Balance Keepers are for."

"All right, all right," Hoyt said impatiently. "The drain pipes are clogged up and the King Fireflies are going all nutso from drinking the nasty water and setting things on fire. We get it. What's that got to do with the Competition?"

Albert had to admit he was wondering the same thing.

"Your challenge today is threefold. Find the Means to Restore Balance, which Trey and I have planted in the Pit, deliver the Means to the top of Copper Peak, and release the Means's contents into the mountain."

"But what *is* the Means to Restore Balance?" Birdie asked. "What are we looking for?"

"Good question, Miss Howell," Professor Flynn said. "Unfortunately, we don't have an answer for Calderon yet—it appears that that part of the Core records has gone missing. What we do know is that the Means to Restore Balance is another liquid that must be released into the mountain."

"Like how Pap uses Drano when the pipes get clogged in the post office?" Albert said, chuckling to himself.

"Exactly, Albert, though we prefer not to think of the Realm as a giant toilet." Professor Flynn winked at Albert. "In the simulation today, you'll be looking for a giant acorn. You Cedarfell boys are familiar with them, I assume?"

"Yes, sir," Albert, Leroy, and Slink said together. Hoyt and Mo mumbled something a little less polite.

"Let's get started, then," Professor Flynn said. "Keep your wits about you, Balance Keepers! Trey! The whistle!"

Trey blew his whistle again, and the Pit reacted even more fiercely than before.

The barrels started to buck even more wildly. Some of them shot more blue fireballs. They'd dealt with fire in the Pit, but it had been stationary before. Seeing it shoot all over the place made Albert a little nervous. In Calderon, it would only be worse. And who knew what other dangers the Imbalance would cause?

"Find the acorn, release its contents in the Peak, and your team wins!" Professor Flynn said. "On my count. Three, two, one. Begin!"

The crowd went wild as Albert, Leroy, and Birdie huddled up together to talk strategy. Hoyt's team did the same.

"All right, guys," Albert said, taking the lead. "This is serious business. Where should we start? Leroy, do you see anything around here, any clues about where the acorn might be?"

"Well, we always had to go up before, so I'm guessing that the chances of the acorn being down here, within our reach, are pretty low," Leroy said. "But those barrels are at least twenty feet over our heads, and getting to the top of the Peak won't be easy."

Albert nodded in agreement.

"So we'll climb the walls," Birdie said. She pointed at the sides of the Pit. They were like giant rock-climbing walls, with foot- and handholes every few feet, though Albert noted that regular rock-climbing walls didn't have fire bursting forth from them at any given moment.

"It looks like the ground is trampoline style again," Leroy noticed, bouncing a little. "If we fall, it's cool. We'll live."

"You're not scared?" Birdie punched him on the shoulder, laughing. "I think our Leroy's growing up."

Leroy's face reddened. "Maybe I am. Besides, today is about proving to Hoyt that I'm not afraid of him."

"Attaboy, Leroy!" Albert said. "Come on, let's do this!"

They ran forward and started climbing the outer walls

of the Pit, side by side. Ten feet up, Albert's foot slipped and landed in Birdie's face.

"Sorry!" Albert cried out.

Birdie shook her head and blinked her eyes a few times. "I'm okay; keep going."

Across from them, Hoyt was already at the top. Albert knew Hoyt's Speed Tile made short order of climbing challenges. He wished all over again that he knew how to make his own Tile help him out. He had certainly done things in the Core that seemed impossible, but he couldn't say for sure those moments had been his Tile at work. And if it *was* his Tile, he certainly didn't know how he was activating its powers.

"What's next?" Birdie asked, halfway to the top. She clung to the wall like a bug. Albert and Leroy climbed up beside her, their muscles tired from hanging on. Blue flames shot out from holes all around them, bursting forth with a sound like a giant blowtorch.

"I guess we jump for it," Leroy said. "First to the barrels, then maybe to the Peak?"

The barrels were spinning around Copper Peak, soaring past in a blur.

"We'll have to time it just right," Albert concluded. "Leroy, you want to call the shots on this one?"

"Now that's a job I can do," Leroy said. "All right, get ready. When I say jump, jump!"

Albert and Birdie watched as the barrels swung past.

If Albert looked at only *one* barrel, it was easier to focus. He counted the seconds, trying to time it just right. He knew Leroy would have it all figured out, so when he heard his friend counting down, and then screaming, *"Jump!"* Albert pushed off the wall, leaped into midair, and crashed into a barrel. Somehow he was able to hang on as the barrel sailed by and to sit astride it like a cowboy as it bucked and swayed. Behind him, Albert heard Leroy's command, and saw Birdie jump from the corner of his eye. Leroy waited a few more seconds, then leaped from the wall and clung to a barrel.

It looked to Albert like Leroy's Texas upbringing was finally paying off. Leroy's horse-riding skills were turning him into a barrel-riding rodeo champion.

"Yeehaw!" Albert screamed, laughing as Leroy soared past like a pro.

Out of nowhere, Albert's barrel went wild. One of the cables snapped and he slid backward, somersaulting into the open air. The rubbery floor of the Pit bounced him back up, and he clung on to the rock wall. He glanced around to see where Hoyt was, but from his position on the wall, he couldn't tell who was who up above. "These teams are neck and neck! It's a new day, ladies and gentlemen!" Professor Flynn shouted. *Well. Better climb faster.*

The crowd, so large in size, was naturally louder than they had been in previous simulations, but also more enthusiastic. People actually knew who Hydra was now, probably from Leroy's massive win in Tiles the night before. Petra was up there again, calling out a Hydra cheer. Albert heard the names of his own team: *Come on, Birdie! Ride that thing, Leroy! Climb, Albert, climb!* The swell of voices told him the crowd was on his side, and it gave him a huge boost of confidence. He climbed with a new purpose and energy, then leaped into the air from the side of the Pit. Albert could not have landed more awkwardly on a barrel, but somehow he'd done it. All three Hydra team members were riding bucking barrels around the Copper Peak. Now they just had to find the acorn. Albert trusted Leroy's guess that it was somewhere up here. He looked closely at the Peak, trying to get a glimpse of *something.*

But the barrels spun wildly, bucking like crazy, and Albert had to concentrate on holding on. Finally, the barrels calmed down a bit and Albert could really look around. He saw that Hoyt, Mo, and Slink were riding behind him. Team Argon was right on their tails.

"Folks, we have ourselves a race!" Professor Flynn yelled.

"Now what do we do?" Albert called to Birdie and Leroy.

The barrels started spitting fire at one another. The one Slink was on shot fire at Albert's. Albert leaped just in time as his barrel burst into blue flames. He landed on

Leroy's barrel. When he did, Leroy's barrel went wild.

"See anything?" Albert shouted into Leroy's ear.

As if in answer to Albert's question, the Copper Peak started to ooze something green and slippery from the rock. Albert knew there had to be something important about this event, but he couldn't quite figure it out.

"I forgot to mention," Professor Flynn suddenly shouted into the MegaHorn, "the bacteria has also caused a strange sludge to ooze from the mountain. Take caution!"

But green ooze was the least of Albert's problems. Suddenly, Slink's barrel came crashing into Albert and Leroy's, and all three players burst into the air like popcorn. With the extra height from the collision, Albert saw a flash of a familiar shape at the very top of the Peak.

Gotcha! Albert said to himself. He knew he'd seen something important and hoped Team Argon hadn't spotted it yet.

He curled into a tight ball and hit the rubbery ground like a wrecking ball. The floor launched him, shooting him high into the air until he reached his arms out and grabbed a barrel flying past.

He spotted the shape again. It was there, at the very top, right where the green goo was spilling out.

Unfortunately, it seemed like Hoyt had caught on, too. Hoyt was shouting commands to his team, instructing them to get to the top of the Copper Peak.

Albert tightened his grip on his barrel as Slink leaped from his own barrel onto the Copper Peak. Slink landed on a slick, narrow pathway that wound around the mountain, but his feet slipped and he fell off in an instant. Albert watched as Hoyt tried next, but he jumped too far, tumbling over the edge and down to the floor of the Pit.

"We need someone with good balance!" Albert yelled.

He looked at Birdie, but she was busy fighting with Mo for a barrel, and didn't look like she had heard Albert. Leroy was way too tall to have great balance, wasn't he?

"I'm not doing that!" Leroy shouted. His glasses were askew on his face. "No way! I've already reached my limit for today!"

Albert took a deep breath, and nodded. *Looks like it's gonna be me.*

The barrels were going even faster, speeding up as the challenge wore on. Around and around they went, tangling into one another. Just as Albert was about to jump, he heard a terrible crash. Mo had finally knocked Birdie off of the barrel, and she was falling.

"Birdie!" Albert screamed. He stretched his free arm for her, but he wasn't quite close enough.

He watched, sick to his stomach, as Birdie hit the floor of the Pit. She cried out at first, but after the Pit had bounced her up and back down two more times, she lay still, crumpled on the floor. *No! She has to be okay. She has to!*

Albert almost leaped from his barrel, but before he could do anything, Professor Flynn rode down in his mechanical cage, scooped Birdie up, and hauled her to the observation level.

Across from Albert, Hoyt's team was laughing, pointing at Birdie as she stepped out of the cage on wobbly legs, then crumpled back down to the floor. Trey helped her up and led her away. At least she was on her feet, out of there safely. That made Albert focus again. He was angry, upset at Mo for hurting his friend, and even more upset at Hoyt for making such a show of her.

Okay, Albert. Now's your chance. Let's do this, for Birdie.

"Go for it, Albert!" Leroy shouted. He was pointing at the Copper Peak. "You can do this!"

Albert waited for the right opportunity. A burst of blue fire shot out of the volcano, and as it cleared, Albert prepared to jump. Slink's barrel was just behind Albert's, and Albert watched in horror as Slink stretched his foot out and kicked Albert's barrel, knocking him into a tailspin. There was nothing he could do.

"Nice try, sucker!" Slink yelled. He pulled a yellow Tile out of his pocket and waved it in Albert's face. It had a triangle on it with a sphere balanced perfectly on top. He slipped it around his neck and leaped. He landed on the narrow path with surprising precision, and started to make his way to the top of the mountain.

How was Albert supposed to compete with Slink

without one of his own Balance Tiles?

Albert wasn't going to lose another simulation. There was *no way* he'd let that happen, especially with Birdie out and possibly injured. Another cable on his barrel snapped. He almost tumbled off, but he held strong.

Albert took a deep breath, readied himself for the jump, and pushed off the barrel. While he leaped, an image popped into his head. It was that strange Balance Cat that Lucinda had given to Leroy when they first entered the Core. He wished he had that now. In midair, something happened to Albert. He had a strange feeling, like he'd just chugged down an entire fizzy soda. He felt lighter, like he was almost completely weightless.

When he landed on the path that wound around the mountain, he was only a few feet behind Slink. At first, Albert felt like he was going to fall right back off. The path was only a few inches wide, thinner than thin, and cool, green ooze flowed down the copper mountainside like neon lava, making the way even more slippery and dangerous. But instead of slipping, his feet felt rooted to the spiral pathway. It felt quite strange, really. There was no time for observations, though—Slink was already a few feet ahead of him. Albert turned sideways, placing his back toward the mountain's side, and began sliding up as fast as he could.

"It's a close race!" Albert heard his dad say, but he was too focused to listen to the rest.

Albert's eyes fell on Hoyt on a barrel across the Pit. The guy was laughing, pointing at Leroy falling from his barrel. For a second, as Hoyt shot past, Albert caught sight of his Tile.

A sideways zigzag symbol.

Focus, Albert. No time for distractions! And as Albert continued forward, desperate to catch up to Slink, he was suddenly *there.* Right behind the guy, in two seconds flat! He had moved fast like Hoyt! Yet here he was, still balanced like Slink. This time, Albert could feel it in his bones. This was his Tile at work, and whatever the reason, it was allowing him *two* skill sets at one time. It should have been impossible, but there was no time for wondering why. Now he had to get around Slink.

All right, Tile, Albert thought. *I need to jump like those Jackalope things, like I did in the second simulation.* He pictured himself leaping high and wide, and as he did, he felt like he'd been plugged into a light socket and powered up. He bent his knees, dodged a ball of cool fire from Hoyt's barrel as it flew by, and jumped.

Everything seemed to move in slow motion. One second, Albert was in midair over Slink's head, and the next, he'd landed sideways on the pathway, perfectly balanced.

"No way!" Hoyt screamed from below. "He's cheating!"

"Hey! Don't accuse my teammate of cheating!" Leroy shouted, and the two got into an argument as they circled round and round.

I'm doing it! Albert thought. He scurried along the side of the wall, making his way closer to the top. Now the Peak was pouring green slime in channels all around him, but Albert expertly moved around every challenge.

And there it was: an acorn the size of a basketball, sitting on the pathway in front of him, right near an opening at the top of the Peak.

Albert scooped the acorn up and carried it with one hand. The barrels seemed to sense that he'd taken the prize, because they all started shooting fireballs in his direction. He ducked and dodged, sometimes leaping to avoid them. One final leap and he was right at the edge of the opening, standing on the last little bit of pathway, looking down as green sludge continued pouring out. Albert risked a quick glance over his shoulder. Slink was only a few feet away now. But what was he supposed to do with the acorn? Just toss it in? Crack it open like they did in Cedarfell? Where was Leroy with his Synapse Tile when Albert needed him? Three more steps and Slink would be on top of him. Time to make a decision. Three, two . . .

Albert cracked the acorn on his own head, and out poured the milky liquid into the Peak's opening.

"Noooooo!" Slink screamed, knocking the acorn shell out of Albert's hands. One second later, both Albert and

Slink had grabbed onto the edge of the opening—the mountain was shaking like a volcano about to erupt. For a moment, Albert thought maybe he'd gotten it all wrong, and without another thought, he turned and leaped, grabbing onto a barrel as it raced by. Slink did the same. Albert rode the barrel once around the Peak, and then jumped, landing on the spongy floor of the Pit next to Leroy. The floor down here was shaking, too.

It was like a science experiment on caffeine.

"Uh-oh," Leroy said, "I think it's gonna blow." Half a second later, the Peak spewed the brightest blue water Albert had ever seen. It doused the fireballs that shot from the barrels and put out the flames bursting from the walls.

Albert was quickly getting soaked, but he turned to Leroy. "Did we just—"

"Hydra wins!" Professor Flynn shouted into his MegaHorn.

The crowd erupted into a roar of cheers, and the water explosion stopped as quickly as it had started. Leroy leaped into the air, tackling Albert with a big bear hug, then started wringing out his baseball cap. Albert shook himself off like a dog coming in from the rain. Across the way, Hoyt groaned and started yelling at Slink and Mo, blaming them for their loss.

Albert and Leroy made their way to a platform,

wringing out their T-shirts. When their platform arrived at the top, Professor Flynn was there to celebrate with them.

"Well done, boys! Well done! You've just logged your very first victory in the Core."

"Where's Birdie? Is she okay?" Albert and Leroy asked together.

Professor Flynn pulled out three copper Medallions and passed them to Leroy and Albert. "One for Miss Howell," he said. "You can visit her in the Infirmary after late lunch, down tunnel three. She's banged up, but she's tough. Birdie will be fine."

"For Birdie," Albert said, holding up his Medallion.

"For Birdie," Leroy agreed.

After the last meal of the day, the boys found the Infirmary. It was a small, warm room with real lightbulbs hanging from the ceiling. An old man with one eye in the middle of his forehead scurried about, tending to several wounded Balance Keepers. A boy lay asleep in one of the beds, his leg in traction. He clearly wouldn't be doing any Competitions for a while. It struck Albert as he walked around: This is serious business. People get hurt in the Core.

Birdie was propped up in a bed in the back of the room, practicing playing Tiles. Farnsworth was there, his head on her lap, his eyes droopy and sad. There was a white bandage wrapped around Birdie's head. A Floppywhippet flew around the bandage, chirping a little song, as if to make Birdie's wound all better. When she saw Albert and Leroy, she groaned.

"It's totally my fault we lost," she said. "I shouldn't have been so careless."

Albert smirked and nudged Leroy. "No worries, right, Leroy?"

"Yeah," Leroy said. He pulled out a Medallion and flipped it onto Birdie's lap. "Maybe you can use this to buy some chocolate or something."

At the sight of the Medallion, Birdie's eyes went wide. "You guys won? If this is a bad joke, I'm *so* gonna pummel you both!"

"It's real," Leroy said. "Made of copper, which is a chemical element, and its symbol on the periodic table is . . ."

"Quit nerding out and hug me already!" Birdie screamed, pulling both boys in.

She scooped up the Medallion and the one-eyed cyclops nurse arrived at the side of the bed.

"Are these boys bothering you?" the old man asked.

Birdie smiled. "No, sir," she said. "I'm the best I've been in days!"

The cyclops nurse turned to Albert and Leroy and pointed at them one at a time. "I've got my eye on you two."

No one could stop giggling when the nurse walked away. Leroy and Albert spent the rest of the evening telling Birdie the story of how they'd won. When Leroy got to the part about Albert's megasuperhero moves, Birdie gasped. "I can't believe I missed that! It's your Tile, Albert! It has to be! I think it's finally kicking in, big-time, just like it did the other day when you swam like me!"

Albert nodded. "I think you're right. I've been going over the simulation again and again. It's like my Tile reacts to my thoughts or something."

"What do you mean?" Leroy asked. He plucked a cup of applesauce off Birdie's bed table and peeled open the lid, then wolfed it down.

Albert shrugged. "I don't know. Sometimes, when I want something *really* bad, and I sort of picture it happening, it just happens."

"So you wanted to swim like me, and suddenly you just could? That doesn't make any sense at all," Birdie said. "Maybe you're just a better swimmer than you thought you were."

"No—I could breathe underwater like you can. Nobody can do that without magic. And I definitely can't run as fast as Hoyt does, but that happened, too, in the Pit today, while I was balancing like Slink. I asked my dad about it the other night—if my Tile could give me multiple powers at once. He said it was impossible."

"Well, it looks like maybe your dad's wrong, doesn't it?" Birdie replied. "We'll just have to try harder to figure this out ourselves."

"But my dad's a professor. He's the one who helps everyone pick their Tiles out of the Waterfall of Fate. If anyone knew something, it would be him. I think he knows something . . . but he's not saying it, for some reason."

"Well then, like I said, we'll just have to figure it out ourselves," Birdie said. Then she turned to Leroy, who was sneaking another cup of applesauce from a nearby sleeping patient. "Leroy! Don't think I didn't see you take mine, too!"

The two of them started arguing like brother and sister. Albert, overwhelmed by them, turned his attention to the corner of the room, where an old TV was playing news from the outside world. Farnsworth hopped down from the bed and joined Albert in front of the screen.

It crackled with fuzz, but Albert gave the TV a good slap, and the image cleared.

It was New York City.

"Guys! Come here and look at this," Albert called over his shoulder.

"It's been showing the same story for the past couple of hours," Birdie said. "Looks like trouble."

Leroy helped Birdie out of bed, and they settled down in front of the TV screen.

"The volcanic ash clouds have taken over Staten Island," the reporter said. *"It seems the ash is coming right out of the Atlantic. All of New York City has shut down for the remainder of the week."*

"That's not good at all," Birdie said. "Albert, I thought your mom said everything was fine?"

"She probably didn't want to scare me." Albert leaned forward to get a closer look. There were snowplows in the streets of Manhattan, scooping up piles and piles of ash. Cabs were stuck in the middle of the streets. Hot-dog stands were covered, and you couldn't even see the fire hydrants anymore. This *definitely* wasn't okay.

The reporter continued:

"If someone doesn't find a solution to this, and fast, the residents of New York City could be in serious danger. Evacuation of the city is imminent."

"It's Calderon," Albert said. "We're going to have to figure out the Means to Restore Balance, and soon. Or who knows what could happen up there?"

"Grey, Aria, and Terran must be exhausted." Birdie nodded. "We've barely seen them recently. And it's only getting worse."

Leroy said what they were all thinking.

"We need to be ready if the First Unit fails."

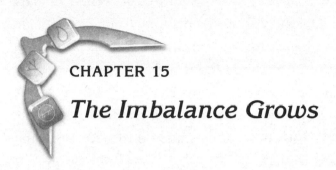

CHAPTER 15

The Imbalance Grows

The next morning after breakfast, Albert, Leroy, and Birdie made their way through the cave to Professor Flynn's office for a specially scheduled lecture.

They passed by the Waterfall of Fate, and Albert felt cool droplets of water on his face. The last time Albert had been here, he'd been completely disappointed by his Tile. But today, he felt like he was walking a little taller. Whatever his Tile actually did, it was starting to work. Maybe not all the time, but when it did, it seemed that it could make Albert do *anything*. And that made Albert feel stronger, like he was really becoming a Balance Keeper.

As they rounded the Waterfall, about fifty or so students came into view. They were all seated on the floor in front of Professor Flynn's desk. When he saw Albert, Professor Flynn winked.

Albert smiled. His dad looked like he was still really proud of him for yesterday's Pit win.

"So, anyone know what this is about?" Birdie asked, as the three of them settled down in the back of the crowd. Petra was there, a big smile on his face, and a fat notebook on his lap.

"Professor Flynn's going to give us *even more info* on Calderon!" Petra squeaked. He had his pencil poised at the ready to take notes.

"That's exactly what we need," Leroy said. "If there's a chance we might be going into Calderon, we've gotta know *more*."

Albert grinned. "Yeah, and with you here, Birdie and I don't even need to pay attention. You'll remember everything."

Birdie rapped Albert across the shoulders anyway and narrowed her blue eyes. "Class is starting. We should *all* pay attention."

"Good morning, students. I'm glad you're all here. Balance Keepers—as you know, it's getting more and more likely the Calderon First Unit will need backup in Calderon. The information I'm sharing today will be vital if you have to enter the Realm. Other students—the Core is your home as much as it is the Balance Keepers'; you deserve to know this stuff, too."

Professor Flynn started off by showing them a hand-drawn map of Calderon. "We can't take photographs there, of course. Most technology doesn't work in the Realms."

Albert craned his neck to see better. It was a huge world, entirely different from his own. Calderon looked like it was laid out in giant rings, starting with a jungle around the edge, then an open field, then, judging by the big, black portion on the map labeled the *Forest of Thorns*, a rather scary forest—Leroy groaned when he saw that—and finally, in the middle, Calderon Peak.

"In the Pit simulations, you've seen only a portion of the things a Balance Keeper might see in the actual Realm," Professor Flynn said. He started talking about all the creatures the Balance Keepers might encounter—Hexabons, Hissengores, and some strange bird the size of a horse that would attack on sight.

"I just love birds," Birdie whispered to Albert and Leroy.

"Not that kind of bird. No way!" Leroy shook his head.

Albert laughed. It felt amazing to have these two friends by his side. Petra smiled at Albert and gave him a thumbs-up.

Okay, three friends.

He exhaled, and turned his focus back on Professor Flynn. His dad was just starting to tell the class about his first time in Calderon, when the alarm bell went off.

The noise came so loud and strong that Albert had to clap his hands over his ears. He looked right at his dad, hoping this was just another drill.

But by the look of horror on Professor Flynn's face, Albert knew it wasn't.

Trey appeared, running around the Waterfall of Fate. His face was red, as if he'd been sprinting across the Core.

"Professor! We need you at once in the Realm. It's a class-four alert!"

"What's happening?" Leroy asked, or at least that's what Albert thought he asked. The alarm was extremely loud and reading lips wasn't his strong suit.

"This is bad. Really, really bad!" Petra yelled. He stood up and ran from the room without another word.

Albert got up and watched as his dad reached into his desk and pulled out his Tile. Professor Flynn strung it over his neck and stood up tall.

"Class dismissed!" he said. "Trey, escort them back to their dorms at once."

Albert tried to break through to the front of the crowd, but everyone was pushing and shoving.

"Dad!" Albert yelled as he watched Professor Flynn and Trey speaking to each other, the expressions on their faces quite grave.

If Professor Flynn was going in, it meant the First Unit couldn't handle whatever was happening on their own. And it meant they might need a training unit to go into the Realm soon, too. This was the worst of the worst. Albert's heart was slamming in his chest, out of control.

"Dad, wait!" Albert called out again, hoping to get a word with him before he left.

Professor Flynn stopped at the sound of Albert's voice. He turned, looked Albert in the eyes, and gave Albert one curt nod. Then he disappeared behind the Waterfall of Fate and out of sight.

As Trey called the students to order, the alarm bell finally stopped. The room fell into a hush. No one said a word, but Albert could see the looks on his friends' faces. At that moment, a horrible thought snuck its way into Albert's mind.

What if he never saw his dad again?

CHAPTER 16

Trouble Ensues

Days passed and Albert still hadn't been able to talk to his dad.

News had come out that Core Researchers had identified three liquid-filled things in the Calderon Realm that could be the Means to Restore Balance: the pod of the Leafless Willow, the seeds of the Fireflowers, and the silver eggs of the Hissengores, though rumor had it that while the silver eggs lasted for centuries, an actual Hissengore nest hadn't been found in generations of Balance Keepers.

Professor Flynn and the Calderon First Unit had been spending their nights in Calderon, searching for these possible Means. Albert, Leroy, and Birdie waited by the door to Calderon every morning before breakfast, and

Albert held his breath each time, only letting it out when he saw that his dad was back safely, though *safely* was a relative term.

When his dad, Grey, Aria, and Terran got back each morning, stumbling through the door at the end of the Calderon river, they were covered in ash, dripping sweat, and so tired they were ready to drop. Professor Flynn looked worse and worse each day. His hair had developed a deeper sheen of gray, and his eyes were purple underneath, as if he hadn't slept. Albert hated to see his dad that way. He knew the Realms took a toll on professors. But to see it in person gave Albert a lump in his throat that he could never quite swallow. Albert didn't have the heart to bother his dad with questions when he knew all he wanted to do was rest.

After a few weeks of failure in Calderon, an announcement was made: Terran was leaving the Core for good. Everyone was shocked. A First Unit member giving up on the Core, especially in such a time of Imbalance? Albert took it as a sign that things were worse than he thought. If Terran, as talented as she was, wanted to give up . . . what was stopping everyone else from doing the same thing?

After the announcement about Terran, the Pit practices intensified. From now on, the training units had to train twice as hard to prepare, in case they were needed. With only Grey and Aria left in the First Unit, it became even more important for the backup units to be ready. Trey took over the training, pushing them through head-on duels. They did underwater drills and climbed moss-covered trees that were as slick as Slip 'N Slides. They swung from cables like Tarzan, side by side, while Hissengores tugged at their ankles. The intensity of the Competitions increased with each passing day.

At night, Albert, Leroy, and Birdie spent time poring over books in the Library, trying to learn as much as they could about Calderon. They studied the creatures, the plants, the weather patterns—anything they could think of. They had to be ready.

The Main Leaderboard remained in Argon's favor at first, but Hydra and all the other teams were close behind. Ecco sustained a series of injuries that slowed them way down, and they were eliminated from the Competitions, which only made the seriousness of the situation increase. Now it was always Argon against Hydra. Hoyt's team kept taunting, but their quips were getting less creative and more antagonistic by the day. Albert could tell: Argon was starting to see Hydra as a real threat.

Albert, Leroy, and Birdie went to the Tiles room every afternoon to distract themselves. Leroy won games left and right. Even Slink tried to beat him once. Leroy won, of course, which only made the Pit Competitions rougher, more heated. Leroy eventually ran out of Tiles opponents—no one wanted to play someone they could never beat.

One night, while the three of them sat watching an intense match between Jack and Ellery, the game was interrupted by an announcement over the Core loudspeaker.

"Attention, please," Trey's voice rang out. "I have an update on the Calderon Realm. Today, Professor Flynn and the Calderon First Unit attempted to cure the Sea Inspire using the pod of the Leafless Willow, but unfortunately found that the pods were all dried up— there was no liquid inside. We can only assume this is further evidence of the Imbalance."

There was a murmur in the Library as everyone whispered about what this could mean.

"But have faith," Trey continued. "The Realm always provides the Means. Tomorrow they begin their search for the seeds of the Fireflower. I will keep you updated. Until then, train hard, Balance Keepers. You may be called on to serve. Thank you."

"That's not good at all," Birdie said, sighing as she ran her fingers through her ponytail. "What happens if the Fireflower seeds don't work? What are the odds of that happening?"

Leroy pushed his glasses farther up on the bridge of his nose. "It's fifty-fifty. And that's not looking good, because if we're on the wrong side of that fifty percent, then we're stuck with the mythical Hissengore eggs as our final option."

"That must be why Terran left." Birdie sighed. "She probably got scared that nothing would ever fix this."

Albert thought about his family back home in the city. He had tried to call his mom yesterday, but the lines were busy. The TV in the Infirmary showed that the ash was getting even worse, making the city streets look like ski slopes.

"What if the Hissengore eggs don't even exist? No one's found a nest in centuries," Albert groaned. For the first time, he felt totally helpless. His dad was exhausted from entering the Realm, his mom was out of reach, and the fate of the world above relied on finding some sort of cure that might not even work.

Just then, Petra walked into the Tiles room. He waved halfheartedly at Hydra. "You guys feeling as down about this Imbalance as I am?"

"Yes," Birdie, Leroy, and Albert said together.

"I can't believe Terran left. She always seemed so . . . focused." Petra slumped down on the floor next to them. "I've spent all day in the Library, reading books on Calderon, in case I found something to help out Grey and Aria. They're probably hurting right now. But I've found nothing. Nothing at all!"

"I haven't either," Leroy said.

"Poor Grey and Aria." Birdie sighed.

"They must be exhausted." Albert nodded in agreement.

As if the day couldn't get any grimmer, Hoyt and his cronies sauntered into the room. The second Hoyt's beady eyes found Hydra, he marched over. "Word is Leroy here thinks he's the best Tiles player around."

Albert sighed. *I'm not in the mood for this today.* "Yeah. He's pretty good, I guess."

Hoyt grimaced. He crossed his arms and pointed at Leroy. "Not good enough to beat me. Let's play."

Leroy stood up and smoothed out his pants. "Actually, Hoyt, we were just leaving."

Albert, Birdie, and Petra stood up to follow, but before they could go anywhere, Hoyt grabbed Leroy's shoulder and whirled him around. "What's wrong? Are you scared, Four Eyes?"

Leroy's jaw tightened. His face flushed a deep shade of red.

"What's your problem? Just beat it, Hoyt, before I sink my fist into your face!" Birdie snapped, stepping in front of Leroy.

"I'm not afraid of a little *girl*." Hoyt laughed, and Slink and Mo stepped up beside him.

Albert joined Birdie. "Hey, guys, come on. Let's just forget about this," he said, trying to stop a fight that didn't need to happen. He pulled Leroy and Birdie away, but Hoyt wasn't done yet.

"You guys think you're better than us, Flynn, but you're all just a bunch of pansies." Hoyt motioned for his cronies to follow him. "We're competing in the Pit tomorrow. And you'll see just how pathetic you are."

Hoyt spun on his heel and marched out of the room, his shoulder slamming Leroy so hard that Leroy tripped. His glasses fell off of his face, and Hoyt's boot crunched over them, shattering the lenses.

"Oops. Didn't see those there." Hoyt laughed.

"Oh man," Leroy whined, as he knelt to pick up the broken glasses. "My mom's gonna be so mad. I can't see. Birdie, where are my glasses?"

At the sight of Leroy and Birdie on the ground, looking totally defeated as they tried to fix the broken glasses, Albert felt his heart race, and heat spread to his cheeks. "That's enough," he said. "I'm tired of this."

He imagined himself being strong, the way he was in the Pit when he lifted Mo off of his body like the guy was weightless. In two strides, Albert was at Hoyt's back. Hoyt turned around and started to laugh at Albert. Albert shoved Hoyt lightly, so he wouldn't really hurt him. But Albert's hands felt all tingly, and suddenly Hoyt went flying across the room.

Hoyt's arm knocked into one of the Tiles boards. The pedestal rocked back and forth for a second, then crashed to the ground and broke in two pieces. Everyone in the room gasped.

"Now you've really done it, Flynn!" Hoyt whined like a baby, clutching his arm. Surprisingly, there was nothing but a tiny scratch there. Slink and Mo tried to help him up, but Hoyt shoved them off and left the room, yelling over his shoulder. "You're going to pay for this!"

Albert's pulse slowed back down. Everyone was staring at him. Some people were smiling, happy someone finally stood up to Hoyt's bullying. But others were looking at Albert like he'd just turned into a werewolf.

"I didn't mean to push him so hard," Albert said. "I hardly touched him, I promise!"

"Albert . . . that was . . . ," Birdie started, but she stopped midsentence. Her eyes went wide, just as Albert felt a hand tighten over his shoulder.

"Young Mr. Flynn," Professor Asante said. She turned Albert around so that he was staring up at her face. She had a new tattoo on her cheek, an eyeball symbol that really gave Albert the creeps. "As impressive as that was, I'm afraid we do not tolerate fighting in the Core. You have earned yourself two hours of detention."

"But Albert was just standing up for Leroy!" Petra squeaked. "Hoyt broke his glasses!"

Professor Asante held up a large, tattooed hand. "I will deal with Mr. Jackson later. And I believe you are late for cleaning duty in the Tower, Petra, are you not? I suggest you head there now. Take Mr. Flynn with you—

he'll be on cleaning duty with you there as punishment for his actions."

Petra sighed, but nodded anyway. "Yes, Professor."

Albert and Petra left the room, leaving Birdie and Leroy behind.

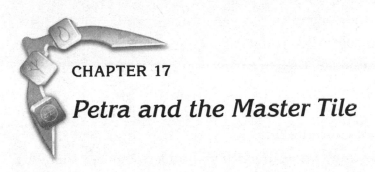

CHAPTER 17

Petra and the Master Tile

D etention with Petra, it turned out, was Albert's favorite part of the day.

"You did the right thing, standing up for Leroy," Petra said. "I mean, throwing Hoyt across the room was a little extreme, but he kind of deserved it."

"I guess so," Albert agreed. "He wasn't hurt that badly, was he?"

"It was practically a paper cut! Imagine if Birdie had gotten ahold of him first. Now *that* would have ended in a serious injury."

Albert followed Petra out of the Library and up a spiral hallway that twisted and turned so much it made Albert dizzy. They stopped before an old wooden door.

"This is the Tower," Petra said. "It's basically the

professors' lounge."

The Tower was a well-sized, rounded-out cave, complete with a natural spring running right through the middle. There was even an old pinball machine in the corner.

There were shelves lining one wall, full of ancient-looking leather books. Another wall held a rack of gleaming swords and other strange weapons. There was a cabinet full of snacks, a glowing pink parrot chirping happily in a wire cage, and several hammocks that hung from one wall to another. Professor Bigglesby was curled up in one of the hammocks, snoring nearly as loud as Leroy.

"Looks like being a professor isn't so bad," Albert said, whistling. "My dad didn't tell me about this place."

"You should see the kitchens. Now *those* are cool!" Petra opened up a cabinet in the corner of the room. He pulled out two mops, a metal bucket, and a bottle of soap.

They set to work, filling the bucket with water from the stream, and started mopping the floors. Albert hated doing chores, but this was different. It was nice to have some peace and quiet, unless you counted Professor Bigglesby's snores, which seemed to get louder the longer he slept.

"It's awesome spending time with a Balance Keeper," Petra said. He was mopping like a champ. Albert wondered if Petra had been cleaning the Core since he could walk. "I wish I was like you."

"I'm not so great," Albert said. "I don't even know how to work my own Tile."

Petra tossed Albert a rag. "We're supposed to shine the weapons twice. And what do you mean you can't work your Tile? I've watched every Competition. You're amazing."

"That's just it," Albert said. "I don't know *how* I'm doing that stuff."

Petra thought on it for a second. "That's the rumor about the Master Tile."

"The *what*?"

Petra stopped mopping. "The Master Tile." He pointed at Albert's black Tile. "You mean no one's told you? I'm sorry, Albert. I guess I figured you knew. I mean, it is *your* Tile."

"My dad never told me my Tile had a name. Or any rumors!"

"Probably because the professors don't believe them. I only know because I've spent loads of time in here, reading these books. Also I'm a Pure, and we sometimes see things differently than people from the outside." He set down his mop and crossed to the bookshelf. He went through the books, finally pulling out a huge, black leather volume. "This is called the Black Book."

"You don't say," Albert quipped with a smirk. Petra

just rolled his eyes.

They sat down on the floor together and opened the Black Book. It was full of Tile symbols, thousands of them, each one with its own unique meaning.

"This one is the symbol for Invisibility." Petra pointed at a symbol that looked an awful lot like those puffy storm clouds that always brought on rain.

"People can be invisible?" Albert gasped.

Petra nodded. He was so excited his hands were shaking as he flipped through the book. *Leroy would love to get his hands on this thing,* Albert thought. There were symbols that gave people superhearing, the ability to go for days without needing to eat, even singing at perfect pitch, which Albert wasn't sure would be all that helpful in the Realms, but what did he know? He'd never been in one.

"So where's this Master Tile thing?" Albert asked.

Petra flipped to the very back of the book and landed on a page denoting a new section. The page was blank but for a few words:

Tiles beyond this point are unconfirmed and, quite possibly, do not exist. If they do exist, they are most likely useless. If these Tiles are genuine, then they are dangerous. Proceed with skepticism. And caution!

Albert sat back with a sigh.

"I can see why my dad wouldn't think much of this Tile," Albert said. "It's a dud, just like Hoyt said."

"I've been in the Core my entire life," Petra said, more serious than ever. "And I'm telling you: I have a feeling about this Tile only Pures can have. I think your Tile might be the greatest of them all."

Albert wanted to laugh. There was no way his Tile was the most powerful one. But he saw the hope in Petra's eyes and nodded for Petra to turn the page.

"It's right here: the Master Balance Keeper symbol." Petra flipped to the next page.

There it was, a matching image of Albert's Tile symbol, with that strange scale-looking shape. Scribbled next to it, in rushed handwriting that Albert could hardly read, were a few scant words:

The Master Tile. Knowledge is the key to its power. Proceed with great caution.

"What's that supposed to mean?" Albert asked. "Knowledge?"

Petra thought on it for a second. "Maybe it means you've got to study?"

"*Study?*" Albert made a face. "Study what?"

"Beats me," Petra replied.

"Well, if I do have to study, that would totally blow, dude," Albert said. "Everyone else gets to have these Tiles that just give them free powers and I have to study to make mine work?"

Petra frowned at Albert. "I've wished for my entire life that someday I'd wake up and become a Balance Keeper.

If I had the opportunity that you have, I'd study until my eyes fell out. Or, you know, something less intense."

Albert sighed. "You're right. I didn't mean it that way. It just hardly seems fair."

"Nothing's fair!" Petra smiled. "That's what makes life interesting!" He flipped through the book again, until he opened up a page that had the water-droplet symbol. "You breathed underwater like Birdie once, didn't you?"

"Well, yeah," Albert said, "but I don't know how. I mean, I knew what her power was, and I just sort of . . . wished I could have a Tile like hers and do what she did, I guess."

Professor Bigglesby snorted, and mumbled something about eating cheese. Petra lowered his voice. "And you also ran fast like Hoyt, balanced like Slink, got superstrong . . ."

"And one time, when Leroy was playing Tiles," Albert remembered, "I felt mega whiz-kid smart. Just for a few seconds, but then it stopped."

"Well, there has to be something connecting all those things," Petra said. "What were you doing before you felt the power of the Synapse Tile?"

"I don't know," Albert replied. "I remember looking at Leroy's Tile and thinking the symbol reminded me of this tree in Herman, and how cool it would be to play Tiles like Leroy so I could beat my Pap."

"And what about when you could balance like Slink?"

"Slink had waved his stupid yellow Tile in my face."

"And before you swam like Birdie?"

"I wanted so badly to help my team it was like I could see Birdie's water droplet in my mind."

"Exactly!" Petra exclaimed. "What if your Tile only works if you know the power well? Like, if you know the symbol for the power and can picture it in your head?"

Albert stood up and started shining the swords again. "But I don't know all the symbols. I guess I knew Leroy's and Birdie's and maybe Hoyt's, but most of the time I just pictured what I wanted to do, like jumping on a trampoline or something, and it happened."

"Hmm . . . ," Petra mused. "Maybe that somehow unlocked only part of the power of the Tile." He began flipping through the book. "How did you do that crazy leap over Slink on the Copper Peak?"

Albert was getting a little tired of all the questioning, but Petra was so excited he decided to humor him. "I think I sort of . . . asked my Tile to help me jump like the Jackalopes in Cedarfell. Totally lame, I know, but it seemed to work."

"And that's when you could *really* leap, right?" Petra said, stopping on the page he had been looking for. "Here's why."

Albert leaned in. The page showed the Jumping Jackalope Tile, complete with a stick figure of the part-rabbit, part-antelope creature.

"So I accidentally pictured this symbol and got the power?" It seemed too easy to Albert. "What about all the other times?"

"You said it yourself, Albert—you were imagining Birdie's symbol and then you could swim like her. With Leroy and Slink, you had just looked at their Tiles, so their symbols were fresh in your mind, even if you didn't *know* the Balance Tile symbol. It says *knowledge*, right there in the book. Albert! Just imagine . . . if you knew *all* the symbols and could picture them at will—"

"I'd be the best Balance Keeper there ever was."

Petra nodded enthusiastically.

"*If* it's true," Albert added.

"There's only one way to find out!" Petra motioned for Albert to join him on the floor in front of the book.

They spent the next few minutes flipping through the book, getting familiar with several symbols. When they'd looked at ten or so, Petra quizzed Albert by covering up the powers with his hand.

"What's this one?" Petra asked, as Albert looked at a symbol of a bird with outstretched wings.

"Easy," Albert replied. "Flying."

"This one?" Petra held up the book on a page with a crescent-moon symbol.

Albert didn't know this one right away. Was it the power to sprout claws like a werewolf or the ability to see in the dark? All this was getting a little boring, even when it was about something as cool as Core powers. But Petra was right. Albert was lucky to be a Balance Keeper. He gritted his teeth and forced himself to focus.

"Night Vision?" Albert guessed.

"Nope," Petra said. "It's Sleeplessness. Going for days without even needing a nap." Petra turned the book now so only he could see it. "Describe the symbol for the Vanishing Tile to me."

Albert knew that one—it was a cloud shape, like the puff of smoke when a magician goes *poof* and disappears. He closed his eyes and could see the symbol clearly. He opened his mouth to describe it to Petra, but before he could say anything, Petra jumped up. Albert opened his eyes at the sound and found Petra pointing at him with wide eyes. His hands were shaking.

"You're . . . gone! Albert, you're *gone*!"

"What are you talking about?" Albert asked. But when he looked down at his toes . . .

There was nothing there.

"I'm invisible!" Albert said, trying not to scream and wake up the professor. It only lasted for a second. As soon as he got distracted and forgot about the Tile symbol, his body reappeared.

"I knew it!" Petra squeaked. "I knew you could do it! Let's try another one!" He flipped to the page for the Diminishing Tile.

All the symbols were swirling around in Albert's head

now, but he focused and imagined a big triangle with a tiny triangle next to it. All of a sudden he was eye to eye with Petra's shoelaces, as tiny as a mouse.

"Awesome!" Albert squeaked. Petra's foot moved then, though, and Albert lost his concentration. He grew back to his normal size in one second flat. Petra was grinning from ear to ear.

"Let's try one more! Picture the symbol for the Creature Speak Tile."

Albert already knew that one—it's was his dad's Tile. He brought the weird megaphone symbol to the front of his mind, then opened his mouth. A strange—and very loud—roar came out. Professor Bigglesby stirred in the hammock. Albert clasped his hands over his mouth.

"I think that's enough for today!" Petra said. He was still bursting with so much energy that he tripped over his own feet as he rushed forward, picked up the book, and shoved it into Albert's arms. "Time for you to study up, Albert Flynn. You'd better learn every symbol in this book if you're going to unlock the power of the Master Tile. You're about to become the best Balance Keeper ever. I can feel it!"

Albert grabbed the book silently. He couldn't believe he really had the Master Tile. As if to convince himself again, he turned to the end of the Black Book and found the page with the warning on it. He flipped the page and looked at his Tile symbol, then realized they hadn't thought to look at the rest of the section. Were there other Tiles as powerful and controversial as his? He flipped the page again.

That was it. He'd reached the back cover of the book. "My Tile is the only one here."

"Like I said." Petra smiled. "Best Balance Keeper ever!"

Albert took a closer look, running his finger along the binding between the back cover and the page his Tile was on. It was there that he found the tiniest evidence of a tattered edge of paper.

The last page of the Black Book had been torn out.

CHAPTER 18

Secret Pit Practices

That evening, Albert found himself lying in his bed in Cedarfell, absently petting Farnsworth's head. The Master Tile. He had the Master Tile.

Why hadn't his dad said anything to him about it before? Professor Flynn acted like he didn't know Albert's Tile even existed. But surely his dad had heard of the Black Book. He'd probably read it loads of times.

Which made Albert wonder: Was the Master Tile really dangerous? In the wrong hands, it could do some serious damage. What if his dad didn't *want* him to learn how to make the Master Tile work? And what was the Tile on the missing page? Albert shivered, even though he was buried under the covers.

Leroy arrived sometime later and flopped down on the

bed opposite Albert. He was wearing a new pair of glasses with red rims. "Lucinda gave me these. She's not bad, except for that snake of hers. Hey, thanks for what you did back there. It was really cool. I should've stood up to Hoyt on my own, but that guy sort of scares me a little."

Albert sat up. "Leroy, I know what my Tile is."

"Say what?"

Albert spent the next few minutes explaining the Master Tile to Leroy. When he got to the part about turning invisible, Leroy looked like Albert had just sprouted a fresh pair of wings. "We need to tell Birdie about this. And we need that book."

"Dude, I've got that covered." Albert hadn't liked the thought of stealing the book from the Tower, but how else was he supposed to harness his powers? He lifted up his pillow, where the Black Book was safely hidden. "I think this calls for a nighttime adventure. How do you feel about breaking a few rules tonight, Leroy?"

Leroy didn't look so sure, but gave Albert two thumbs-up. "Where were you thinking of going?"

Albert grinned slyly. "Same place we always go, only we're going in at night."

A half hour later, with Farnsworth in the lead, Leroy and Albert stood in the shadows before the doors of Treefare. "Time to go on a mission, little buddy," Albert whispered to Farnsworth. He tucked a letter into the dog's collar.

"Go inside and find Birdie. Don't bark, okay? You have to be sneaky."

Farnsworth wagged his tail, his flashlight eyes alight like he understood Albert's every word. Leroy opened the door to Treefare and Farnsworth scurried inside.

"Now we wait," Albert said. He and Leroy sank back into the shadows.

A few minutes later the door to Treefare swung open. Birdie came rushing out, the letter clutched in her hands. "Albert? Leroy?"

Albert and Leroy emerged from their hiding spot. Birdie jumped, and slapped Leroy over the head with the letter.

"Ouch! Stop it, Birdie, it's *me*!"

"You scared me half to death!" Birdie held out the letter. "Someone better be on fire or something, because I was totally asleep. What's this about?"

Leroy smiled. "The Master Tile."

"The what?" Birdie crossed her arms.

"We know what Albert's Tile is, and we're going to sneak to the Pit right now so Albert can practice and show us what it can really do."

Albert explained the story to Birdie with as much detail as possible, though she kept demanding more answers. They got to the Pit undetected, thanks to Farnsworth's super dog hearing.

The Pit looked exactly the same as it did in the daytime,

but the room was colder. "We shouldn't be here," Leroy said. "We could get in serious trouble."

"I think it's exactly where we need to be!" Birdie smiled as the three of them stepped onto the platform. It carried them down to the floor of the Pit. Albert clutched the Black Book tightly in his arms, eager to open it up and show his friends all the powers he could harness.

As soon as their feet touched the Pit floor, it sprang to life.

The ground started to tremble, and Albert yanked Birdie aside just in time before the Pit floor opened up and a metal tree sprouted right out of the ground. It rose higher and higher, stopping when its tallest branches were slightly above the mouth of the Pit.

"Well, that's something we haven't seen before," Albert observed.

There was a rumble, and a Melatrix appeared out of a hole in the wall. "But we *have* seen that thing," Leroy groaned.

It didn't bother them until Albert touched the trunk of the metal tree. Then the Melatrix came full speed toward him.

Birdie kicked at it and the Melatrix soared away. She smiled triumphantly. "All right, Albert. It was your idea to come here, so let's get to work."

They pored over the pages of the Black Book, picking a few choice powers for Albert to focus on. There were so many to choose from. Albert would *never* learn all of them. It seemed impossible.

The key was to know the symbol well enough that he could concentrate on it while doing other things. When he felt like he'd gotten a few symbols down, Albert ran to the tree and started to climb. The Melatrix came at him with a vengeance, knocking its way through the metal branches until it was bumping Albert's heels, trying to throw him from the tree.

"Okay, Albert," Birdie called out. "Try concentrating on the power for Double Vision!"

Albert thought hard, focusing on the symbol he'd just studied. At first, nothing happened. The Melatrix was really getting on Albert's nerves, coming at him from odd angles. His hand slipped, and he nearly fell.

Focus, Albert. Double Vision. Double Vision . . . He saw the symbol in his mind, an eye with four pupils, and amazingly, he was looking in two directions at once.

"Uh . . . guys? Please tell me I don't have eyes in the back of my head, because if I do, I think I'm going to be sick."

"No eyes!" Birdie said. "Can you see us, though?"

In front of him, Albert could see his hands gripping on to the metal tree branch. But he could also, impossibly, see *behind* him. He saw Birdie and Leroy staring up at him from below. He also saw the Melatrix coming at him full speed. Albert watched, timing it just right, and when the Melatrix swooped in, he let go of the branch and dropped to the next-lowest one.

"That's it, Albert! You did it!" Leroy clapped. The feeling was incredible. Albert was controlling the Master Tile! He practiced for a few more minutes, but before long, Albert's head felt like it was going to explode.

He lost focus, forgetting to keep the image of the symbol in his head, and the Double Vision went away. Albert dropped to the floor.

"It changed," Leroy said.

"What are you talking about?" Birdie asked as she came in close.

"Albert's Tile symbol. It changed. I saw it."

Albert thought as hard as he could about the four-pupiled eye until his vision doubled again.

"There it goes!" Birdie said, pointing to Albert's black Tile.

He zeroed in on his Tile, holding it in front of his face. Then he let the power he was focused on drift away. His normal vision returned and he was able to watch the symbol on his Tile change back to its resting place: the Master Balance Keeper symbol.

"When it looks like this, it has no power at all," Albert said with wonder. "It keeps the powers secret. It hides them."

"Dang, Albert, that is one seriously cool Tile," Leroy said.

Birdie agreed, but for the first time Albert felt nervous about how much power he was holding in his Tile. How much could he unlock? And if there was another Tile as powerful as his, how much could someone *else* unlock?

A week passed. News came that Professor Flynn and the Calderon First Unit had reached the Fireflower field hoping to gather seeds, only to discover that it had been burned to a crisp. Now they were on the hunt for the infamous Hissengore eggs. Albert was getting worried about his dad—he knew the Realm took its toll on him.

At first, Albert spent nights studying the Black Book and being quizzed by Leroy in their tent (never in his life did he think he'd study this much over the summer), but after an unfortunate incident in which Albert accidentally set their tent on fire, the boys determined that the Pit was the only safe place to study—and the best way to keep their secret, too. They had decided they didn't want anyone to know the true power of Albert's Tile—not yet, anyway. Albert and Leroy snuck out every night along with Birdie so Albert could practice harnessing his powers.

They learned that the Tile required even more precision than Professor Bigglesby did in their weapons lessons. One time, Albert thought he had pictured the symbol for the Tall Tile, a spear-like arrow pointing up, but apparently his symbol was more spear than arrow, and he ended up with a giant cut across his leg. Luckily, he conjured the image of a fat plus sign, the Healer symbol, before things got too out of control.

While in the Pit, Leroy and Birdie practiced beating the simulations, too. It was looking more and more like a training unit would have to enter the Realm, and while they had beaten Argon twice in the Pit in the last week, Argon was still ahead on the leaderboard. They needed to strengthen their own physical skills if they had any chance of entering Calderon.

One night late in the Pit, Hydra was practicing dives through looped vines over what looked like a big, black hole in the floor.

"Whoever does the most flips wins!" Birdie yelled. She did three flips in the air and landed on her toes on the other side of the hole. Leroy stepped up, took a deep breath, and flipped four times.

"Nice one!" Albert said. Leroy was getting braver at stuff, slowly. "My turn. I hope I can beat four, but we'll see!"

"Try Antigravity," Leroy said. He knew every power in the Black Book.

"Remember . . . keep the symbol in your head at all times!" Birdie added.

Albert knew the Antigravity symbol—a bunch of black and gray circles stacked on top of one another that got lighter in color from bottom to top. He focused on the feeling of his Tile around his neck and watched as his Master Tile symbol changed.

"I got this one," Albert said with a smile. He bent his knees, jumped softly, and tucked his body into a ball. Albert felt himself flipping over and over. When he landed, Birdie and Leroy were both staring at him with their mouths hanging open.

"Seven flips, Albert!" Leroy said. *"Seven!"*

Ding! Ding! Ding! The sound rang out as soon as Leroy was done speaking.

"What was that?" Albert asked, brushing himself off.

"I think it's the scoreboard. . . ." Birdie pointed up, behind Albert. "But it's not supposed to be on."

There on the side wall of the Pit where the Competitions scores were held, a bright blue light was flashing.

"What does that mean?" Albert asked. The blinking light was on Hydra's side instead of Argon's. After a moment, it went away. Albert looked at Leroy and Birdie. "Must have been a wiring issue or something."

They left the Pit without a second thought about it.

CHAPTER 19

Hydra's Time Comes

Early Saturday morning, Team Hydra was milling around in the Canteen, considering what to purchase with some Medallions they'd won at another game of Tiles—someone had finally agreed to play Leroy.

"Hey, guys, I'll be back in a few. I'm going to call home," Albert said. Normally at this time of the morning, he'd be waiting for his dad to come back from Calderon, but it was the same every morning—his dad came through the door, shook his head at Trey, and went straight to his dorm to rest. Albert hardly saw a reason to be there anymore. Today he figured that if he couldn't say good morning to his dad, he might as well say good morning to his mom.

He made his way to the Phone Booth and pressed his Medallion into the little slot. When the Path Hider answered, Albert gave his mom's number, and waited as the familiar dial tone came.

The phone rang and rang, but no one picked up. *That's strange. Mom always answers the phone.*

Albert hung up and tried again, thankful that Leroy had won them so many Medallions lately. This time, when the phone rang, a voice answered.

It was one of those computer recordings. *All circuits are busy. Please hang up and try again later.*

Albert tried three more times. No one ever answered but the recording, and on the third time, the phone didn't even ring at all.

"Oh man, this isn't good," Albert said out loud.

Something was seriously wrong. If the phones weren't working, that might mean New York City was completely shut down. He ran back to the Canteen, but Leroy and Birdie were nowhere to be seen. He finally found them in one of the spare study rooms, where Leroy was trying to help Birdie improve at Tiles. They were arguing, as they had been lately.

"I get that you're saying that stacking this Tile on that Tile should be my next move, but I don't understand *why* that's the best move." Birdie glared at Leroy. "You're not explaining it well enough!"

"And you're not listening well enough!" Leroy snapped back.

"Guys!" Albert clapped his hands to get their attention. "I can't get ahold of my mom. New York is way worse; I can feel it."

Birdie started to say something, but at that moment, Albert heard a commotion outside the Library. There were shouts, and a monkey screeching in the distance. Farnsworth ran up to Albert and started tugging on his shoelaces, trying to pull him away.

"What's going on out there?" Birdie asked. She and Leroy stood up.

"Come on, let's go see," Albert said.

By the time Hydra got to the Main Chamber, the alarm bell had gone off, and something told Albert this wasn't a drill. A large group had gathered, including Trey, waiting for the Calderon First Unit to come back from the Realm.

All those mornings waiting for his dad to come back, Albert had looked closely at the door to Calderon. But today, looking at the symbol of the mountain with a sea beneath on the Calderon door, it all felt really, really ominous. He gulped, and thought of his mom and dad. Both of them were in trouble, one in an Imbalanced Realm, the other in a city filling with ash.

"The Calderon First Unit should be arriving," Trey began, speaking up so all could hear, and looking at a timepiece on his wrist. "In exactly fifteen seconds."

Albert counted the time in his head. But when the fifteen seconds were up, nothing happened.

"Where are they?" Albert asked, inching closer to the door until he was standing right before Trey. His stomach did a flip-flop.

"Give it a moment," Trey said nervously.

But two minutes later, the door remained closed.

"This isn't good," Trey said, more to himself than anyone else. "We're very precise about schedules in the Realms."

More Balance Keepers and Core workers had started to gather at the river's edge, watching Calderon's door. At one point, Farnsworth sprinted off, disappearing down a tunnel. Albert could hear his barks echoing from far away. Doors slammed in the distance, and in minutes, Farnsworth came back with the other three Professors and their Apprentices. They pushed their way through to Trey.

"What's going on?" Professor Asante asked Trey. She had a fresh cut on her cheek—it looked like a creature had attacked her. Her tattoos looked extra fierce on her muscular arms. Tussy, her Apprentice, stood beside her, quiet and sullen.

"The Calderon First Unit is late," Professor Bigglesby said, sniffing the air. His eyes were as crafty as ever as he glanced at the door to Calderon.

He started to say something, but Trey stopped him, pulling all the Professors and Apprentices into a closed circle. They spoke in hushed tones and glanced at the gathering nervously.

The entire time, Albert had a lump in his throat. Where were his dad and the First Unit? What if they weren't okay?

"It's fine," Birdie said beside him. "Everything is okay."

But she didn't look like she believed what she was saying.

"It's eighteen minutes and seventeen seconds past the usual time," Leroy said. "They've never been this late. . . ."

Finally, the Professors and Apprentices turned to the swelling mass of Balance Keepers and Core workers. It was so quiet in the Main Chamber, Albert wondered if everyone could hear his heart slamming in his chest.

Professor Bigglesby looked up. (He was the shortest person in the Main Chamber.) Then he addressed the crowd.

"The Code of the Core states the following: if a First Unit goes missing—"

There was an audible murmuring among the crowd as everyone tried to guess what Bigglesby was about to say. Apparently it was unprecedented for a First Unit to vanish as Grey and Aria had. *Especially* with a Professor's help inside the Realm.

Professor Asante held up her hands to silence the crowd, and picked up where Bigglesby had started: "If a First Unit goes missing, all training teams who have trained for that Realm shall be eligible to enter as backup. The team with the most points shall be the team that goes in."

Hoyt stepped forward out of the crowd.

"My team is ready," Hoyt said proudly. "Just say the word."

"I like your determination," Trey said. "But all the same, I think we had better check the score, don't you think?"

Trey held out his fist and revealed a round ball in his palm. He tapped the top with his free hand, and a holographic image of the Main Leaderboard appeared in the air. Tiny blue balls of flame appeared in columns above the team names, one team at a time.

Ecco had twelve fireballs.

Team Fury had fourteen fireballs.

Terra and Sapphire were deadlocked at sixteen.

Argon had eighteen fireballs.

Finally, Hydra's score appeared. They had thirty-seven fireballs.

The Main Chamber burst into chatter.

"How is that possible?" Albert whispered to Leroy.

For the first time ever, Leroy didn't have an answer. He just took off his glasses and cleaned the lenses on his shirt, like maybe he was seeing the scoreboard wrong.

"There's no way we've earned so many points," Birdie said, shaking her head. "No way at all."

She was right; Albert had to agree. They hadn't even competed in the Pit that many times. Sure, they'd been practicing at night, but those scores weren't counted. . . .

Were they?

"They cheated!" Hoyt yelled above the din. The crowd gasped. He turned to Hydra and gave them all a pointed glare. "And besides, we're way better than them!"

"Enough, Hoyt!" Trey silenced him. Then he turned to Albert, Leroy, and Birdie. "Curious, wouldn't you say, that you've come so far ahead of Team Argon? You've competed twenty-eight times in the Pit. How is it that you've gained thirty-seven wins?"

A silence fell over the proceedings, and then someone stepped forward from the crowd.

"Professors?"

Albert turned. It was Slink, and his face was white like a sheet of paper.

"Hydra's been practicing at night. I've seen them sneaking out."

"Hydra, is this true?" Trey spun around to face the three of them, but looked straight at Albert, his expression registering somewhere between admiration and disappointment.

"Well, yes, but . . . ," Albert began.

"Sir, I've also read all one thousand seven hundred and eighty-six pages of the Core Code." Slink stepped out of the crowd. "It *never* states that a team cannot practice during their free time."

The crowd gasped again. Hoyt gave Slink a nasty look. Albert gave him a nod of thanks. Slink sure was full of surprises.

Hoyt shouted out complaints. "But they snuck out! They should be expelled!"

But Professor Bigglesby spoke, cutting him off.

"The leaderboard rules above all. It is decided that Hydra will enter the Calderon Realm in search of the First Unit."

Everyone clapped and cheered for Hydra, thrilled to see the underdogs getting their day. A first-level training team was going to enter the Calderon Realm.

"We're really going in?" Birdie asked Trey.

"Yeah, you're really going in."

"I don't feel so good," Leroy said, clutching his stomach.

Albert wrapped his hand around his Tile and closed his eyes.

Please, he thought. *Help us find Grey and Aria.*

And help me find my dad.

CHAPTER 20

Entering the Realm

Trey spent the next thirty minutes briefing Albert, Leroy, and Birdie on the Calderon Realm. They holed up in Professor Flynn's office, poring over maps, reviewing what Professor Flynn had started to teach them that day the alarm bell went off. *The last time I really saw my dad*, Albert thought. His absence now was like a big, black hole in the pit of Albert's stomach. He had to find him. And soon.

Trey told them how after they passed through the entrance tunnel to the Realm, they'd go through the Ring of Entry, and then the Ring of Gold, where they would be followed by things they didn't want to encounter— they shouldn't turn back once they began crossing.

"You'll want to keep a good pace, too," Trey said,

"and don't jump—there are many things that could fly overhead. All of them are sharp clawed and good at grabbing jumping Balance Keepers."

"Who signed me up for this?" Leroy asked, his voice suddenly trembling. "And can I unsign?"

"It's going to be fine, Leroy. Stop making a scene," Birdie said. But even *she* looked terrified.

Albert patted Leroy on the back and gave him a look that said: *We got this, bro. Settle down.*

Trey continued. "When you clear the Ring of Gold you will come upon the Forest of Thorns. There you will find the biggest, blackest, oldest tree in Calderon: the Tree of Cinder. Hissengores are known to sleep there— real Hissengores that will kill you, not just knock you out with their bad breath—so beware."

"*Kill* us?" Leroy gasped.

"Leroy, you're freaking me out! Stop it," Birdie said, but she grabbed his hand anyway, and squeezed it tight.

Trey went on, showing no sympathy about the anxiety he was creating. "Beyond the Tree of Cinder, there are dangers of every kind, including some we probably don't know about. It's likely the First Unit is trapped or lost somewhere beyond this point."

"So our mission is to get through the two Rings and the Forest of Thorns, and find Professor Flynn and the First Unit," Leroy said, checking things off on his fingers. He seemed a little less anxious now that he had a to-do list.

"Yes," Trey said, "but that's only part of it. Ideally, you'll find the Hissengore eggs and restore Balance to Calderon, too."

"But even Grey and Aria haven't been able to do that!" Birdie said. *Professor Flynn* hasn't been able to do that. It's the whole reason Terran left!"

"And the Hissengore eggs might not even exist!" Leroy said, shaking his head.

"Terran left because she lost her courage," Trey replied to Birdie. He turned to Leroy. "You three must have faith—the Realm always provides the Means." Now he turned to Albert, too. "And you three are some of the most talented Balance Keepers I've seen yet."

"Why can't you come with us?" Albert asked. Birdie and Leroy nodded.

Trey smiled sadly. "An Apprentice is bound to the Core. If I could go with you, I would, but I have to stay here and care for the others. You have no choice but to enter the Realm. The entire world above is counting on you three."

The weight of Trey's words hit Albert in the gut like a semitruck.

All his life, his parents were there to protect him. Now the tables were turned, and it was up to Albert to save them all.

"What if we screw up?" Albert asked. "What if we don't make it out of there?"

Trey swallowed, hard. "If you do not discover Professor Flynn and the First Unit, and restore Balance, the destruction above will spread past New York, and fast. This must be contained at once."

"What if we get lost?" Leroy exclaimed.

"With your Synapse Tile, Leroy, I doubt you will allow your team to get lost." He looked pointedly at Albert for a moment before he spoke again.

"Professor Flynn needs you. Grey and Aria need you. Whatever the circumstance, whatever you run into inside of Calderon, the three of you *must* be brave."

Trey turned back to the maps. He handed them to Leroy. "This is your time to shine, Leroy. You are more talented than you know."

Leroy gulped, but he nodded. Albert gave him an encouraging pat on the back. Leroy and Birdie both looked as scared as Albert felt. He smiled at them. "We've worked hard, you guys. We're ready." He hoped they believed his words. He hoped *he* believed his words.

Ten minutes later, Hydra returned to the Main Chamber, where everyone from the Core waited. Even Argon was there, Hoyt and Slink separated by Mo in the middle.

"Don't get knocked out by King Fireflies, Hydra," Hoyt said, a half sneer on his face. "But if you do, I mean, that's cool with me."

"Shove off, Hoyt," Jack ordered, from the back of the

group. "In case you haven't heard, Hydra *earned* this shot."

Hoyt rolled his eyes. "When these three fail, it's going to be up to me and my team to clean up their mess."

"Ignore him," Albert whispered to Leroy. "He's just trying to rattle us." Albert stood up tall and took in the scene.

The Professors were lined up near the river to Calderon, and behind them, all the students and workers stood waiting. Even the companion creatures had come. There were bright-colored birds soaring around the massive chandelier, a pink monkey swinging from one of the pipes, and a lizard with two heads and four orange eyes blinking at Albert, Leroy, and Birdie.

Albert felt his stomach turn a somersault as they walked up to the entrance to Calderon. The huge door was like an impenetrable wall that stood between them and what Albert knew would be the biggest adventure of their young lives. Professor Bigglesby approached Hydra, a silver box cradled in his hands.

"This is for you," he said, holding the box out. "I hope you won't have to use it."

Albert took the box and lifted the lid. A dagger lay inside, glowing like a pale star. When Albert closed his fingers around the hilt, the dagger lit up a bright green. It felt as if the weapon was alive in his hand.

"The blade was forged in a powerful poison," Professor

Asante said, handing Albert a leather sheath. "It won't kill any creatures you encounter, but it *will* paralyze them for a short time. Don't let it touch your skin. You'll be sorry if you do."

Albert carefully holstered the blade into the leather sheath. "I think you should keep it, Leroy," he said. "So you can fight off whatever comes your way. You've always wanted to be a ninja. Now's your chance."

Leroy nodded gratefully, then tucked the sheath into his boot and stood at attention.

"Are you three ready?" Trey asked. "Remember what you've learned?"

"Don't die," Leroy said.

"Keep our wits about us," Birdie added.

"And find my dad," Albert said.

Trey looked worried. He leaned in and lowered his voice.

"Remember, the entire *world* is counting on you three. Find the First Unit and the Professor, and restore Balance. If you don't come back in six hours, I'll send in Team Argon."

"Thanks for the vote of confidence," Leroy said.

The river in front of Albert's, Birdie's, and Leroy's feet began to swirl like a whirlpool and the water started to bubble and steam. A wave rose up, rushing toward the door to Calderon. It crashed against the old wood with a loud *whoosh!* Albert ducked, thinking the water was going to drench everyone around the door. But instead, the water was sucked into a wide hole that had appeared near the bottom of the door. When the rush of water subsided, the hole in the door remained.

On the other side was nothing but deep, dark emptiness.

"Bravery is a Balance Keeper's greatest attribute," Trey said, placing a hand on Albert's shoulder. He looked at Leroy and nodded, then to Birdie, and gave her a faint smile. Albert realized Trey thought he might never see the trio again. The very thought gave Albert chills down to his toes.

Birdie grabbed Albert's hand, then Leroy's. Farnsworth scurried through the crowd and let out a good-bye howl. His eyes shone like blue fire on their backs.

Trey looked at the timepiece on his wrist.

"Your six hours begins *now*. Make the most of it."

Albert looked at the hole in the giant door and thought of what Trey had said: *first the Ring of Entry, then the Ring of Gold.*

Albert squeezed Leroy's and Birdie's hands, and together, Hydra stepped through the hole in the door and entered Calderon for the very first time.

It didn't take long for them to realize the water had traveled down a twisting, turning tunnel that got darker as it went. After a few tentative steps inside, they went more boldly, touching the slick walls as they put one foot in front of the other. Behind them, they could hear the hole in the door where they'd entered begin to close up, the walls caving in from the top, and turned to look. When little more than a shaft of light was left of the outside world, they saw Farnsworth's eyes flash to life. The dog jumped through the small opening that remained in the nick of time, and arrived at their sides with his bright blue eyes shining upward.

"You're staying with me," Albert said, kneeling down and hugging Farnsworth to his side. "Don't go wandering off like you did in the forest outside of Herman, little guy. This place isn't safe like it is there."

They continued on. As they walked, Albert could feel Birdie and Leroy both shivering on either side of him—the air around them was freezing, like a snowy New York night.

"When will it end?" Birdie asked through chattering teeth as they turned this way and that, unable to see more than a few feet ahead. Even Farnsworth's lighted vision seemed to evaporate into the dense darkness of the tunnel walls.

"I'm pretending like I'm eating a big bowl of Fruity Pebbles right now," Leroy said. "Everything is cool. We're not in a narrow, dark, creepy tunnel that might turn out to be the way into a monster's stomach. I'm just chowing down on sweet cereal. I'm good."

"Just keep walking," Albert said. "It's got to end sometime."

The air started to get warmer, and soon, Albert was wiping sweat from his brow. His Hydra shirt was sticking to him like wet paper.

"We're close," Birdie said. "I can feel it!"

The darkness began to clear, first to a deep gray, then to a color as pale as ash. The walls of the tunnel seemed to fall away, leaving a gray hue that went on and on like a stormy sky.

They had emerged into a charred clearing, where trees had been burned away. Ash floated through the air, falling across Albert's shoulders like snow.

"You guys," Albert said, taking in the sight. "We're standing in Calderon."

Beyond the burned-out trees, in a wide circle, was a lush jungle. The paintings back in Professor Flynn's office had been so green and bright that Albert had expected Calderon to be . . . well, not like this. With all the ash, the colors were muted and dampened, as if the world had begun to wither away.

Despite all of that, Calderon was still wildly beautiful.

Vines crisscrossed their way through the trees. Neon butterflies the size of birds flitted back and forth in the canopies. A Hexabon monkey lounged on a low tree branch, its hairy belly no doubt full from the fresh bananas that hung overhead. The creature dropped a peel to the ground and burped loudly, looking down at the gaggle of three intruders and their dog as if to say: *What are you lookin' at?*

"Over there, you guys," Albert said, wiping ash from his brow. He pointed beyond the jungle, in the far distance. "Calderon Peak."

It was incredibly narrow and tall, twisting high up into an ash-filled "sky." It was more the color of a sheet of metal than the blue, cloud-spotted skies they were used to on the surface. Light appeared to be coming from everywhere and nowhere at once, leaking in from openings in the distant ceiling of stone.

"I wonder if the light comes from the surface or somewhere else?" Leroy asked out loud. He was terribly curious about everything he saw, but they were on the most important mission of their lives. Studying the wonders of the Calderon Realm would have to wait.

"The Peak is a lot taller in here than it was in the Pit," Birdie observed nervously.

"Yeah, this place is way bigger than I imagined." Albert nodded.

"And dangerous," Leroy groaned. He pointed his long, skinny arm into the sky. There at the very top, high above the ash and the twisting spiral of the mountain, was an angry, whirling mass of gray.

"New York must be up there. This is bad, dudes," Albert said.

"I'm not a dude," Birdie said. "We should get moving. Six hours isn't much time. It looks like it will take us at least that long just to climb the mountain, assuming we find the Means to Restore Balance before that."

"Oh!" Albert said, and reached into his pocket, pulling out a piece of folded paper. "I almost forgot. Petra gave me this. I asked him to do some research on the silver eggs while he was on cleaning duty in the restricted area."

"Albert," Leroy said, "that was an excellent idea. How come you didn't tell us before?"

"I didn't want to get your hopes up," Albert replied. "And I still don't. I haven't read this myself."

The three of them gathered around the note.

It looked like Petra had copied out a section from the journal of a Balance Keeper named Roderick Heckleson from 1597:

> *". . . the shining orbs were found in the Forest of Thorns and retrieved after a great toiling . . ."*

Beneath that, Petra had written,

> *Shining orbs = silver eggs?*

"Sounds good to me," Birdie said. They kept reading. From the same journal, dated 1599:

> *". . . saddens me that the Forest of Thorns has burned to the ground . . ."*

Petra had written,

> *So no more eggs?*

"See," Albert said, "I didn't want to get your hopes

up. If the silver orbs *were* the eggs, they wouldn't have survived this fire anyway. I guess we're back to square one."

"Hold on, Albert," Birdie replied, "Leroy's up to something."

They turned to Leroy, who had a look of intense concentration on his face. After a moment, he nodded to himself and looked up at them.

"Whatcha got, Leroy?" Albert said.

"The silver eggs are in the Tree of Cinder." Leroy smiled.

"But Petra says the Forest burned to the ground," Birdie said.

"It did," Leroy replied. Albert suddenly saw a spark back in Leroy's eyes that he hadn't seen since Leroy was forced to stop playing Tiles. "But Trey said the Tree of Cinder was the biggest, oldest, blackest tree in the whole forest. Black because it's been burned, and oldest because it survived while new trees grew up all around it. It's likely the Hissengores made their nests in the tree, because it was the only safe, established place at the time."

"You're a genius, Leroy," Birdie said, giving Leroy a quick hug.

"All right," Albert said. "We have a plan! Let's find the eggs first, and hope we see my dad and the First Unit along the way."

"All right, boys," Birdie said. "To the Tree of Cinder!"

She forged ahead across the burned-out landscape, Albert and Leroy behind her. They were at the edge of the jungle in no time.

The Ring of Entry was heavy with warm humidity that made it hard to breathe. A high canopy of jungle trees towered overhead, and the underbrush was thick at their feet. Albert felt like he was trying to tunnel through a thousand tangled ropes. He put Farnsworth in his backpack and zipped it up tight, so just the dog's head poked out.

"Stay in there, please," Albert said. Farnsworth whimpered, but winked a bright blue eye.

"Hey, guys, watch this!"

Leroy and Albert looked overhead and saw that Birdie had climbed halfway up into a tree with curvy branches. Now Birdie leaped out into the open air, grabbed a hanging vine, and began swinging.

"This is going to be a faster way through this jungle," she said, latching on to a vine even farther away. "And a lot more fun."

"That girl is *always* right," Leroy said.

"Let's get up there," Albert said, and in a flash they were both climbing the same tree Birdie had scaled moments before.

Once they understood how to pass through the Ring

of Entry, the three of them swung their way through the jungle, flying over branches and mud bogs that surely would have threatened to suck the boots right off their feet. They were most of the way through the Ring of Entry when they came upon a wide bog that contained no trees at all.

"We'll either have to go around or walk this part," Albert said when they were all standing together on the same limb of the same tree.

"Looks muddy down there," Leroy said, but they all looked around the sides and saw how far it was around the bog. If they could cross without sinking, it would be the faster way by far. They hopped off the tree and started across.

Some of the bog bubbled with wet mud like a prehistoric tar pit. Other parts were sloppy like quicksand. Albert tested it out, stepping with one foot into the bog. He sank at once, and when Leroy and Birdie helped pull him out, he'd nearly lost a boot.

"We can't go in there," Albert reasoned. "We'll sink, or drown, or something."

"I won't drown," Birdie reminded him. She turned to Leroy. "Isn't there some kind of power that Albert can use?"

Leroy thought for a moment, then nodded. "Weightlessness. You remember the symbol, right, Albert?"

Albert went through the list in his mind. *Weightlessness.* "It's a symbol in the shape of a square, with an *O* in the center?"

"That's the one." Leroy nodded.

Albert had an idea. If he tried really, really hard, he might be able to imagine two symbols at once. He'd been planning to try it out in the Pit next week, but they'd been called on to enter Calderon first. He didn't even know if it was possible. But as he thought of the problem, a symbol popped into his mind. Unity—two triangles, interlocking.

"Grab my hands," Albert said to his friends. He closed his eyes and pictured Weightlessness in his mind. Slowly, he felt himself growing light as air.

"Albert," Birdie started, but Leroy shushed her.

Then Albert pictured Unity. Instantly, the Weightlessness went away. *Picture them together. The square, the triangles . . .*

The symbols appeared inside his head, drifting together until Albert saw something entirely new. Two interlocking triangles, with the square in the center.

"Your Tile is doing weird stuff, Albert," Leroy said. "You're getting the wrong symbol."

"Omigosh!" Birdie yelped.

"Albert, what did you *do* to me?" Leroy exclaimed. "I feel like I'm full of bubbles!"

Albert kept his eyes closed, but he could feel his

Master Tile working its magic. "Step forward. Guide me across, but don't you dare let go of my hands. I'm using two powers at once, guys, so we can all be Weightless together. Hurry. I can't keep this up for long."

Slowly, Leroy and Birdie walked across, guiding Albert, who focused so hard he felt like his brain was going to explode. They stepped forward onto the bog, their bodies so light that they might as well have been made entirely of air. With each step, the mud stuck to their feet, but they were able to keep moving without getting sucked under.

Keep the symbols in your head. Don't you dare let it fade, or the three of us will sink!

Finally, Albert felt his feet touch solid ground.

"We made it, man. You can stop now."

Albert opened his eyes. He crumpled to the ground, gasping for air as his Master Tile changed back. There were white spots in his vision, as if he'd just been smacked across the back of the head.

But he'd done it.

"That was really something, Albert." Leroy knelt down beside him. "Your dad would be proud. You okay?"

The pounding in Albert's head was already fading. "I'm fine. No worries."

"You guys?" Birdie said beside them. She stooped down and plucked something out of the thick goo.

"Oh man," Leroy said. He helped Albert up, and then

moved in beside Birdie to get a closer look. When Birdie held out her palm so they could lean in, Albert felt his heart drop to his toes.

It was his dad's Tile.

CHAPTER 21

Jadar the Guildacker

The Tile was etched with that strange megaphone shape. Albert would never forget that symbol.

"It's all right, buddy," Leroy said, when he saw Albert's frown. "He probably just did some amazing flip and lost it on the way. No big deal."

"Guys, my dad is a *Professor*. He would never lose his Tile. We all know he wouldn't," Albert said.

Birdie put a hand on Albert's shoulder. "We'll find your dad, okay? And we'll give him back his Tile. He's fine, Albert. I'm sure of it."

Albert wanted to believe Birdie, but his stomach ached, and his heart kept banging harder and harder against his chest. He was more afraid than he'd ever been before. Albert took the Tile and strung it around his neck. It settled against his own with a soft *clink*.

Wherever you are, Dad, please hang in there. I'm coming for you. I'll find you, I promise.

"The best thing we can do for your dad right now is keep moving," Leroy said. "I don't like the looks of this. None of us do. But we've got to stay on track."

"You're right," Albert said. "Let's look for more clues."

There were footprints that led out of the mud, but they were going in all directions, like the First Unit and Professor Flynn had been in a moment of complete chaos.

"What happened to all of them?" Birdie asked. "So close to the Calderon entrance?"

"And where are they now?" Albert wondered out loud.

"Well, we won't know unless we keep moving," Birdie said. "The Peak is a long way off and six hours will be gone before we know it."

"More like five," Leroy said, glancing at his timepiece. "We've already burned an hour."

"All we need to do is get the silver eggs," Albert said. "Then we'll run to the Peak and restore Balance."

"Somehow I doubt it will be that simple." Birdie shook her head.

"We have to rescue the First Unit, too," Leroy said. "Don't forget about that."

Albert nodded and stared up at the Peak far overhead. "And we don't even know where they are."

Suddenly, there was a blast of wind, and a fresh plume of smoke appeared in the sky not far from where they were—more creatures must be infected and blowing fire. The whole experience was strange. Ash kept falling on Albert's nose. It almost felt like he was in some huge, burning jungle, far across the sea in the real world.

But this was Calderon. The sky was not a sky, and the wind was not wind—at least not the kind of wind Albert knew up above. He had to keep reminding himself of that.

As they made their way along, hopping through trees and swinging on vines, the jungle slowly started to thin out. Soon Hydra was standing on the edge of what Albert knew was the second ring of Calderon.

Before them lay a field with golden grass taller than the trio's heads.

"It's the Ring of Gold," Leroy said. "That wasn't so bad. We're really moving."

But Albert wasn't nearly as upbeat about their prospects. He was sure the terrain would become more treacherous and difficult to pass as they got closer to the mountain itself.

The tall grass, like the jungle before it, grew in a ring around the entire Realm.

"It's like walking through a thick cornfield back home in Oregon," Birdie said. "I hate not being able to see in front of me."

"Or behind," Leroy said, glancing over his shoulder and listening. "Uh-oh . . . I think something is following us."

Albert heard the noise—a rustling in the grass, coming from directly behind them. The noise got louder. Farnsworth started to growl from Albert's backpack, just as the grass bent and two massive hairy feet appeared.

"Run!" Albert cried.

He took off at a steady pace, his friends following close behind. Huge blades of grass slapped him in the face, and he couldn't see where he was going, but he didn't dare stop.

"Just keep going, straight like an arrow!" Birdie called from behind him. "Remember what Trey said. Don't turn back once we start crossing."

"Oh man, oh man, I don't like this part!" Leroy shouted. He sprinted past Albert like an Olympian.

Other creatures flew low overhead, doing flybys as if they could tell someone had entered the Realm. Their shadows were dark and wide, fast as lightning. Whatever they were, they made no sounds other than the flapping of huge, leathery wings. Farnsworth barked from Albert's backpack as if to ward the creatures off, but still they flew overhead. Albert thought about jumping to take a look, but Trey's warning rang clearly in his head: *Don't jump. There are many things that could fly overhead. All of them are sharp clawed and good at grabbing jumping Balance Keepers.* Whatever made the rustling noise pursued them all the way to the end of the Ring of Gold. By the time the grass started to thin, Albert was nearly out of breath. Leroy burst through the edge of the field first. He stopped so abruptly that Albert and Birdie smacked right into him. They all tumbled to the ground. Albert braced himself, waiting for the creature to burst forth from the Ring of Gold . . . but the creature never came.

"That was terrible," Birdie said, through gasps for air. "I'm good at swimming, not running!"

"Sorry about that one, guys. But I wasn't about to run in *there*," Leroy said.

Albert stood up and brushed himself off. When he saw what stood before him, he felt his jaw drop. Goose bumps lined his arms as he took it all in.

"The Forest of Thorns," Birdie breathed beside Albert.

It was full of skeletal trees with twisting trunks and spidery branches. Glowing, red vines hung from the trees like threads of string, moving slowly on a hot breeze. The trees themselves were blanketed with sharp thorns as long as drumsticks and—Albert swallowed hard— around some of these thorns were long Hissengores snaking in every direction.

"Talk about spooky," Leroy said, shivering. "Why couldn't it be called the Forest of Fluffy Bunnies or something?"

Leroy was right. Albert watched the shapes and shadows that moved every so often in the Forest of

Thorns, as if there were living things stalking in the darkness.

A mournful howl broke the silence, carrying toward them from the forest. They all stepped backward into the tall, golden grass.

"That didn't sound inviting," Birdie said, fixing the laces on her boots.

"Neither does *that*," Albert said, because the rustling in the cornstalks was back. This time, Albert could tell that something large and heavy was pounding toward them.

"Guys," Albert said, "I think we should—"

Suddenly, Farnsworth leaped from Albert's backpack down to the ground and bolted out into the open floor of the Forest of Thorns.

"Farnsworth!" Birdie cried. She chased after the dog. Albert chased after Birdie, but Leroy stayed frozen in place.

Albert skidded to a stop. "Come on, Leroy! We gotta move!" Albert yelled. He saw Birdie getting farther and farther ahead. *"Leroy! Now!"*

To Albert's right, a cluster of cockroaches the size of mice scurried across charred earth with a strange clicking sound. Hissengores slithered and hissed in the trees overhead. From Leroy's direction, Albert heard the mournful roar again, only closer now.

"Let's go!" Albert called.

He whirled around again, just in time to see a dark shadow move in the tall grass behind his friend. Albert watched, horrified, as a giant, three-clawed hand covered in matted fur came down toward Leroy's head.

Almost without even trying, the Speed symbol popped into Albert's head, and he was by Leroy's side in a flash.

"Look out!" Albert cried. He grabbed Leroy by the wrist, and hauled him out of the way. The beast roared, and Albert lost the symbol, but it didn't matter—they were already far away, sprinting into the Forest of Thorns in the direction Birdie had gone, or at least, the direction they thought she had gone.

"I don't want to know what that was!" Leroy said, breathless, when they finally slowed down. "But thanks."

"No big deal. I'm getting good at Speed. But we shouldn't have split up. *That* was a bad idea!" Albert groaned. "Come on, look for clues; we have to find Birdie and Farnsworth."

Leroy took the lead, watching the forest floor for signs of footprints. Albert was impressed. Leroy tracked like a hunter, using his Tile to help them catch on to Birdie's trail. They spotted footprints—four paws and two human boots. Finally, they heard Birdie's shouts in the distance.

Albert started running again. They rounded a large tree the size of a bus. Birdie stood on the other side. "Watch out!" Birdie called. "Overhead!"

There was the sound of rushing wings above them.

Albert saw the look of terror on Birdie's face and he realized he was in serious danger.

He turned, afraid of what he might see, but curious all the same. He recognized the beast from their research in the Library. It was a Gullpacker. Or Gillnacker? Guildacker—that was it—a flying beast with wide wings and sharp talons. He thought Guildackers rarely left the sky over the Ring of Gold, but this one was either brave or remarkably angry. Albert dove to the side and rolled to his feet, just as the beast stretched its claws for Leroy.

Leroy flattened himself to the forest floor not a second too late.

Albert was about to take off running again, when Birdie cried out.

"Don't move an inch!" Birdie hissed, standing perfectly still. Albert froze on his feet (Leroy froze facedown in the dirt), but Farnsworth didn't get the memo. Instead, the little dog turned and began barking at the Guildacker, pointing his eyes up into the creature's face like headlights from an oncoming car.

"Farnsworth, no!" Albert yelled, but it was too late.

Albert gasped as the Guildacker reached its talons down toward Farnsworth and snapped them shut, missing by a hair. Albert had no choice. He dove forward, scooped up Farnsworth, and backed away slowly.

The Guildacker kept snapping, trying to reach them, but apparently, the light from Farnsworth's eyes had momentarily blinded it. The creature turned wildly off course, missing Leroy by several feet.

Albert watched as the beast veered close to one of the trees, connected hard with a flurry of thorns, and ripped long tears into its right side. The Guildacker careened into another tree, taking more damage, and then slammed into the ground, tumbling end over end. It was immediately attacked by every Hissengore within a hundred feet.

"This is our chance!" Birdie yelled. "Run!"

Farnsworth leaped from Albert's arms and took off through the trees.

"Not again!" Albert chased after him, zigzagging between thorny trees, jumping long and hard over roots pushing out of the earth. He started to picture the Speed Tile again, and he wanted so badly to leave the Guildacker in the dust. But Albert forced himself not to use his Tile. He wouldn't leave his friends behind to face the danger alone.

This is just like Herman. I'm just following Farnsworth to deliver a letter. There isn't a giant Guildacker on my tail, trying to eat me. Everything is going to be okay!

Birdie followed in his wake, then Leroy, until they were far enough away that it seemed safe to stop.

"At least the Hissengores were good for something," Albert said when they stopped for a breath.

"I can't believe that just happened!" Birdie said, fixing

her ponytail back up on her head.

Leroy's face was caked in dirt, but he still smiled beneath it. "We just escaped a freaking *Guildacker*."

Albert slowed to a walk as he noticed a towering black tree in front of him. It looked as if it had been burned to a crisp a thousand times over, growing harder and more impossible to destroy with each successive torching. Birdie and Leroy came to a stop beside him.

"I think we've found the Tree of Cinder," Albert whispered, breathless.

There were black vines in the shadowy light all around them, like strands of thick hair hanging off the head of a giant ogre.

"This reminds me of our first Realm simulation," Birdie said. "The one with the bell at the top. Remember?"

"It's kind of like that silver tree, too, where Albert learned how to use Double Vision," Leroy added.

The three of them stood staring up into the Tree of Cinder, mesmerized by how *big* it was. Albert didn't even know where they'd start looking for the silver eggs. "Hey, guys." Leroy broke the silence. "Where's Farnsworth?"

Albert looked every which way on the ground, but the dog was nowhere to be found. Suddenly he heard a whimpering noise, followed by a bark. Both sounds were coming from high above, up in the Tree of Cinder. Albert craned his neck, searching through the gloom.

A few seconds later, they saw all too well what was

up there. Everything about the scene was like their first Realm simulation in the Pit, but instead of a bell at the top, there was something trapped in the clutches of a dozen Hissengores, and that something had eyes like headlights pointing down at them.

Albert's heart sank. The slithering monsters had grabbed the easiest prey they could find and hauled it up into the tree. "No way," Leroy said. "We are not letting Farnsworth get eaten alive by Hissengores."

"Where's the threat from the simulation? The thing that's supposed to attack us?" Birdie asked.

Almost as if in response to Birdie's words, a buzzing sound, like an approaching swarm of killer bees, came toward them through the gloom.

"Oh man. I was afraid of this," Albert said, wiping his sweaty hands on his shorts. "Climb! Now!"

Everyone grabbed a swaying black vine and started the ascent as a King Firefly broke through the trees. This one was *huge*, with four silvery wings that spread twenty feet across. Its body was oval shaped, and on its tail end a piercing light shone so bright Albert, Leroy, and Birdie had to look away. This was no Guildacker that couldn't navigate the many obstacles in the Forest of Thorns. This was a King Firefly that could swerve expertly back and forth, perfectly dodging everything it came across. When it saw Albert and the rest of the Hydra team racing into the scorched branches of the

Tree of Cinder, the creature's big bug eyes turned to slits.

Leroy froze on his vine, his face a mask of terror as he watched the Firefly. The creature buzzed, staring Leroy in the face.

"I'm gonna puke!" Leroy called out over his shoulder. His thin arms were starting to tremble. He scooted up his vine, trying to get away, but the King Firefly followed suit.

"Hey, up here, little Firefly!" Albert called out, trying to get the Firefly's attention away from Leroy. "No need to get testy. Can't we talk about this?"

The King Firefly buzzed angrily. The light on its tail end grew brighter and its eyes flamed from black to bloodred.

"It's getting really angry!" Albert shouted, just as the beast opened its mouth and coughed up a ball of flames right in Albert's direction.

"Swing!" Birdie screamed. "Rock back and forth like in the Pit!"

Albert swung on his vine just in time, then grabbed on to another as the ball of fire flew by. He turned and watched what was left of the vine he'd been on as it sizzled and dropped to the ground.

Below him, Leroy had scurried down to the forest floor. He looked so terrified that Albert knew his friend wasn't going to be of any help right now.

"Move fast, Birdie!" Albert said. "Just like the simulations! Pretend it's a race!"

They scurried up their vines, leaping from one to another as the King Firefly flew a circle around the sprawling limbs of the tree.

But it was no use. Every time they got close to Farnsworth, the King Firefly shot another fireball, and they were pushed back down.

Albert had an idea. "Keep it distracted! Make it mad!"

Birdie began swinging back and forth on her vine, shifting her weight in the hot, ashen breeze blowing off the fires elsewhere in the Realm.

"All right, Firefly," Birdie said. "Let's dance!"

Just when Albert was about to tell her *not* to do what he thought she was about to do, Birdie swung from her vine. She soared through the air, a look of sheer determination on her face. Albert nearly lost hold of his own vine as he whipped around to see her land right on the back of the King Firefly.

"You're crazy!" Leroy shouted from the forest floor as he watched her fly past.

The King Firefly started bucking like a wild bronco. Albert saw Birdie wrap one arm around the King Firefly's neck.

"What are you doing?" Albert cried out. Birdie had always been brave, but this was an entirely new level of courage—one that might be more dangerous than useful.

The King Firefly, which seemed to be possessed by an evil plan to kill everything it saw, laid eyes on something in the distance.

The Guildacker had found them through the trees, and it was heading right for the Tree of Cinder.

"Birdie, it's going for the Guildacker! Let go!" Albert cried again.

He watched, helpless, as the leather-winged Guildacker locked eyes with the Firefly. A battle of winged beasts was about to begin, and Albert's friend was right in the middle of it.

Now she couldn't let go. She was way too high. She could break a leg or an arm, so Albert watched, holding his breath, as Birdie held on. The Firefly whizzed off through the trees, with the Guildacker on its tail.

Albert tried to think of a symbol that would allow him to help Birdie, but in the heat of the moment, he drew a blank. He grabbed his Tile and his dad's, and closed his eyes. *Come on. Please, we've come too far. Please, help me find a way to fix this.*

Albert opened his mouth, intending to say, "Don't hurt her!" but instead of his own voice, a strangled roar came out.

The Guildacker turned just before it was out of view.

It locked eyes with Albert and let out a deep, ground-shaking roar. *Use the dagger,* Albert heard it say. Then the Guildacker took off through the trees after Birdie and the Firefly.

"No!" Albert and Leroy screamed together.

"I'm okaaaaay!" Birdie called back. "Get Faaaarrnswooooorth!"

Albert didn't like the idea of not pursuing Birdie, but he didn't know how else to help. Had the Guildacker understood his plea? And what was that about using the dagger?

"Leroy!" Albert called down. "I think we better stay here, get Farnsworth, and look for the silver eggs."

"I can't do it, man," Leroy said. His face was white as chalk. "I just can't."

Albert shimmied down the vine and joined Leroy at the base of the tree. "You've come so far, Leroy. You've trained hard for this moment."

Leroy nodded, but said nothing, so Albert continued.

"Think of Birdie. She's counting on us right now to succeed. Think of how proud you'll feel about yourself!" Then, for good measure, he added, "Just picture Hoyt's face when we get back to the Core, and you prove to him that you're a *real* Balance Keeper."

Leroy looked up at Albert. He took a deep breath and nodded. He straightened his new glasses on his face, cracked his knuckles, and turned his hat backward.

"Okay! Let's do this! For Birdie!"

"For Birdie," Albert said, and it took him back to that moment in the Pit, where Leroy and Albert were on their own, and they won the simulation together as a team. "Let's go."

With renewed determination, Albert and Leroy bolted up the tree, reaching Farnsworth and the snapping Hissengores in no time. As Albert and Leroy turned toward them, the Hissengores began spitting green sulfur. Albert grabbed a black vine, kicked off the trunk of the tree, and spun in a wide circle around Leroy and the Hissengores. As Leroy grabbed a vine and did the same, the Guildacker's voice rang in Albert's ears. *Use the dagger.*

Of course! Use the dagger against the Hissengores! "Leroy! The dagger! Use the dagger!"

Leroy nodded. For a second, he looked like he wasn't going to do it. But a look of calm came over his face, and Albert watched as Leroy pulled the dagger out of his boot.

"Leave our dog alone!" Leroy yelled as he swung back toward the Hissengores. He held the dagger out in front of him and sliced through the air as he swung past. The blade touched more than one Hissengore, slicing through their thick skin. One by one, the Hissengores released Farnsworth and tumbled toward the ground. The paralyzing poison had worked!

"You're a natural!" Albert cried out.

Several of the Hissengores that hadn't been struck

moved off, afraid of Leroy and his blade of steel, but one remained, unwilling to let go of its prey.

Luckily for Farnsworth, he was a smart dog, and when a smart dog is trapped by only one Hissengore, it senses an advantage. Farnsworth bit into that last Hissengore with all he was worth, sinking his teeth into snakeskin as his eyes burned blue.

The last Hissengore shrieked wildly, uncoiled, and tumbled to the ground.

"Good boy!" Albert shouted.

Farnsworth barked and wagged his tail happily, searching for a way off the wide limb he stood on.

"Don't go doing anything crazy, Farnsworth," Leroy said. "It's a long way to the bottom."

Leroy and Albert swung close to the limb and tried to reach out and grab Farnsworth, but he moved back, just out of their reach, and kept barking.

"What is it, boy?" Albert asked.

"Maybe he likes it up here," Leroy guessed. "Probably the safest place in Calderon, even with the Hissengores."

"Come *on*, Farnsworth," Albert said, reaching for the dog. "We're going to look for the silver eggs down below, but we can't leave you up here. We don't know when the Hissengores will return."

"We gotta move fast," Leroy said. "Rescuing a dog and having Birdie fly off on a giant King Firefly wasn't exactly in the plan."

Albert felt a new sense of urgency at the sound of Birdie's name. Farnsworth wasn't the only one that might need saving, and they were burning way too much time in the Forest of Thorns, even if they might find the eggs there.

"Why won't he let us save him?" Leroy groaned as he tried and failed once more to swing close and grab Farnsworth off the branch.

This time, Farnsworth began pawing the trunk, like he wanted to climb up it and go even higher in the tree.

"This dog is losing his marbles," Leroy said as he gave up the vine and landed on the branch, carefully balancing a few feet away from Farnsworth.

Albert landed beside him. "I think he's trying to tell us something."

Both boys took a step forward, holding their arms out at their sides to help them balance, and followed the path of blue light from Farnsworth's eyes up farther into the tree. It was even darker and thicker with branches and thorns above. Albert didn't want to go up there if they didn't have to, but then he looked back down at Farnsworth.

"Leroy," Albert said. "I think he can smell something that we can't. See how he's sniffing up the tree?"

"Pizza?" Leroy asked, turning toward Albert on the limb.

Albert gave Leroy *that* look. "Dude. Not now. What if

it's the silver eggs?" Albert said, hardly daring to believe that they could be so close to finding the Means to Restore Balance.

"Oooooooohhhh," Leroy half whispered, gazing back up into the tree. "Let's go for it." He dug into his pocket and pulled something out. It was the strange cat statue Lucinda had given Leroy when they first entered the Core.

"I can't believe you thought to bring that!" Albert said.

"Hey, I don't have the Master Tile like you." Leroy laughed, and Albert watched, amazed, as Leroy walked along the tree branch with catlike precision. Albert focused on the symbol for Balance, and they started the ascent.

Climbing the Cinder Tree was tricky business. For starters, the higher they climbed, the more the tree felt like it had been torched a thousand times over, which maybe it had. The bark was cooked like charcoal, and it broke off in their hands more than once. By the time they looked down and saw Farnsworth twenty feet below on the limb, they were covered in soot.

"I feel like a hamburger hot off the grill," Leroy said, holding up his blackened hands.

"It's amazing it's stayed alive so long," Albert said, stopping abruptly at a knothole in the tree the size of a basketball.

"Who said it was alive?" Leroy said.

"*I* said it was alive," Albert said. "And it totally is. Look." He moved aside so Leroy could peer in, too.

Bright green vines snaked around the inside of the tree. There was a soft, green glow filling the hollow space.

"Pretty cool," Leroy had to admit. "Where's the light coming from?"

"Down there," Albert said, peering into the vast inside of the tallest tree in the Forest of Thorns. He closed his eyes and pictured the eyeball-shaped symbol for Enhanced Vision, and when he opened them, it was like he was looking through binoculars. Far below, at the very, very bottom of the tree in a protective cage of tangled roots, sat four silver eggs the size of baseballs. They glowed brightly, like small, silver suns.

"Dude," Albert whispered, "this is it. The silver eggs."

"No way." Leroy leaned back against the tree trunk. "I mean, I know I said this is where they'd be, but I'm not sure I really believed they existed. This is just getting too weird for words. What can you see down there?"

Albert swallowed hard. "There's only one way to retrieve those things." He looked at the hole, then at Leroy. "I'm guessing you aren't going to climb down there with me?" Albert asked.

Leroy shook his head. "No way, Jose. Nope. Not a chance."

Albert stared down into the hole.

"We could send Farnsworth, but he's all the way down there," Leroy said.

"I don't think we want to entrust the antidote for saving the world to a dog."

Farnsworth barked as if his feelings had been hurt, and Albert looked down.

"Dude," he said. "We've got company."

More Hissengores than ever were hissing at the base of the Tree of Cinder, and some of them were starting to slither up the tree. There was a roar in the distance. Was the Guildacker coming back for them? Was Birdie all right?

"Better hurry," Leroy said. "Birdie might need us. There's no way we can let her face those monsters alone."

The Guildacker roared again. It sounded like it was getting closer.

"Here goes nothing!" Albert patted Leroy on the back. He took a deep breath and grabbed his Tile and his dad's. Somehow, having a piece of his dad made Albert feel braver. He would do this. For his dad, for Grey and Aria, and for everyone else on Earth. Albert reached into the hole, and grabbed ahold of a green vine as thick as his wrist. He pulled himself inside the tree and held on for dear life. When he looked up, he saw that the tree narrowed quickly—he was near the very top. But looking down, he saw how far he could fall.

"I'm inside a tree," Albert said. "This is nuts."

Leroy poked his head inside. "Enough with the shock and awe. You gotta move! The Hissengores aren't going to stay down there much longer. And I think I might see the Guildacker!"

Albert started working his way down through thick tangles of green as quickly as he could. It was like descending a miniature version of Jack's beanstalk, with soft light that turned everything lime colored.

"Those silver eggs really put off some light!" Albert shouted up to Leroy, moving faster as he grew more used to his surroundings. He slipped once, and nearly crashed down to the bottom of the tree, but at the last second, his instincts kicked in, and he found a handhold and pulled himself back up.

"Steady, Albert," he told himself.

After a few more seconds of climbing, Albert saw that the thick vine he was on stopped in midair. He looked around for another one to grab, but from here, all the vines were tiny; they certainly wouldn't hold his weight. The eggs were at least fifteen feet below, sitting on the ground at the bottom of the tree's hollow trunk. He hung from one arm and tried to reach the eggs with his free hand, but they were way too far down.

I can't jump down there or I won't be able to make it back up.

Unless . . . the Jumping Jackalope symbol! He could

picture it and jump back to the vines.

Albert took a deep breath, let go of the vine he was on, and dropped to the bottom of the tree.

"We've gotta go!" Leroy cried out, his voice echoing down to Albert.

"Drop the knife!" Albert called down. He scooted safely against the edge of the tree. The knife landed with a twang on the ground beside him.

Quickly, Albert cut the eggs free one at a time. He couldn't hold them and climb, so he put them in his pack. With each silver egg he hid away, the inside of the tree grew darker, until the last egg was in his hand and he could barely see two feet in front of his face.

"Hurry up down there!" Leroy called. "They're on the move big-time!"

Albert dropped the last of the four silver eggs into his backpack and everything went dark. "You can do this, Albert," he said. "Just leap. The vine is right there, waiting for you."

And so he did, picturing the Jackalope. Once on the vine, Albert knew he had to move fast. He pictured Hoyt's Speed Tile. *Funny how that guy's power has helped me out so many times* . . . When he reached the hole, Leroy was freaking out.

"There's, like, a hundred of them!" Leroy said. "And they're halfway to Farnsworth!"

Farnsworth was barking down at the Hissengores, acting a lot bigger than he was.

"Hold this," Albert said, handing his pack through the hole.

By the time Albert squeezed through and put his pack back on, it looked like more than two hundred Hissengores were slithering up the tree.

"Oh man! Maybe Hoyt was right about us," Leroy said, looking very afraid. Albert didn't know what to say, so he didn't say anything. And in that brief moment of silence, he closed his eyes and heard a sound.

"Do you hear that?" he asked.

"Yeah, I hear it," Leroy said. "That's the sound of a hundred Hissengores coming to choke the life out of us."

"No, not that," Albert said. He touched Leroy on the shoulder, closed his eyes, and listened. "*That*."

Leroy inhaled a sharp breath and Albert knew he heard it, too: a growl, deep and heavy, coming closer by the second.

Albert held out the dagger. Leroy balled his fists. They stood side by side, ready to face whatever was coming their way.

Albert had always known Birdie was tough. But to see her coming full speed ahead, riding a Guildacker like it was a leather-winged dragon, gave him an entirely new perspective on just *how* tough she was.

"Hit those Hissengores with all you've got, Jadar!" Birdie cried out.

The Guildacker reared back on Birdie's command and let fly a series of fireballs that shook the roots of the tree.

"I guess it's true King Fireflies aren't the only things in Calderon that can breathe fire," Albert said, not quite believing what he was seeing.

Albert and Leroy held on to the Tree of Cinder as Jadar, the Guildacker tamed (and named) by a girl of the Core, flew circles around the pack of Hissengores. Fireball after fireball rocked the base of the tree, until every Hissengore had scattered into the jungle, possibly never to return.

"Birdie!" Albert screamed, pointing into the air below. "There!"

Farnsworth had finally lost his footing. He was falling through the air, and not like a cat with nine lives. Birdie lowered her head with determination, swooped Jadar under the tumbling dog just in time, and caught him in her arms.

Albert and Leroy scrambled down the tree until they could reach vines, and after that they were on the ground in no time, though Albert had to take a bit of extra care with his backpack—he was holding the Means to save the world, after all. They stared at Birdie as she prepared to land the Guildacker beside them.

"Whoa, boy," Birdie said.

Jadar came to a stop, shaking his head back and forth. Birdie slid off of his side, and patted the creature on his head. He made some deep growling noises, like a wolf awaiting its next command.

"Good job, Jadar," Birdie said. She turned to face the boys. "Why are you staring at me like that?"

"You're *alive*!" Leroy said. "And you caught the dog! And you have a new pet. That part is freaking me out a little bit."

"I knew it!" Albert said. "I *knew* he heard me speak to him! I told the Guildacker to protect you, Birdie, and I think he listened!" He watched as the Guildacker nuzzled Birdie's side with his huge head. "He likes you!"

"He chased me on the King Firefly," Birdie said, petting Jadar's leathery, folded wing. "It's amazing how fast he moves. I jumped on him in midair and the King Firefly just flew away!"

There were a couple of cuts on Birdie's arms, and a jagged scratch on her cheek, but she was okay. Albert and Leroy couldn't help it. They came in for a group hug, all smiles and excitement.

"Let's try and stay together for the rest of this journey," Albert said.

"Deal," Birdie said.

Farnsworth joined in with two loud barks.

Birdie noticed Albert handling his pack carefully when he pulled away.

"What's in the bag?"

Leroy and Albert gave each other a look. They'd been having some success of their own while she was off taming a Guildacker in the faraway corners of Calderon.

CHAPTER 22

Calderon Peak

Team Hydra had passed through the Ring of Entry and the Ring of Gold, found the antidote that could fix Calderon, and tamed a Guildacker. But they were down to three hours, and the numerous fires set by the King Fireflies were still pushing an endless cloud of ash up into the world outside. Ash was starting to fall around them like a blizzard. There was no real sign of the First Unit or Albert's dad. Time was running out with the biggest tasks still ahead of them.

"How much weight do you think Jadar can carry?" Albert asked, wondering whether or not a Guildacker might be the safest and fastest way out of the Forest of Thorns.

"Approximately four hundred thirty-four pounds," Leroy said.

"Well, that was more specific than I was looking for," Albert replied, elbowing Leroy in the arm, "but it'll work."

"Down, Jadar," Birdie said. The mighty Guildacker bowed his head, stooping low to the ground so Birdie could climb on. Then she looked down at Albert and Leroy. "Ready to board?"

It took some coaxing with Jadar, who seemed less sure about the boys than Birdie, but after a few moments, he stopped growling and let Albert and Leroy climb on behind her. They moved Farnsworth into her backpack so he could stick his head out over her shoulder and provide some serious headlights in the darkness to come. "This is perfect!" Albert shouted.

"He's kind of furry," Leroy said, running his hand along Jadar's back. "Who'd have thought?"

"Good for holding on to," Birdie said, "which is what you should do right now." She leaned to the right, where Calderon Peak rose high into the air, gave a little kick, and pulled up on Jadar's neck.

"Let's ride, Jadar!"

Jadar let out a wolfish howl, then shot into the sky. Wind rushed into Albert's face, and he held on for dear life. They soared through the canopy of the Forest of Thorns, over the tops of the blackened trees, leaving the Hissengores behind.

Even in the ash storm, they could see a blue stream

sparkling far beneath them like the riverbed was covered in diamonds. Hexabons swung between the trees below, disappearing into strange jungles of green and yellow. And the view of orange goo flowing down the mountain, from way up in the sky, was breathtaking, even though Albert knew it was evidence of the great Imbalance wreaking havoc on the Realm.

As if to drive that point home, there was an explosion from inside the Peak. Channels of steaming, toxic, orange sludge ran down the side of the mountain and out into the valley floor. It was clear that if it kept up much longer, the sludge would burn all of Calderon, including every tree and all the underbrush they'd tried to cross through. Albert could only imagine that that much sludge would affect other creatures in Calderon, too. What if they were poisoned, too, and started breathing fire like the King Fireflies? And the Ring of Gold was a tinderbox of dry grass, just waiting to burst into an endless, smoke-filled flame. New York wouldn't stand a chance if all that smoke and ash poured out into the city.

Over the roar of the wind, Birdie said what Albert was thinking.

"If this whole place goes up in smoke, it's not just New York that will be in trouble. We could lose the Core and the other Realms, too. Maybe even the whole world."

"We can't let that happen," Leroy said. "We have to restore the Balance!"

Birdie increased their speed, driving them ever closer to Calderon Peak.

"Albert," Leroy shouted, "what's the plan for the eggs when we get there?"

"Good question. I think we'll have to make a decision once we see what we're working with."

"Got it," Leroy replied. "Just let me know how I can help."

Jadar swooped closer, and more details of the mountain came into view—even more when Albert used the power of Enhanced Vision.

"It's like the Peak in the simulations," Albert said. "Leroy, keep an eye out for any openings or cracks in the surface as we circle this thing. We can go in, find the Sea Inspire, and figure out where to drop the eggs."

"Will do," Leroy said. His Hydra baseball cap was turned backward and wedged on tight, but as they came very near the mountainside, the flowing, orange sludge put off a ton of heat and glowing light. A wind blew and more ash fell from the sky, obstructing their view. Leroy turned the hat around, pulled it down supertight, and used the visor to shield the light as he scanned the top third of the mountain while Jadar circled.

"There!" Leroy yelled, pointing toward the mountain.

"I see it, too!" Albert said.

"And another opening, right there," Birdie said.

Albert spied giant holes in the side of the mountain,

with overhanging rock formations that made the sludge flow around the edges.

"Keep circling, Jadar," Birdie said. "I think we've found what we're looking for."

As Birdie guided Jadar all the way around, they saw a total of four wide holes, all of them at the same level on the oozing mountain.

"What do you think—are they big enough for Jadar to fly into?" Albert asked as he turned to Leroy.

"I'd say yes," Leroy answered. "Because *those* things can get out."

When Albert turned back to the mountain he saw what Leroy was talking about. King Fireflies, which were just as big as Jadar was, were pouring out of the holes like hornets from a nest.

"They're acting weird," Birdie said.

It was true. The King Fireflies were flying haphazardly, bouncing off one another and wobbling from side to side. Two of them crashed together and fell into the sludge flow, rolling down in a burning mass of flaming ooze. The remaining King Fireflies caught sight of Jadar and their whole bodies turned red as flames.

"They've spotted us!" Leroy said. He turned his baseball cap backward again and leaned in low toward Birdie. "See if you can navigate past them and aim for one of the holes. We need to get in there and get to the Sea Inspire fast!"

Birdie took the command and ran with it, guiding Jadar like a top-notch Air Force pilot. Albert's Double Vision helped them notice every opportunity to get hit by a fireball. Leroy acted as navigator.

"Left!" Leroy screamed. "Right!"

A new wave of fireballs came in, and Birdie followed Leroy's commands.

"Go down, go down!" Leroy cried out.

Birdie pushed down on Jadar's neck and the Guildacker dove, narrowly avoiding a sky filled with flame.

"Take us in!" Albert yelled, and Birdie guided Jadar up, aiming directly for one of the four holes in the mountainside. The closer they got, the hotter the mountain felt and the more ash rained down, until they all had to close their eyes and shield their faces.

They were going in blind.

Albert opened his eyes again when he felt a cool breeze on his face; the heat had evaporated along with the light as soon as they entered the hole. He was suddenly grateful they had brought Farnsworth with them—if it weren't for his eyes acting as headlights, they would have been traveling through total darkness.

Leroy shifted forward on Jadar's back, craning to get a better look.

"Keep the lights on, Rudolph!" Leroy yelled. Farnsworth howled in response. "Let's see if we can find the Sea Inspire."

The tunnel widened out, but it was also a labyrinth that twisted and turned in many directions. Albert craned his neck backward, and his stomach dropped.

"We haven't lost them yet!"

A pack of angry King Fireflies was right behind them, tailing their every move.

They exited through one of the other holes and shot back into the smoky skies of Calderon. Once the King Fireflies had exited, too, they doubled back and entered the mountain again. Jadar was amazing, so fast and precise in his movements. If Albert hadn't known any better, he would have thought Birdie had a Creature Taming Tile.

Three more times they entered and exited the mountain, and each time it seemed more confusing to Albert. *We entered over there, then went through there, made a left, a right—no, that wasn't right. . . .*

But Leroy was there to keep them on track, guiding them with his Synapse Tile like he was reading straight from a map.

"We've got a light source," Birdie said. "There."

She pointed down as they passed over a small opening inside the rock that revealed two more tubes of stone crossing through a wide space below. Orange goo was floating on the surface of a sea of water, hissing and gurgling wildly beneath them. They passed over and continued through the dark tunnels, pursued by King

Fireflies once more.

"That's gotta be the Sea Inspire back there!" Albert said. "That's where we need to release the silver eggs!"

They continued flying through the labyrinth of tunnels, searching for the way into the center of the hollow mountain.

Once more, they burst back out into the open air around Calderon Peak. The heat was even worse than before and Jadar was clearly getting tired.

"Hey, guys," Leroy said.

"Whatcha got, Leroy?" Albert asked.

"I've been memorizing every path we've taken through the mountain. I have it now—I know the way to the Sea Inspire!"

"I love your photographic memory!" Birdie said, turning Jadar on a hard path back toward the mountain. "You tell us what to do; we'll do it."

Jadar let fly a series of fireballs, clearing a path.

"Take that hole right there," Leroy pointed. "Then I'll give you directions."

"On it!" Birdie yelled, aiming Jadar and closing her eyes. Albert closed his, too. When they cleared the heat of the toxic sludge, Leroy started guiding: Left here, right here, down fast! Left, left again, up hard!

A flurry of commands followed and they lost all the King Fireflies. Then Leroy gave a final command.

"Down hard! Now!"

Birdie guided Jadar straight down into a narrow opening that forced the Guildacker to fold his wings and take the shape of an arrow. They shot through the hole at the bottom, and Jadar's wings spread once more, holding them aloft in a soft circle.

When Albert opened his eyes, they were floating over a sea of bubbling, orange goo. In the very center, a column of stone rose up into the middle of the open cave. And there, on the shelf of the column of stone, was the best thing Albert could have hoped to find.

"Dad! Dad! It's us. It's Hydra! Grey! Aria!"

Albert's heart leaped as Grey and Professor Flynn cheered, and Jadar came in for a soft landing. Albert leaned down and embraced his dad, dismounting Jadar in the process.

"But how . . . ," Professor Flynn started to ask. His clothing was torn and singed, and his hair was nearly all white, but he had the biggest smile on his face. "I didn't think anyone would ever find us."

"I know, right?" Leroy said, jumping down from Jadar's back and embracing Grey. "You guys are way in here."

Albert suddenly realized that Aria was still on the floor.

Birdie knelt beside her unconscious figure. "Is she okay?"

"Yes. Well, no, but she will be as soon as we get back to

the Core," Professor Flynn said. "She's badly dehydrated."

Phew, Albert thought. *Could be worse.*

Albert turned to his dad. "How did you end up in here?" Albert asked.

Grey stepped forward, covered in cuts and bruises. "It was the King Fireflies. They scooped us up while we were looking for Hissengore eggs in the Circle of Entry. We didn't even stand a chance."

"I tried to speak with them," Professor Flynn said, picking up where Grey had left off. "But in the chaos, I'd lost my Tile. It was pointless by then."

Albert touched the place where his Master Tile hung, right beside his dad's. Albert removed Professor Flynn's Tile from around his neck.

"I think this belongs to you, Dad."

Albert's dad beamed with pride as Albert handed him back his lost Tile.

"We thought the Kings might kill us," Grey said, completing the story. "But they carried us here, to their home. Sometimes they come back and look at us, but they don't actually seem to want to do us real harm."

"They know, even in their madness, that we are friends," Professor Flynn said.

"If only we could have discovered the Means in time," Grey said angrily. "They brought us right to the Sea Inspire. Right where the eggs need to be used. It would have been so perfect."

Albert took off his pack and opened it up. Soft light leaked out into the chamber.

"I think we may have found what you've been looking for."

Everyone except Aria gathered close as Albert took out one of the silver eggs and held it up.

"You guys really are something," Albert's dad said, astonished. He looked at the eggs as if they were holy relics. "I wasn't even sure these were real. Where did you find them?"

"*Inside* the Tree of Cinder," Leroy said. "The opening is way at the top. Can you believe it?"

Farnsworth barked, and Birdie took him out of her pack and set him on the ground.

"Okay, fine," Leroy said. "*Farnsworth* found them. But Albert went inside and got them. He's the egg man."

Professor Flynn looked at Albert. "That's my boy."

Albert beamed. He had waited for *so* long to hear those words. But there wasn't time to celebrate yet. Albert set the silver egg back inside the bag and pulled it shut for safekeeping.

"We have four. Now we just need to release their contents into the four tunnels."

Birdie was standing at the edge of the shelf, staring down into the water. She appeared to be contemplating the situation.

Professor Flynn looked out over the goo-filled surface

of the Sea Inspire and sighed. "The four tunnels are deep under the water; that's all we know. No one's been down there in centuries."

Everyone was gathered at one edge of the stone shelf, staring down at the orange goo clinging to the sides of the pillar.

Everyone, that is, but Birdie.

Albert whirled around too late. "Birdie! No!" he shouted, but she was already diving through the air.

"Birdie!" Leroy yelled, too, running to the other side of the stone pillar. He got down on his hands and knees and peered over the side, right as she disappeared into the Sea Inspire with a splash. "She did *not* just do that!"

But she had. Albert's knees went weak. Wasn't losing Birdie once in a day enough? He dropped his pack at his feet, then scrambled over to the edge next to Leroy. One second later, he heard his dad gasp. "The silver eggs are gone," Professor Flynn said, picking up Albert's pack. "She's taken them."

"Oh man!" Leroy said. "Now we're really in trouble." He got up and began pacing back and forth. "What if the goo stuff burned her? What if she's *dead*?"

"She should be fine in the water, I think," Professor Flynn said, but didn't look entirely sure himself.

As Albert stared into the water, he remembered the last time he'd waited for Birdie to surface back at the Waterfall of Fate, and the dread in his stomach disappeared. He stood back up. "Guys! This is Birdie Howell we're talking about here. She can stay underwater for as long as it takes. If anyone can do this, it's Birdie, right, Grey?"

Grey and Professor Flynn glanced nervously at each other.

"There's something else," Grey said, shaking his head. He looked terrified beyond words. The confidence Albert had just found left as quickly as it had come.

"What? What is it?" Albert asked.

It was Professor Flynn that told him. "A treacherous monster called the Hendeca swims in the Sea Inspire. Birdie has just entered its domain."

"What?" Leroy jumped up, too. "We didn't read about any creature in our research at the Library. I'd definitely remember that."

"It's been asleep for centuries," Professor Flynn explained, "for so long that Balance Keepers stopped thinking of it as a threat. But it seems this Imbalance has awakened it. We wouldn't believe it either, but Grey and I saw its tentacles break the surface this morning."

"That's it," Albert said. "I'm going in, too."

"I can't let you do that, Albert," Professor Flynn said. "You'd never make it out alive."

"Actually, Dad, I will," Albert said. "I have the Master Tile, and I've figured out how to use it."

His dad shook his head sadly. "Whatever you've heard about that Tile, don't believe it."

"I can't explain how it works right now, Dad," Albert said. "But you have to trust me. Whatever you think you know about the Master Tile, it's probably wrong. I"— Albert looked at Leroy—"*we* unlocked its powers, and now I'm going to use it to save my friend."

Professor Flynn started to say something, but Albert closed his eyes and the symbol on his Master Tile began to change. Professor Flynn watched in amazement, speechless at what he was seeing.

Then Albert turned, ignoring the cries of his dad and Grey, and dove off the pillar, toward the Sea Inspire and the monster Hendeca.

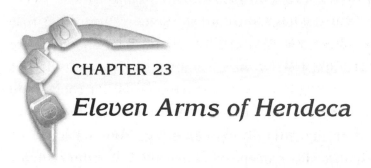

CHAPTER 23

Eleven Arms of Hendeca

The first thing Albert noticed after passing through the orange goo was that his body felt as light as a cloud. He opened his mouth and blew bubbles, and he found, amazingly, that he didn't feel like he needed to breathe. Even though he'd done this before, the feeling was still strange.

Albert looked up at the surface overhead. It was covered in orange goo in every direction. The Sea Inspire had protected him from burns as he dove in . . . but getting out would be a different story.

I've really done it this time, Albert thought to himself. *I'm trapped down here until I heal the Sea. I hope I can do this.*

But then he thought of why he'd come down here in the first place. He had to find Birdie and get her out of here, quick. *I hope the Hendeca hasn't found her first.*

He swam a circle around the stone column that rose through the middle of the Sea. It ended far above, where his dad and friends were trapped. The water itself was warm up here, but as Albert dove deeper, it cooled and took on a richer shade of blue. It was a wide, deep space, and what light there was came from four holes in the depths. He swam deeper and felt the cool water turn icy on his skin.

This must be the place, Albert thought as he arrived twenty or so feet in front of an opening large enough to walk through. He turned and spotted three more such holes on the same level, scattered around the stone walls of the deep.

The water was murky, but Albert still turned in a circle to see if he could spot Birdie. Still, every way he turned, Birdie was nowhere to be found. Neither was the Hendeca.

Albert swam nearer to one of the holes. The water here was stagnant and warm, almost like it was feverish. The closer he got to the holes, the warmer the water became.

He moved off to the side and slowly swam closer still. The light that emerged from the hole was swirly and sickly green, as if the depths of the hole were full of gunk.

Suddenly, Albert saw something that made his heart freeze like a block of ice.

On the bottom of the Sea Inspire, glowing far below him, sat the four silver eggs.

Had the Hendeca taken Birdie? Where *was* she?

Albert swam down, fast as a dolphin, and grabbed the eggs. He took the first of the four eggs and felt its warmth in his palm. Its light was even brighter down so deep, and holding it out, Albert could see all the way across the Sea Inspire. Something big was moving slowly in the faraway shadows.

That has to be the Hendeca.

The goo on the surface was growing brighter, shining light down onto Albert. He had to go after the monster . . . but the entire world depended on Albert right now.

Have faith in Birdie. She's smart. She'll be okay until I find her. Restore the Balance first. Albert turned back to his work, slamming the silver egg into the rock wall. The egg began to leak silvery fluid that looked like flowing mercury. The contents of the egg emptied out into the tunnel as if they knew where they were going. Albert let the eggshell go and it vanished into the hole, too.

Albert took the precaution of moving farther to the side of the hole, just in case something did change, and it was lucky he did. Light began to radiate from the tunnel, shedding a wide band of brightness across the water. A current began flowing, increasing tenfold by the second. Even from his spot against the wall some thirty feet away, Albert felt he might be sucked in. The green color of the water was sucked away, too, and it faded to a calm, beautiful blue. He peered farther down below, in the deepest depths of the sea, and watched as a second hole of light appeared.

It's flowing again. It's working!

He felt the water grow colder still, rising up from his feet, and then he sprang into action. There wasn't much time.

Albert made sure to stay along the wall, afraid to pass in front of the hole he'd just fixed. When he'd swam far enough along the curved stone, he was careful to swing wide and land on the opposite side of the next hole. That way, he could keep going around the outer edge until all the eggs were used, without passing in front of a current strong enough to suck him into oblivion. As he approached the second tunnel, he glanced toward the stone pillar and saw giant shadows swirling once more.

Finish the mission, Albert, and fast!

Albert made quick business of the tasks at the second hole, and when he was done, the Sea Inspire became lighter still. It was then that he saw what had been hidden in shadow before.

An eleven-tentacled squid of massive proportions was slowly moving toward him. It was black as night, like an endless oil slick moving across the sea. *What I wouldn't give for this to all be a very bad dream right now.*

Albert reached down and untied the laces on his boots,

kicking them off so he could swim faster, and raced for the next hole. The giant Hendeca that shared his space wasn't the only thing Albert saw. As the water became even colder, he saw millions of silver fish swimming up from far below, released from some prison they'd been held captive inside of. They almost looked like the sparkling lights in the Cave of Souls, rising up to meet him. The Hendeca shadowed Albert in the circle he was making around the Sea Inspire, but it stayed near the middle, obviously aware of the powerful current it might become ensnared in if it got too close to the outer wall.

When Albert completed the third healing, the silver fish had reached the level he was at, and he had a better idea of how deep the Sea was. The fish swam all around him. Some of them were sucked into the hole he was nearest to, only to reappear far below. It was so deep— miles, it seemed—and so bright and clear that Albert could see all the way to the bottom.

He made his way to the fourth tunnel, the final egg cradled in his arm like a football, his eyes trained on the Hendeca the whole time. He prepared to toss the egg in, but it slipped through his hands. Albert scrambled to grab hold of the egg and in that moment, took his eyes off the Hendeca.

Not a second later, the Hendeca's eleven tentacles had surrounded him, pinning him to the wall. Its one huge eye peered down, blinking at Albert as it observed its prey. Albert felt his heart skip a beat. He twisted to find a way out.

That's when Albert saw Birdie, wrapped up in one of the tentacles. She was squirming, trying to fight her way out, but the Hendeca was the size of a two-story house.

"Birdie!" Albert screamed, but it just came out like a muddled groan underwater.

Her eyes met Albert's. When she saw him, she looked shocked for a moment, but then she nodded her head once, as if to say:

Get the egg where it needs to go. Then you can help me.

Albert hit the final egg against the wall and watched its contents drizzle into the hole like silver honey. He felt a black tentacle surrounding him, wrapping around his waist, squeezing. Albert fought and kicked, but the squid was too strong. It pulled him away from the wall, looked at him once more with the giant eye, and drew Albert near. And then, with greater speed than he thought any creature could move in the water, the squid as big as a whale burst into action, its black body shimmering against the Sea.

It was carting them off toward a hole on the opposite side. Albert knew that he and Birdie only had seconds to get free.

We are your friends! Albert tried to call out, picturing his dad's Creature Speak symbol, but the Hendeca didn't make any noise. *Please! Let us go!*

The tentacle holding Birdie swung closer to the one holding Albert, so that they were side by side.

Birdie was trying to say something to Albert, but he couldn't understand. She kept looking pointedly at Albert's ankle.

The paralyzing dagger!

Albert stretched as best he could. The beast was almost to the entrance of one of the holes when Albert's fingertips brushed the handle of the dagger.

He grabbed it, twisted it around, and stabbed it into the Hendeca's tentacle.

Nothing happened. Albert pulled it out and saw that the Sea had washed the poison off. And the knife was so small compared to the Hendeca; the stab hadn't even fazed it.

Albert began to panic. He ran through a mental list of Tile symbols, trying to settle on one that would help him save Birdie.

Finally, just before the Hendeca reached the cave, a symbol appeared in Albert's mind.

It was one he hadn't practiced yet; in fact, he thought it sounded pretty lame.

Sonar Speak.

Albert focused, hard, on the symbol's shape, the way it looked like an open, toothless mouth, screaming. When he felt the strength inside of him, Albert opened his mouth and let out an incredibly loud and piercing sonar scream. The Hendeca began to quiver and shake.

The creature released Albert, but not Birdie. Birdie covered her ears and closed her eyes as Albert tried harder, screaming so loud that the silver fish all darted into holes and hid. Soon the Hendeca's entire body started to quake. Albert didn't know how much longer he could keep screaming—he felt his throat getting tired, and his mind growing weary. Finally, after one last tremor, the Hendeca released Birdie and darted off into the shadows.

Albert and Birdie locked hands and swam backward as fast as they could as they watched the Hendeca disappear into the hole, fading into the darkness.

Now what?

Birdie pointed at the floor of the Sea Inspire. Albert nodded, and they swam downward together.

As soon as their feet touched the sandy bottom, Birdie looked at Albert and pointed upward toward the surface, where they were happy to see that the goo had disappeared, cleared away by the now-flowing water.

Leap! Birdie mouthed, and luckily, Albert understood her.

Together, they bent their knees, pushed upward as hard as they could, and torpedo-swam all the way to the top.

As they shot through the surface, Jadar swooped down. They landed on his back, and the creature took them to the pillar of stone, where everyone stood waiting.

"Oh man!" Leroy cried out, pulling his friends into a

hug as they slid from Jadar's back. "You did it!"

Professor Flynn hugged Albert, too, and soon, Grey joined in. Albert was glad to see that Aria was awake, dizzy on her feet, but smiling nonetheless. Farnsworth barked and yipped around their ankles.

Birdie coughed up a little water and pulled away from the group hug. "Albert did it," she said. "He saved me from a giant squid with eleven arms. It was bigger than a house. He used . . . I don't know, sonar or something to scare the Hendeca away! Am I right, Albert?"

Albert nodded. He'd never call sonar lame again.

"No Balance Keeper has ever survived the Hendeca, Albert," said Professor Flynn, "let alone saved another Balance Keeper from its tentacles. Well done."

Professor Flynn took hold of the Master Tile around Albert's neck and looked at it with amazement, at the power his son had figured out how to harness.

"I thought it was a useless legend," Professor Flynn said. "We all did. You proved us wrong."

"Professor Flynn," Aria piped up, "look!" She pointed out into the cavernous space.

The King Fireflies were buzzing again, flying around and then diving down to the Sea Inspire and drinking from its surface. Albert watched, his breath held, as they swooped close to the pillar. But not a single one turned red or angry. The King Fireflies were back to normal again.

"Balance has been restored," Professor Flynn said with a smile. He looked at everyone on Team Hydra, his eyes landing finally on his son.

"It's time we went home."

CHAPTER 24

Upon Leaving for Home

"I still can't believe you battled the Hendeca," Leroy said to Albert as they flew on Jadar's back toward the exit of Calderon. "You've got mad Balance Keeper skills!"

"It was crazy, no doubt," Albert said. "When that last hole was healed, the Hendeca started taking us away, like it was going to pull us into its lair. It was chilling."

"That's when Albert used the paralyzing knife." Birdie beamed as she guided Jadar toward home. "And when that didn't work, he used his Master Tile to scare it away."

She'd told that part five or six times already, but Albert didn't mind. It *was* pretty cool, what he'd done.

"I'm glad you scared him off, Albert. I'd miss you guys if you hadn't made it," Leroy said.

"What makes you think the Hendeca is a he?" Birdie argued with Leroy, and Albert couldn't help but laugh. Farnsworth yipped from Albert's backpack, clearly enjoying the ride.

Everything was back to normal again.

Albert waved at his dad, who was flying on a King Firefly not far from Jadar. His dad waved back. Albert didn't want this moment to be over—he had grown to love Calderon with all its mysteries and dangers—but they were nearly at the far edge of the Realm. He didn't know for sure when he and his friends would be back.

When they were close to the tunnel that would lead them back to the Core, Jadar touched down and then hopped and bobbed, taking a breather from all the flying he'd done.

Albert, Leroy, and Birdie slid from his back. Professor Flynn, Grey, and Aria landed beside them. Their King Fireflies buzzed and took flight again, heading back toward their hive.

Professor Flynn looked at Birdie. "You are forever linked to this beast now," Professor Flynn said, seeing the concern on her face as she watched the Guildacker. Albert knew she didn't want to leave him. "He will long for you while you are away, and he will never betray you. That is the way of companion beasts from the Realms."

"Wait, are you saying Jadar can come with me?" Birdie asked, her voice revealing how much she wished it were true. "Back into the Core?"

Professor Flynn nodded encouragingly. "You can't take him home, but you can keep him in Treefare."

Birdie beamed. "But the Core *is* my home."

"You are all residents of two homes now," Professor Flynn said. "The Core, and the one you left behind. We're approaching a time when you must return to the surface, to your old life."

"When?" Leroy asked.

"We'll see," Professor Flynn answered. "Only the Libryam knows—unless you've been keeping track, Mr. Jones?"

"Nope," Leroy replied, "I've tried, but that's one thing my Tile won't let me do."

"Well, it won't be long now," Professor Flynn said. "You've been down here awhile."

They were at the entrance to the tunnel now.

Albert turned around and looked one last time at Calderon.

"Thank you," he whispered, though he wasn't quite sure who he was thanking. Then he turned and ran down the tunnel to catch up with the others.

When they reached the door to the Core twenty minutes later, Professor Flynn positioned Albert, Leroy, and Birdie in front, followed by the First Unit and himself behind. But before Albert could reach out to open the door, it opened unexpectedly.

"Let's clean up Hydra's mess!"

Albert looked at the timepiece on his wrist.

"Five hours, fifty-six minutes, and twelve seconds, Hoyt," Albert said. "You're leaving a little early, aren't you? We still have four minutes."

"Chickened out, huh?" Hoyt said. "I expected as much. Step out of the way and let a *real* team through."

"Gladly," Albert said, moving forward into the Core. "But you'll have to make some room for my friends."

Everyone from the Core was there, and they went silent as Albert, Leroy, and Birdie entered. Albert felt the crowd take in the state of the three of them—battle worn and weary, and in Albert's case, missing boots. Albert grabbed his Tile and made sure it was visible. He didn't want to hide it now.

"What a bunch of losers," Hoyt said, turning to Slink and Mo, who didn't look nearly as gung-ho as he was. "Come on, guys, let's do it right!"

Hoyt turned for the door to Calderon and found Professor Flynn standing there. Every man and beast in the Core gasped with excitement. Grey and Aria came out next. The cheers intensified.

Hoyt turned on Birdie.

"Bet you didn't restore Balance, though, did you? You and your Hydra lame-os aren't that good. No way."

"Uh, Hoyt?" Slink asked.

"Shut up, Slink! I'm busy here."

Albert watched as Jadar tapped Hoyt on the shoulder. Albert's grin widened as Hoyt turned around and let out a high-pitched whimper. "Better be nice to my friend's bird," Leroy said. "He's very protective."

But it was too late. Jadar leaped into the air and picked up Hoyt with his claws, grabbing Hoyt by the back of his shirt like a mouse that had been caught. Hoyt screamed as Jadar carried him around the Main Chamber and dropped him into one of the silvery streams.

The Core erupted with laughter.

"Balance has been restored to Calderon!" Trey yelled, beside Professor Flynn. "Hydra has done it!"

Farnsworth barked.

"And Farnsworth!"

Albert, Leroy, and Birdie never endured so many backslaps and high fives as they did that afternoon. It was the best day of Albert's life. They told the stories over and over again, ate until they were bursting, laughed endlessly. They'd saved the world and lived to tell about it.

Did it get any better than that?

A couple of days later, Albert and Leroy met Birdie and Jadar at the door to Cedarfell. Birdie turned to Jadar and stroked the feathers on his black head. She ran her hand along his black beak and the Guildacker closed his eyes.

"I will miss you, too," she said. "Every single day, until I return."

They all watched Jadar fly off, high over the cedars, already howling Birdie's name to the wind.

A tear slipped down her cheek.

"I knew deep down you were a softy," Leroy said.

Birdie couldn't help herself. She burst into laughter, and soon all three of them were laughing as they headed toward the Main Chamber, just like old times.

It was true what Professor Flynn had said: time was short. That morning, just two days after they restored Balance to Calderon, Albert, Birdie, and Leroy had stepped on the Libryam scale. It had said the same thing for each of them: they were down to only a few hours before they'd have to return home. If they stayed any longer, they could never leave the Core again.

"Maybe one day we'll decide to stay," Leroy had said when he stepped off the Libryam. "And then we can live in the Core forever."

"But not today," Professor Flynn said. "Today you're going home, and so are we."

He had put an arm around Albert and they both smiled.

Now the three friends were standing on the same bridge they had crossed on their first day in the Core.

"When do we get to come back again?" Birdie asked.

"Trey said next summer," Leroy replied, tossing a pebble into the river below.

"And you'll be taking our spots," Grey said, coming up

beside them at the railing, with Aria in tow.

All of their cuts and bruises were gone. Albert noticed, too, that they were holding hands. They both smiled at Hydra like they had never been prouder.

"It's time we left this place and didn't come back," Aria said. "That trip into Calderon was our last mission. At least we ended on a high note."

"I'll say," Albert agreed. "But won't you miss it?"

"Won't you miss *us*?" Birdie chimed in.

Grey looked at Aria and smiled. "We've had our time and done our part. If we come back again, it will have to be for good, as Professors or Core workers. That's how it is when you get a bit older. You'll see. In a couple of years, you'll have to decide, too."

"We're deciding it's time to be together," Aria said. "Up there."

Albert felt a small pang in his heart. Was it because he had started to like Aria, and Grey, too? Or was it because he knew that somewhere in the not-so-distant future, he, too, would have to decide where to spend the rest of his life?

"You three are going to make a great Calderon First Unit," Grey said. "To be honest, I don't think we're needed like we used to be. You've given us the confidence to leave."

"Wait," Albert piped up. "I thought we were going to train for another Realm next term."

"Yeah," Leroy said, adjusting his cap. "Second Terms can't be First Units. That's not how it works."

"Leroy . . . ," Birdie whined, "has *anything* been normal since we got here?" She turned to Aria. "We'll train for another Realm *and* be First Unit for Calderon?"

Aria nodded. "It will be double the work, double the action. But you can do it. You guys are going to be great."

"Obviously," Birdie said. She was so pumped she was bouncing up and down.

"Thanks, guys," Leroy said, and offered Grey and Aria low fives. Albert gave them quick hugs. He couldn't believe they were going to be First Unit.

Grey and Aria lingered a little longer, and then they had a nice send-off from everyone in the Main Chamber, including Professor Flynn and Trey. Eventually, they exited through the same double doors through which Albert, Birdie, and Leroy had arrived seventy-four days earlier.

Professor Flynn turned toward Team Hydra. "You three are next."

"What about you?" Albert asked his dad.

"I'll follow along in another day or two," Professor Flynn said, looking at Albert. "Then we'll grab your Pap and have a barbecue. We'll have plenty of time to talk about your Tile, kiddo. I've got lots of questions. Oh, and Albert? Farnsworth will be lonely here. He can go with you to the surface, as long as he promises to keep his eyes turned off."

"Really?" Albert beamed. He was going to have a real live piece of the Core with him, until he returned again. Farnsworth thumped his tail across Albert's ankles. He let out a yip, and his eyes faded to a normal-dog blue.

"Dad?" Albert asked. "How much time do we have left before we absolutely have to go?"

"About forty-five minutes. Why?"

"I have something I want to show Birdie and Leroy," Albert replied, hoping his dad was catching on.

"Go on, then, Albert." His dad winked. "Just make sure you're out of the Path Hider's tree in forty-five minutes—I don't want to have to explain to the post office why all the undeliverable mail has piled up if you get stuck down here."

Then Professor Flynn and Trey left. Trey turned back and smiled encouragingly. This was one Apprentice who was very impressed with his team.

"Come on, you guys," Albert said, grabbing Leroy and Birdie by the hands. "You have to see this before we go."

In the Cave of Souls, Albert, Leroy, and Birdie were silent for several minutes. Albert eventually spoke up.

"There are three flames up there, one for each of us," Albert explained. "I bet you they're always floating around up there, together, causing trouble and stuff."

"It's nice to have real friends, for the first time ever."

Birdie laughed. "I don't know if I've told you guys this, but I've always had trouble making friends. Apparently I intimidate some people."

"Not really," Leroy said with a smirk, nudging Birdie's shoulder. "You've softened up a bit in here, I think."

Birdie nodded. "I'm glad I have you guys."

Albert thought he saw another tear in her eye. He nodded. "Me too. I've never had friends like you guys. Heck, I've never *been* a friend like I've been to you two. I don't think I knew how."

"You're an amazing friend, Albert," Leroy said. He wrapped his fingers around his Tile, and held it tight. "I don't want to leave this place. I feel different here, braver than in the real world, you know? What if all that goes away up there?"

Birdie turned to face Leroy. "I don't think that's gonna happen, Leroy."

She looked at Albert and winked. Albert caught on at once.

"Birdie's right. I think it's *you* who's made yourself braver. Not your Tile."

"Thanks, guys." Leroy sighed.

They sat in silence for a few more minutes, watching the flames dance overhead, proof that there was an entire world full of people down here, and in turn, people on the earth above, whose lives had all been affected by the Core. "You guys going to be okay without me?" Birdie said. "Up there, on the surface?"

"I'll text you if I need a bodyguard," Leroy said with a smile. Albert nodded in agreement. They'd stay in touch aboveground. And soon enough, they'd be back for bigger, better adventures.

"Uh, guys," Albert suddenly said, "we have to be out of the Path Hider's tree in ten minutes!"

The three set off, leaving Balance Keeper souls blinking behind them.

Once back at the double doors, they pushed through and jumped in the gondola, Farnsworth hopping in behind them.

"Something tells me this is going to be the wildest ride of our lives," Leroy said as the gondola jerked forward.

Seven minutes (and one upchucked Core meal) later, they passed through the secret Realm of the Path Hider and found themselves standing in the woods.

"Well, I guess this is it," Birdie said. "See you goofballs next year."

Then she ran forward and gave both boys a quick kiss on their cheeks.

"Okay, now you're a little *too* soft," Leroy joked, but he smiled anyway as Birdie headed into the trees.

"Albert," Leroy said, holding a hand out. "You're one righteous Balance Keeper. I'll see you soon." He, too, headed off into the woods.

Albert was surprised to feel a lump in his throat.

He began walking, looking back every few seconds and seeing his friends waving as they walked in different directions. The third time he looked back, they were gone, and it was just Albert and Farnsworth alone in the deep of the woods.

Just like old times.

"Well, now, haven't seen you in quite a while," Pap said. Albert stood on the steps and watched the old guys play Tiles. "It's about time for you to get on home to New York, ain't it?"

"Yeah, just a few more days," Albert said, imagining his old Pap as a Balance Keeper and wondering what adventures he'd had long ago. "I wish I could stay. But I miss home, too."

"I know just how you feel," Pap said, a glimmer in his eye. He went back to playing his game and Albert watched as the Tiles stacked up. He thought of how great Leroy was at the game, and suddenly missed his buddy.

"I hear they've had clear skies over New York for days," Pap said, playing a Tile as he uttered the words. "I wonder what could have caused that?"

Albert shrugged. He didn't feel like telling Pap about everything just yet.

Pap moved the Tiles around in front of him, organizing them just so. "That's a unique necklace you have there, son."

Pap looked up from his Tiles and winked at Albert. Farnsworth growled playfully.

"Have you ever seen it before?" Albert asked.

"Wouldn't remember if I had," Pap said, but Albert saw, for the first time, that Pap had a cord around his neck. He guessed that Pap's old Balance Keeper Tile was concealed just under his flannel shirt.

Later that week they would barbecue some burgers and play Tiles, all three Flynn men, while Farnsworth slept at Albert's feet. Albert would also write a thank-you note addressed to the one friend he had had to leave behind in the Core. He might not have been here without Petra's help.

But for now, for just that moment, Albert could be alone and walk and think about all that had happened. He touched the Master Tile around his neck. He might have discovered what it was, and what it could do. But it was still the strangest of them all. It made him wonder: *Am I destined to live in the Core for the rest of my life?*

The thought of it saddened him then, because he did so love the town of Herman, Wyoming. He brightened at the thought of Guildackers and King Fireflies and besting Hoyt's team, though. He didn't have to make a decision now. Albert looked down at Farnsworth and smiled.

"What do you say we go have some fruitcake, huh, boy?"

* * *

As Albert returned home to his mom in New York City, two figures were meeting in the shadows of the Core. One was a man who wore a long, black cloak. No one had seen him in a very long time. The mere mention of his name was cause for concern, and so he was rarely mentioned at all, even in the highest ranks of the Core. The other was a person who everyone in the Core was aware of. The fact that this person was there, speaking to the most notorious man who had ever entered the Core, was a mystery.

The man in the black cloak spoke first.

"You were right to inform me of the Master Tile's appearance after all these years."

"Thank you, your grace."

"The boy is strong," the one in the black cloak said. "Stronger than I expected."

"He's not so special."

"And yet he made short order of all my work in Calderon. He orchestrated quite a save."

"I suppose he did."

The two moved farther back in the shadows, near the door to an unseen Realm of the Core.

The cloaked man continued: "The longer Albert Flynn has the Master Tile, the more powerful he becomes. And you and I both know the only way *we* can control the Master Tile is if the boy dies in one of the Realms."

"Timing must be perfect, your grace," the other voice

said. "Or the power will not transfer from him to you."

"Let's see how he does when the Ponderay Realm is in chaos and his First Unit has fled."

"That will take some time and planning."

A gruesome smile appeared on the cloaked man's face.

"So start planning."

The cloaked man began walking toward the entry to the Realm of Ponderay, and as he went he pulled his own Tile out and observed its shiny black surface.

The Core fell silent but for an echoing laughter that rang through the night, which ended with the sound of a slamming door.

Acknowledgments

I've dreamed about writing an acknowledgments section in a book since I was a little girl. Now it's here, and it's actually REAL, and there are so many people I have to thank for it. Thank you to my stupid years of illness, which led me to writing. Here's to you, chronic fatigue: I WIN. YOU LOSE. HAHAHA!

To my lord and savior Jesus Christ, who gave me the drive to never, never quit.

A million thanks and hugs to my amazing editors, Katie Bignell and Katherine Tegen, who changed my life and made my dreams come true when they said YES to Albert's story. You both have put so much love and care into this, and into my writing career. Working with you has been above and beyond RIDICULOUSLY AWESOME.

To my dear friend, author Patrick Carman, whose genius goes without saying, who looked at a little "nobody" like me and decided to give me a chance. You are my Yoda, my Mr. Miyagi, my Magic 8 ball with all the right answers.

To my agent, Louise Fury, who is a book goddess as well as a book rock star. You are the dream agent—an answer to many prayers, and I'll forever consider you a part of my family! You are the BEST agent in the entire world!

To Peter Rubie, who helped make this all happen. Thank you!

To the cover designers, Joel Tippie and Tom Forget at Katherine Tegen Books, who are amazing. To the illustrator, Kevin Keele, for being ridiculously talented.

The entire team at Katherine Tegen books, who made this book SHINY.

To my best friend, Cherie Stewart, who helps keep me sane and reads all my early drafts. To my husband, Josh Price, who listens to my ramblings about the publishing world for hours without interrupting. To Abby Haxel and Landon Davies, for being beautiful book nerds. To Karen, Lauren, and Don Cummings, for all of your endless love and support. To the Ryan family, aka the in-laws, for more love and support! To my extended family for all the prayer and support. Thanks to Jen Gray, who is my soul sister and Mini-Me. I love you, girly! To my dogs Hurley, Kai, and Kimber, who were the inspiration behind Farnsworth.

Many thanks to the ladies at my Tuesday bible study, for praying for me for so many years. To DFWcon, my Texas bookish group (you ladies rock), the YA Valentines, and the YA Rebels. The Burleson family, for being so supportive of my dreams. The book-blogging community, for rocking at life. And special thanks to my army of #Booknerdigans. You know who you are, and you've made this journey a blast!

Thank you. Thank you. Thank you.